North. Am. Fiction
signed

6 50

22.50

D0773555

the circle leads home

the circle leads home

by

Mary Anderson Parks

university press of colorado

Published by the University Press of Colorado
P.O. Box 849
Niwot, Colorado 80544

The University Press of Colorado is a cooperative publishing enterprise
supported, in part, by Adams State College, Colorado State University, Fort
Lewis College, Mesa State College, Metropolitan State College of Denver,
University of Colorado, University of Northern Colorado, University of
Southern Colorado, and Western State College of Colorado.

The paper used in this publication meets the minimum requirements of the
American National Standard for Information Sciences — Permanence of
Paper for Printed Library Materials. ANSI Z39.48-1984

Library of Congress Cataloging-in-Publication Data

Parks, Mary Anderson, 1938–
     The circle leads home / Mary Anderson Parks.
        p.   cm.
     ISBN 0-87081-488-5 (alk. paper)
     1. Indians of North America—Washington State—Fiction.
     I. Title.
     PS3566.A734C57   1998
     813'.54—dc21   97-48793
                                                                        CIP

07 06 05 04 03 02 01 00 99 98   10 9 8 7 6 5 4 3 2 1

in gratitude to

my husband
my daughters
Terry Sherf, publishing consultant and inspiration
Berkeley writing group
Tio's writing practice
Steve Murray
Tiina Nunnally
all the people I have worked with and been guided by in the
    Indian community
all my ancestors
all my friends
all my relations

the circle leads home

chapter 1

I run plum gloss over my lips and press them together, savoring the feel and taste. As I replace the gloss in my middle desk drawer, *Pride and Prejudice* stares up at me. Monday I'll finish it during lunch, then on Tuesday I can swing by the library and get books for Tony, too. I switch off the computer and cover it with its plastic protector, then slide the scotch tape into a neat row with the stapler and paper-clip holder. Leaning forward from the hips, I shake my head so my hair swishes against my cheekbones.

"Katherine?"

Allen stands in the doorway to his office. He looks harried, as usual, but there is something else in his eyes, something that makes my back muscles stiffen.

"I wondered ..." He pauses and scrunches his mouth, a habit he has.

"I've got tickets to a concert. I know this sounds corny, but somebody gave them to me at the last minute. A violin concerto? Would you be free tomorrow night?"

Asking that, he looks like a little boy. He reminds me of dozens of men and boys asking such questions. He does have his own style, though. He is thirty-eight, only six years older than I am, but bending over law books has given him a permanent stoop.

"It was just a thought," he says. He must see something in my face that stops him. Maybe he sees me thinking I know where this is heading and I don't want to go down that path. But that's not what I tell him.

"Allen, you're forgetting," I say. "I've got a thirteen-year-old and girls have discovered him. I don't dare leave him alone."

1

It's not quite the truth, but close. I smile, knowing he'll forgive me if I smile in just that way.

He ducks his head and looks sheepish, maybe even relieved. "Ann's still at her sister's." He sighs. "I have no idea when she'll be back."

"It'll work out, Allen," I tell him. I get up, go to the coat tree, and pull down my green suede jacket. "Whatever's supposed to happen." I want to change the subject, get away from all this that takes us right to the edge. "I wonder if it's still raining."

His expression takes on more confidence, more energy. "Who knows! This crazy spring weather, switches on us every ten minutes." He grins at me. "Someday we'll get us an office with windows, babe, and we'll know what's happenin'!" He sails smoothly into the Bogie style he often hides behind. He actually does resemble Bogart: intelligent face so ugly it fascinates, and a kind heart. I brush past him, careful not to pass too close, as he holds the door open. It makes me laugh inside, knowing he likes being several inches taller than I am. All my life I've wished I were tall and slim and model material, but I'm barely three inches over five feet, and I have to watch my weight. I push away the image of my mother, even shorter, and round and bristling as a hedgehog all those years ago when we last saw each other. At least I haven't slept with Allen. And we're alone together in this tiny office all day, except when clients come in. No married men, that's one standard I've kept to!

There've been close calls, like the time he surprised me when I was writing a poem. "What's it about?" he asked, and I could feel the pull I exerted on him, an electric connection that wasn't only physical, it was my mind drawing him. I lifted the sheet of paper for him to take and saw his white hand tremble when it touched my brown fingers. So I started talking in a way that would keep a distance. "I read in the paper," I told him, "about an Indian tribe that worked thirty years to reestablish claim to their land and be recognized by the feds." "You wrote about that?" He sounded surprised. "No," I told him, "I wrote about growing up on my reservation and how my bare, five-year-old feet knew the earth under us belonged to my tribe." I watched him read the lines, I watched his face to see if he understood anything of what

2

I was trying to say. He laid down the poem. "I'm from the tribe that's wandered the earth for centuries," he said, "and I haven't made it to Israel yet. So I wouldn't know the feeling. I think you've got it, though. I think you've got the feeling right there in those eight lines." I wondered if the sudden moisture in his eyes was from emotion, or if his allergies were bothering him again. Then he asked me, "Remember that writing sample you submitted when you applied for this job?" "Yes," I told him, "and I felt embarrassed after I gave it to you—I wanted to grab it back." He flashed me a grin. "My only worry was you'd turn my legalese into poetry and have judges in tears. Maybe not a bad idea, hey?"

He knows so little about my life, though I've worked for him four years, and during those years Larry wasted away and died. He doesn't even know my husband was black. Or would Larry be calling himself African-American?

"Have a good weekend, Allen." The words are meaningless, but make him feel cared about. He'll come back and work on the weekend. There are times he needs me to work on a Saturday, but this morning I finished the appellate brief and sent it off. He'll find some reason, though, to come back and work. I take the steps for the five flights down, feeling agile despite high heels, enjoying the movement in my calves and thighs, glad not to be a workaholic. I feel a smile touch my face, relaxing the muscles. It is cool, Seattle-gray daylight outside, a couple of hours yet before dark. My bus to Beacon Hill comes right away, and I find a seat by the window. A good feeling to be on the bus, away from both my lives, in blissful suspension.

A huge figure looms over me. "Mind if I sit here?" He seats himself as he asks, and presses his thigh against mine. I edge closer to the window, but the man moves with me. He is white, pasty-complexioned, with scraggly hair and a soiled shirt that doesn't quite cover his bulging belly. "You're too good-lookin' to be alone on a Friday night, squaw girl," he says. "Yuh know that?"

It's best to move quickly. I get up and force my way past the bumpy knees that stick out, blocking me. The bus lurches, and I catch hold of a pole. Finally I make my way to the front, where I squeeze into a small space on the bench behind the driver. You look like an Indian Jessica Lange, Allen told me the morning after he and his wife saw "Blue Skies." He'd responded to my questioning glance with an embarrassed flush. "Something in your eyes. Maybe the shape of them." Remembering his words almost blots out the sound in my ears of "squaw girl." I yearn to be home.

chapter 2

I step aside to let an ancient Asian woman exit ahead of me. I reach out to steady the woman. Her elbow feels bony in my hand. I stay close behind as she creeps down the steps of the bus and onto the curb. The tiny old woman's acknowledgment is like an elder's of my own tribe might be, a slight inclination of the head. Then she darts her sharp beetle eyes from side to side and scuttles off, impervious to the heavy mist and the young gangster-types lounging nearby amid discarded food containers and flattened beer cans. They barely give the woman a glance. Maybe, if I ever get that old, maybe the reward will be peace in the midst of danger.

The marijuana stench fills my nostrils with a sweet-sour sting as I approach the knot of black teenagers, eight or ten of them, leaning on the bus shelter and somebody's fence. To avoid their notice I try to walk with a minimum of movement through the cloud of smoke, which gets denser as I near the heart of the knot. I keep my eyes straight ahead and shift my shoulder bag to the street side. Then I wonder if that is a mistake. Will they take it as a sign of fear?

"Hey, bitch."

The muscles tighten in my back and legs. I quicken my steps.

One of the boys detaches himself from the mob and grasps me by the shoulder. "Hey, bitch, I'm talkin' to you!"

"Leave her alone, man. She's Victor's mom." The second voice cuts in and thwarts the move. Even as my breath comes easier, I feel a new fear take hold, twisting my insides. How do they know Victor? The color blue waves in my mind, seizing my attention. I remember dashing out last week to give Victor his

lunch money that he'd forgotten on the kitchen counter. I
reached the sidewalk on the run, in time to see him disappear
around the corner, the blue thing streaming out of his hip
pocket. It hadn't been there when he left the house. I hurry
on, not taking the chance of slowing to confirm what I glimpsed,
the flashes of blue showing from pockets and waistbands.
Neighbors have been talking about gangs moving in. It would
be great if once in a while two and two didn't add up.

I approach our house, feeling eager to get there, and find
a pile of dog shit on the front walk. A laugh wells up inside.
The perfect symbol! It is huge, obscene, a thing that had been
hidden from view, rotting away inside. Then it comes out and
you have to deal with it because there it is in your face. Should
I laugh or cry? I insert my key in the lock. Automatically, I've
been holding it in readiness all the way from the corner. I let
myself in and close the deadbolt, then hang my bag and damp
suede jacket on the hook by the door. Coffee would help. A
thick, oily brew sits on the stove, left over from morning. I
turn the electric on under the metal pot, then totter into the
front room and collapse on the couch, careful to avoid the
spring that has popped through the upholstery. My high-heeled
pumps clunk one by one onto the wood floor. It is heaven to
be home early and have some quiet. The boys will come in and
turn on the television. Will I have the energy to tell them to
turn it off until their homework is done? I'm drifting off into a
sweet, still, dreamy space, floating there, when an indignant
yell claims me back.

"Mom, you burned the coffeepot!"

"Put hot water in it!" I've done it so often the bottom has
worn thin. At work there is a nice glass coffeemaker and somehow, there, I remember to turn it off.

"Hey, Mom, I brought a friend. We want to watch TV."

Careful to pull my short, straight skirt over my knees, I sit
up, rub my eyes, and swing my feet to the floor. Then I look at
the boy standing by my son in the doorway and wish I were still
dreaming. Victor is tall for thirteen, but this boy towers over him
by a good five or six inches. An expensive designer jacket accen-
tuates his broad shoulders, and he wears a smile I don't trust. I

steel myself against the easy charm in his eyes, flashing there, appraising me. I've seen it before, I know to be careful and put up my guard. But how to tell Victor any of this? Victor saunters into the room, trying to look cool, walking that way a lot of the guys do, a way I have never seen him move before.

"Victor ..." I catch myself. I want to bring whatever gentility I can to this encounter. "What's your friend's name?"

"Rodney, ma'am. Pleased t'meet yuh." The boy has a deep voice one could be reassured by, lulled. It has the Deep South somewhere in its depths.

"Hi, Rodney. Do you live around here?"

"No ma'am. I live over the other sida the hill." He means the project, he doesn't want to say so. Neither did I when we lived there.

"You boys met at school then?"

"Sorta." Victor ducks his head away from me.

"And what does that mean, Victor?" I am learning to ask the hard questions, the ones to which I'm not sure I want the answers. At least Rodney isn't wearing blue anywhere. My mind pockets the observation, taking comfort from it. So Victor's probably just a wannabe. I've read about that in the papers. Kids who want to be in a gang but aren't. How long can that last?

"We met near the schoolground, Mom. Rodney's older. He don't go to school anymore."

"You don't have homework then, do you, Rodney, that you have to get done on time? Like Victor does?" I feel my senses sharpening. Mother fox, foxy lady, am I both in one? I really don't like the look in this boy's eyes.

"I sure don't, ma'am." He laughs. It isn't insolent. It is something else, not all that far from insolent. He turns to Victor suddenly, locking me out. "Hey, man, let's go someplace, okay? I don't want to be botherin' your family." Then, in a lower voice, "You said she wouldn't be home."

Victor scuffs his tennis shoe against the base of an armchair. "Mom, we're goin' out for a while, okay?"

"Where are you going?"

"Oh, just hang out. You know."

Do I have a choice? Could I say "No" and be obeyed? I feel

7

terribly alone. "Be back at six, Victor. I'll have dinner ready. Then you can do your homework. You'll have to miss those shows you watch in the evening."

"Hell, Mom, I don't care about those shows." The way his body turns away from me as he speaks, the twist to his mouth, the rolling of his eyes to the side—all are new, all speak of his embarrassment with every word that comes out of my mouth.

Stubborn, I persist. "What do you do, Rodney? I mean, if you're not in school. Do you work?"

"Oh, I make good money, ma'am, that I do." Rodney aims an evil grin at me. "We'll be on our way now. Nice meetin' yuh." I hear his voice faintly as they go out the front door. "She's a looker, your mom."

For a long time after they leave I stare at the stain on the wall where I threw a pot of coffee three days after Larry and the boys and I moved here. That's how long it took the losers who called themselves his friends to find Larry in his new home and come, just as before, night after night, and take him away. Tony's footsteps on the porch cut into the memory. I hear the door open and call out to him.

"Come in here, baby!"

"Hi, Mom. Who's that with Victor?"

"Are they still out there?"

"Kind of. They were sort of leaving ..." From the way Tony looks in every direction but at me, I guess they must be smoking. I hope it isn't pot. If I weren't trying to cut down, I'd light a cigarette right now.

"Tony, make some coffee, will you? Clean the pot out first. I fell asleep and it burned to the bottom again."

He throws down his bookbag and runs to the kitchen, eager as always to help. A good age, nine. A teenager is new territory. When we moved here, two years ago, I never expected to do it alone. Four months later Larry was dead. It's the good side of the hill. I held up a lot of hopes based on that. No crack houses, no dealers in doorways, a neighborhood of families living in houses with yards, most with dogs. The knot of boys at the bus stop intrudes into my thoughts, then the pile of dog shit. It has to be the Doberman. He's the biggest dog around. We haven't been broken into, though, and the house with the Doberman has. The burglars threw him meat and went right past him. I stare through the coffee stain at memories that feel more real than anything in the present. Sometimes I have the weird sense that truth comes right out of this wall and hits me between the eyes. Larry started heavy into drugs when Victor turned ten. Was it that he couldn't bear to see his own youth leaving him? To see his son become a man, because then who was he and how could he justify not being able to get a job?

"Tony, come and tell me about school when the coffee's ready. And get yourself some pop."

"I'll have orange juice, okay?"

"Sure. We've got enough. I go to the store tomorrow." Saturday. When I was a kid Saturday was a happy day. All the kids on the reservation ran around in packs and felt free to go to any house to use the bathroom or ask for something to eat or drink. Most everybody was related, or close to it. Now I've come to fear Saturdays. Sundays, too. All that free time and kids ... Wanting to shut off my mind, I switch on the television, then click it off. We should talk, Tony and I. He loves it when I take time to listen. Somehow I have to find the secret to keeping the lines between us open. I remember sitting in the lap of my father's mother, Ferntree. You could tell her anything and she would smile or grow sad with you, but never pass judgment. Maybe if Ferntree had still been alive when I came into my teens, I could have told her about seeing my father with the blonde woman, about seeing the blonde woman lay her hands against his cheeks. It would have helped to have someone I could tell. Even though it concerned her own son, Ferntree would have listened, not judging. Why then do I, the daughter, presume to judge? I back off from that.

Victor has quit talking to me about school. In my dreams even, I worry about what goes on there, where he still has four more years, and then I wake to read in the paper worse things than I dreamed. Mainly, I can tell how it is by the change in his eyes. The hope has gone out of them. A tight ball of frustration boils up in me, thinking of the flatness in his eyes. My brother Harry was about the same age as Victor when he had the hope

9

driven out of him, too.

Tony comes in with a steaming mug of coffee and a glass of orange juice. He hands me the mug and sits down on the couch, careful not to bounce. The spring sticks up right in the middle, between us, like an old friend.

"So how was school today?"

Tony stares at the wall. Is he too thinking about his father? Larry shielded him from the drug craziness to a point that hardly seemed possible, but Tony heard and saw my rage when I threw the coffeepot.

"Tony?" I say his name gently, trying to pull him back.

"I won't be going to school that much longer, Mom, probably."

"What on earth?" I choke on the hot coffee. "What do you mean?"

"Mrs. Jorgenson told us today most Indian kids drop out by ninth grade, or even sooner." His eyes travel down the wall. "She said it's a real tragedy."

"Well, what the fuck does she know about it, the old bag!" The words burst out. I make an effort, try to grab control of thoughts bouncing off walls like a slammed ping-pong ball. "Tony, that lady is not in touch. That's kids who don't have anybody who cares about them." I search his face, trying to gauge if I am reaching him. "I mean some Indian kids do drop out of school, but it won't be you because you like school. You know how important it is to get an education, so you'll have choices of what to do with your life." Who can I point to as an example? "That man, Nighthorse, who got elected to Congress, remember?" Thank God I thought of him!

"I'll never be in Congress, Mom." Tony looks at me as if I just landed from the moon.

I take a sip of coffee, holding onto the mug with both hands, to stop them from quivering. "The point is, with an education you'll be able to do whatever you want. You'll have choices."

Tony's mouth tightens into the stubborn line that means he feels thwarted, pushed around, confused. I stare at his fine-boned, handsome profile.

"Anyway, I'm not Indian," he says. "I'm black."

Hysterical laughter threatens to break from some reservoir deep inside me and, without knowing I am going to, suddenly I am hugging him, pulling his thin body up close. He does look something like his father, though only slightly, and several shades lighter. It is Victor who looks like Larry, with his wide eyes and generous mouth and nose, and dusky black skin color. Tony's more chiseled features are those of my own father, jumped down a generation. Big Jim Jack, descendant of Canadian Indian carvers, handsome and doomed. And again I see the blonde woman, her soft, plump white hands up against Big Jim's lean brown cheekbones.

"Well, get after that homework, Tony. You show that Mrs. Jorgenson who the hell is a good student." I take my coffee to the kitchen and stand drinking it until the cup is drained; then I get out the twenty-pound bag of rice and scoop some into a saucepan. I add water and swish it around with my hand to wash it. The grains are like time running out; they are the minutes Victor is out there doing whatever he is doing with Rodney, learning whatever he is learning. I check the clock. Five-fifteen

chapter 3

After dinner, when there still is no sign of Victor, I tell Tony I'll read him another chapter of *Treasure Island* before he goes to sleep. He loves that.

"Two, Mom, read two! Please?"

I smile. "Maybe two. We'll see."

The phone rings. I answer on the second ring.

"Baby?" At the sound of the huskiness in Red's voice, something in me that has lain dormant lurches into life. My free hand smooths its way down over my left hip, sculpting the shape of it.

"Yeah, it's me. Who else?" So suddenly there is a man. I allow the rush of need for him, the wish to have him take over my body and ease away thought, push worry about Victor into some place deeper inside.

"You free tonight?"

"I guess." I smile at Tony, who is watching me steadily, soberly. "I was just going to read to Tony—maybe in an hour or two?"

"Can't he read to himself?"

"That's not the point, Red." I feel a stir of anger, but with Tony listening to every word, I am careful what I say. "I'll expect you around nine." As I hang up, I know I should be remembering something, there is something I need to be careful about, but worry over Victor has merged into the need to forget, to be with a man and forget.

I follow Tony into his room, not much bigger than a large closet but a place he can call his own. It is comforting to lie down on his bed and gaze at the walls covered with baseball posters. It feels safe and right to be here on Tony's soft bed, and for a moment I wish no man were going to intrude on us.

"Tony, honey, go take your bath. I'll rest here and wait for you."

"Okay, Mom." He pulls out *Treasure Island* from his bookshelf and lays it next to me, then scampers off, sliding in his socks on the bare wood floor of the hallway. The baseball players' familiar faces, larger than life, spin around me and close in as I drift away from thought.

Tony returns in a small rush of excitement, dressed in his Batman pajamas, thin wrists and ankles sticking out from sleeves and pantlegs that have grown too short. He needs new pajamas. I rouse myself and try not to hurry through the reading. I fight to give it my full attention. Tony always senses if I don't and elbows me in the ribs. We sit up side by side in his narrow bed, propped against pillows. Part of my mind is planning a long, hot bath, so I'll be ready by the time Red arrives. Victor can let himself in with his key. If Red and I are shut away in my bedroom, he'll go straight to his own room, or the kitchen. He knows what it means when my bedroom door is shut. But he is never out this late without my knowing where he is. I finish the last of the chapters, kiss Tony and cover him up, then head toward the front door to look out and see if Victor is coming.

"Why isn't Victor home yet?" The sleepy wisp of a voice trails me out of the room.

"I guess he's still with that Rodney."

"You don't like him, do you?"

"Rodney?"

"Yeah. You don't like him, do you, Mom?"

"No, I guess I really don't."

"Why?"

"He's too old for Victor to be hanging with. He seems trouble."

"What kind of trouble?" Tony's voice awakens, becomes anxious. I sigh.

"I'm not sure. Goodnight, Tony. I'm shutting your door now. Okay?"

"Because that man Red is coming?"

"Well, in a way, yes, so we'll have some privacy, and so we won't bother you."

"Leave it open a crack, please, Mom?"

13

"No, Tony, I'm shutting it." I run back and give him another quick kiss on the forehead. "It won't matter. You'll be asleep in a minute."

"I like it open though, best."

Feeling guilty, I shut the door behind me as quietly as I can. Then I go to the front door, unbolt it, and step out into the chilly night air. The dampness of the cement porch penetrates the thin nylon on my stockinged feet. A light rain is falling. There are no people on the sidewalk, only dark shadows between cars parked along both sides of the street. Everything seems to be happening far away. A siren fires up, then comes to an abrupt stop. Tires screech on wet pavement. For a moment I think I hear someone yelling in the distance, and I stop breathing, straining to listen, but all that comes to my ears is the moan of a far-off train whistle. A gust of wind sweeps across the porch. My sense of isolation, of removal from the scene of action, makes it hard to imagine Red striding up this walk, a big, solid man with reddish-brown hair held back in a ponytail. He once told me his mother was Welsh and his father was black and Indian and Chinese, with a wee bit of Irish. I stare into the shadows, shivering, remembering his moods, how unpredictable he can be, then shut off my mind before it travels farther down that trail. Quickly I go back in, lock the door, and escape into the luxury of a hot tub of water perfumed by bubble bath. The confrontation with Victor can wait till morning.

I am in my black, lacy nightgown with my old green chenille robe over it when I hear Red's heavy step on the porch and then his loud knocking. I hope the noise doesn't wake Tony.

chapter 4

When I get the locks unbolted and see him there, his trade-
mark red bandanna wound around the long, post-hippie tail of
hair, I feel a tightening in my groin and then a loosening all
over, a kind of giving way, a caving in to his masculinity. He
senses it, of course. He's always been tuned in to that side of
me.

"You've missed me, eh?" His grin, a little lopsided, and his
eyes, too close together, are familiar and mysterious. I feel the
excitement all the way to my toes.

"I guess you're not afraid of being mistaken for a gang member. Wearing that red bandanna." My voice comes out shaky.

He pulls my robe open, to fondle my breasts. "Nice
nightgown."

"Wait! Let's go in my room."

"Whatever you say, baby." Red strides past, towering over
me, his boots heavy on the wood floor. I follow him into the
bedroom and press my back against the door to close it firmly.
He doesn't ask about the kids.

Watching him pull off his boots and unfasten his jeans and
let them drop to the floor, I feel my throat go dry. Quickly, I
shrug out of the robe.

"Come on over here, baby. It's been too long, hasn't it?" His
voice is deep with longing, and his eyes glimmer and pierce right
into me and connect to my own desire deep down in my womb,
pulling me to him until we are belly to belly, feeling each other's
need pulse between us, and we fuse together in a timeless rhythmic thrusting, a rise and fall that builds on its own momentum
until we are both riding on it and finally we spill out into each

other, clinging onto each other until we fall away, satisfied. And I am already wanting something else.

I want to talk. A grown-up to talk to is not something I have every night of the week. I prop myself against a pillow and pull my knees up. The short, black nightgown is silky on my skin. I am glad we didn't have time to take it off. It hides the purplish bruise I got on my hip from bumping into a table edge, roaming the house on a sleepless night. Bruises on my brown skin don't last long, but I'm anxious to be free of it. Conscious of creating an effect, I shake my hair so it fans out behind me, black on the white pillow. But Red is already bringing a bottle out from the pocket of the jacket he flung over the chair next to the bed. It's not a good sign, to start drinking so early. Usually we make love again before we take our first drink, and once, the best time ever, he forgot to bring the bottle out at all and I didn't think of it either.

He takes a long swig straight from the bottle and hands it to me as he eases back into bed.

"Remember how I used to be a milk drinker?"

"Yes, I remember," I say. I tip the bottle and take a long swallow. "That's what attracted me to you. When Larry was doing more and more drugs, it felt so good to be with you then." I stop speaking, aware that the whiskey has gone straight to my head. Too late I sense the dangerous ground I tread. Larry was the bond that brought us together. Red was Larry's one friend who didn't use drugs or alcohol. And Red always stayed faithful to Larry, except for the one thing. The thing of fucking his wife. If Red gets drunk enough, he'll remember how he hates himself, and me, for that. Sex and alcohol work their effect, loosening my mind and body, and almost against my will I remember what I have blocked. I told him the last time he was here not to come back. We were both drunk, and maybe he doesn't even remember, but if he does, he must remember, too, that it wasn't the first time I said it. He left me with bruises and a black eye. The bruises I could conceal with makeup, but I had to wear sunglasses when I recovered enough to go back to work. Allen had looked sad. He understands now what these unexplained absences mean. I make up for the lapses by turning out even more perfect work, and we both slide around the subject. In my mind, too, I slide around it, trying to believe Red and I can still have nights when the drinking and the remembering won't pull us down.

Already, Red is halfway through the bottle. I take it from him and drain down as much as I can, wanting to forget the worry running through my brain, not wanting him to get ahead of me too much in the drinking. If I drink some, there's less for him, right? He never has more than the one bottle with him and I don't keep any in the house.

He takes the bottle back again and puts it to his mouth. Then he holds it off and looks at it with eyes that are no longer focused.

"That's what started me on this fucking stuff, him dying."

I feel the room go out from under me. It spins in whirling circles. Trying to clear my head, I yank on handfuls of hair. It was a mistake to drink so fast. He pushes the bottle at me.

"No. I don't want any more. Just let me be."

"Let you be?" His voice is thick and mocking. "Why would I do that?" He butts his heavy head against my throat. I move away but he is on top of me, crushing me with his entire weight, thrusting deep inside me, and I try to feel nothing until finally he rolls off.

"You're a fuckin' whore, you know that, don't you?" He grabs the bottle from the floor and finishes it in one steady, long gulp that stuns me into clarity. I want to pull on my robe and cover myself, but I hesitate to move and draw his attention. "You always were a whore. Larry never knew, poor slob. Sleepin' together right under his nose and him so zonked out he never knew."

"It wasn't under his nose. It wasn't like that."

"Oh, what was it like?" He shakes the empty bottle in my face. There is a mad, lost look in his eyes. "Huh? What was it like? You tell me that!"

"It was good for a while. I thought you were my salvation."

"Well, we sure as hell weren't Larry's salvation. Were we?" He thrusts his face closer. "Were we?"

"Nobody could have been, Red." I force gentleness into my voice, to try to calm him.

17

He begins to cry. There is a whole predictable series of reactions that will follow. How could I forget? Did I need a man that much?

He burrows his head into his hands, sobbing. "He was my friend. How could we do that to him? It was one time in my life I felt good about myself, helpin' him kick drugs."

I sit next to him, rigid, the nightgown pulled tight around my knees. There is no room for my own feelings. My mind tells me that as I wait for him to pass through the stages. His face emerges, his eyes bleary, his mouth twisted.

"It's you! You were his wife. How could you let me sleep with you?" His eyes circle the room. He picks up the bottle.

"Bitch!" Red yells the word. "How could you?" He throws the bottle and it crashes into the lamp. Glass explodes with a popping sound.

"I'm going to sleep." I say it low and quiet, in the silence that follows. "You try to sleep, too, Red." Sometimes that works. I turn over and bury my head in the pillow. I hear him crying. He won't hit me now. I am safe from that. If he's crying, it means the danger has subsided. My heart is pounding. I am glad to have something to focus on: the fear of my heart beating out of control, something to live through other than the past. Then, in one unguarded instant, I feel anger at myself so intense I imagine it driving me from the bed and over to the broken glass to clench it in my hands, to puncture my wrists and see blood spurt out. Another image comes, of Tony in the morning, walking in and finding my body in a pool of thickening blood. I roll out of bed. It takes a moment to find my robe and pull it tight around me and tie the sash. I go to the wall switch and flick on the overhead light.

From the doorway, I speak to him. "Red, I'm going to lock myself in the bathroom and when I come back, you be out of here." My voice surprises me with its calmness.

In the bathroom I stand swaying at the sink, unsteady on cold, bare feet. Irony washes over me with a wave of nausea. He'll be gone, because he's gotten what he wanted.

It is a relief to cleanse myself and wash my hands and face and brush my teeth. I avoid looking in the mirror. Finally I come

18

out and check to be sure the house is empty of Red. Then I lock the front door behind him, sweep up the broken glass, and pour it from the dustpan into the garbage. All these things I do very carefully, with the deliberateness of intoxication, not allowing thoughts to pass through my mind. I lie down, staying on my side of the bed, facing away from the lingering male smell of him, and pull the covers up high.

chapter 5

The sun streaming through the window promises a wonderful day, but I've felt that before. First thoughts, filtering through, as I awaken from sleep like the dead. This terrible optimism pops up every morning, like what? Toast in a toaster? Morning glories opening ever-innocent faces? More like them, the morning glories, ready and waiting, expectant as brides, for whatever blows may befall them. I lie quiet in the bed, glad to be alone here. Ecstatic, even. I sent him home in the middle of the night. I felt the power that sometimes comes, but rarely. And here I am now with morning sun flooding in. Can this be Seattle? And what is the pull at the edge of my consciousness?

Victor. My mind suddenly clouds over. A sour taste lingers in my mouth, the cheap whiskey Red brought. I remembered to throw him out but forgot my boy wasn't home. How can I be a mother and forget my kid? Did he even have a key with him? He went out with Rodney, Rodney the rod; I stop myself, then let my mind, still groggy from whiskey, finish the thought in an image of Rodney. Can't worry about all this, can I? I breathe in and exhale slowly, then roll over and out of the bed. I slip into the worn chenille robe and pad down the hall, wondering why I can't feel with my bare feet whether my child is there in his room, sleeping, or out on the streets. I open his door and see the empty bed, unnaturally neat, unslept-in, and only then do I know how every muscle in my body aches for him to be there.

"I've been lucky too many times." I say it aloud. "It's gone to my head. This could kill us." I feel it now, in the bare bones of my feet, that my son is on the streets.

I am scoring zero in the quest for peace. I pass Tony's room. His thin voice drifts out to me like a bell on a clear morning.

"Are we having pancakes, Mom? It's Saturday."

Is it really Saturday? Well, thank God. At least I don't have to go to work. I have to stop this kind of thing, don't I? So far, most of the time, I've made it in to work, and on time, too, defying all stereotypes. I smile. There it is again, the terrible, irrational optimism.

"And sausages? Are we having sausages?"

"We're having pancakes, honey. No sausage."

"Why not?"

"Come on out here, why don't you, so we don't have to yell." It hurts my head to raise my voice. I put coffee on and get out the box of pancake mix. Where can he be? There's no one out there who cares about him, no one who would take him in. It's not like it was for me, growing up on the rez, where there was always the safety net of relatives and neighbors. Rising up on my toes, I reach into the back of the cabinet for the pack of cigarettes hidden behind the plates. I finger one out and rummage in the junk drawer for a book of matches. When I turn around, inhaling deeply, Tony is sitting on a chair at the kitchen table.

"I didn't hear you come in!" I say it on the exhale.

"I'm quiet. Like Victor. He says you never hear him come in."

I pour mix into a bowl and add water. My throat is unbearably dry. I hold a glass under the faucet, fill it to the brim, and drink it down in gulps. In a series of quick puffs I finish the cigarette and grind it out in the sink.

"Is Victor still sleeping?" Tony asks.

"No."

"Well, where is he then?"

"Tony, look, we'll have the pancakes, real quick, okay? Then we'll get dressed, and then ..." I stop.

"Then what, Mom? Where's Victor?"

"I'm not sure. He's ... out with Rodney, I think."

"But it's morning." Tony's face is puzzled, innocent. There's really no way to keep it like that much longer, is there? Unless it is like my optimism.

"Yes," I say, "and I'm angry with him about that, about staying out like that." Is it best to be honest, all the time? I throw blobs of batter in the skillet and sink into a chair across from

21

Tony. "I'm scared," I say. "I'm much more scared than angry." I stare at the table, the scratched, scarred wood of it. It has become like my mother's table at home.

"We're going home." I don't know I've said the words aloud until Tony answers.

"We *are* home, Mom. This is home." His laugh is uncertain.

"We're packing, Tony." I get up and flip the pancakes. "After we eat we're packing, you and I. Pack everything you wear often and everything you like to have near you. Bring a whole bunch of everything."

"But where are we going?"

"I'll tell you when Victor gets here. He'll get here while we're packing, I know he will. If he doesn't ..."

"What, Mom?"

"We'll go look for him."

"Where? Where will we look?"

"Where does Rodney live, do you know which house it is in the project? Did Victor ever show you?"

"Yeah, but I think some nights Rodney stays somewhere else."

"What do you mean?" Fear hangs around me like fog that will close in if I don't keep purposeful and active. I fork pancakes onto Tony's plate.

"Maybe he's at that crack house."

I'm going crazy. I sit down and feel myself sink down deeper and deeper, as if I were falling into a hole. It takes a moment before I can speak. "What is a crack house, Tony? You don't even know, do you?"

"It's where they smoke dope."

chapter 6

Location is everything. Why are those words zinging in lunatic circles in my head? The project has the feel I remember, of humanity packed together in close quarters, each unit maintaining a degree of separateness, and a powder-keg quality to the whole of it. A mother, standing at a stove with a spatula, swivels her head to watch us pass. In other windows, where curtains are drawn back, the only light is the flicker of a television screen. I whisper to Tony to tell me which building is Rodney's. They all look alike, of course, and of course he knows which one it is, I have stopped being surprised at what he knows.

Like the others, this building has four apartments downstairs and four above, with a narrow porch running the length of the top level. A tall, very skinny black woman in a long red housecoat strides out onto the porch while we are staring at the building and stares back at us, comes out just to do that, with her hands on her hips and her eyes blazing. I turn away, grab Tony's hand, and wheel him around with me. I hadn't known it would be this hard to ask where my son is on a Saturday morning. The woman calls out as we start to walk off with quick steps, our backs stiff.

"Hey! You Victor's mom?"

I pivot, as if the deep voice has jerked me on a string, like a puppet. I nod my head.

When the woman smiles, white teeth gleam in the darkness of her face, and gentleness comes into her eyes. "He's a nice boy, your Victor."

"I know," I say.

"You lookin' for him?"

"Yes. I was hoping he might be here?"

"No. No, he isn't. I'm real sorry."

I keep my eyes on the woman's face. I want Victor to be here, in someone's home, eating breakfast. My mind needs a moment to give up that hope. The woman shrugs her thin shoulders.

"My boy don't come home much anymore," the woman says.

"I'm sorry." I turn and walk away, still gripping Tony's hand. More than anything, I want to be sitting at my kitchen table with a cup of hot coffee and a cigarette. I let go of Tony's hand and zip my black fleece pullover against the breeze, then crouch down to snap Tony's parka closed at the neck. Part of my mind sorts through words, feelings, ways to reach him. The fastening of snaps and zippers is a comforting delay. I linger over the familiarity of it and remain kneeling in front of Tony's trusting, bundled-up form to ask what I have to ask. I struggle to sound calm. "Come on, honey. Show me where the crack house is."

"Aw, Mom. Victor said I wasn't s'posed to tell." Tony turns pleading eyes to me.

What can I say to make him understand? Slowly, I straighten up. "Victor could be shooting drugs, Tony. He could overdose. He could die." And then, "You don't know what I'm talking about, do you?"

"Yes, I do." Tony looks up at me, his eyes anxious for respect for what he knows or anxious about Victor—I'm not sure which.

"I know all about shooting. I seen them do it once at our house."

I fight panic, try to keep it out of my voice. "When was that? When, Tony?"

"I wasn't s'posed to tell." He is shamefaced now, no doubt picturing Victor calling him a big butthead baby, or worse. Well, Victor can call Tony anything he wants. Just let him be safe. He can call him a ring-tailed son of a jackrabbit. Larry talking now. Is my whole life going to pass before my eyes?

"I can't talk about it, Mom. He'll kill me." He peers up at me with round eyes.

"Look. All I ask is for you to take me to the crack house, all right? All right, Tony?"

His eyes change focus, direct themselves inward.

24

"Are you scared?"

He nods, reluctantly.

"Look, just take me there. I'm too worn out with this to talk to you. I have to get Victor out of here, before he gets too—We'll never get him out unless we—" No more words are needed. I see from Tony's wide, listening eyes that he is caving in to my desperation.

"Okay, Mom. I'll show you. It's just up the hill. A few blocks up from Rainier. It's on our way home." Now he looks proud of himself, probably for knowing so much more than I do. But when we reach the house with boarded-up windows, both of us out of breath from several blocks of fast walking and then hurrying up the hill, Tony hangs back.

"I don't want to go in, Mom. He'll blame me for everything."

"Tony." I kneel in front of him, my blue jeans pulled taut against my thighs. I look straight into his eyes, shimmering dark pools of trust. "I don't want to see Victor die." I grasp his shoulders. "We'll work everything else out later. Right now we have to rescue him, even if we have to drag him out screaming and kicking."

Tony's forehead creases in a frown. "That's what he'll do, Mom."

"No more talking," I say. "We're going in! Just like the L.A. cops."

I look up the steep flight of steps and then higher, to the sky, a neutral expanse of bluish gray in which a pale morning sun glows behind scattering clouds, promising a good, warm day to come. And suddenly, beside me, there is a tree. Offering itself! A response to the mute plea I have thrown to the sky. It stands at the foot of the steps, growing straight and solid out of roots deep under the sidewalk. I place the palms of my hands against the rough bark, and the tree responds to my touch with the pulse of a living thing. I lay my forehead against it and pray to the tree's spirit to lend me its strength. Where does it come from, this impulse to pray, falling out of a blue-gray sky with clouds scudding away?

"I'll go in alone," I say. "You stay here. Don't talk to anybody. Don't move." Tony locks eyes with me and I feel my power, the tree's power, going into him, a good, clean surge of power from deep inside the earth. His eyes say yes, without blinking.

I run up the steps and knock. The door rattles, as though not firmly closed. A muffled sound comes from inside. I push the door. It swings open and I step in. The room is lit by one very dim electric bulb in the ceiling. I see a syringe on a formica table, and a long-handled spoon. A man and a girl sit slumped at the table. The man raises unfocused eyes and blinks rapidly against the shock of daylight from the momentarily open door. Someone is asleep, or passed out, on a mattress. Bottles lie in a corner, some of them broken. The sickly sweet smell of the room invades my nostrils, my hair, my pores. The air is thick and heavy, permeated with smoke and alcohol. One smell, stronger than the others, separates out and dominates. I gag and put a hand to my throat. Someone has vomited.

"Hey, chick, come over here." It is the man sitting at the table who speaks. Pimples dot his unnaturally white face. It makes me feel sick again, just to look at him. The redheaded girl who is slumped over at the table nods her head uncontrollably on bony shoulders. Her ribs show through an unclean undershirt. The veins on her arms are bruised. For a brief moment, her glazed blue eyes meet mine.

"Rodney!" the boy calls out. He is very young, maybe nineteen. "Come look what we got here for yuh." An awful smile appears among the pimples. "You gonna like this one."

Rodney appears in the doorway, wearing jeans that gape open at the crotch, and nothing else. Slowly he zips up his fly. "Shut up, Paul," he says, his eyes on me. "Shut up, asshole. You wouldn't know yours if it ran around in circles and did cartwheels." Paul's smile disappears.

"I want Victor," I say, willing my voice not to tremble.

Rodney feigns disgust. "You can have the little shit. Hell, who'd want him? He puked all over me last night." He whips around and yells into the room behind him. "Get your ass out here, Washington!" Behind Rodney appears Victor, wavering on his feet. Victor's eyes light on me, then roll away. I stretch out my arms but the rest of me doesn't move. Rodney reaches back, grabs hold of Victor, and heaves him toward me.

26

"Here he is, your little pukin' baby. Tell 'im to come back when he's a man."

I take a step forward and catch Victor before he falls. He leans on me and I help him toward the door.

"Man, I wanted her," Paul moans.

"Asshole, you can't do anything with 'em when you get 'em," Rodney snickers. Then he pushes past me, moving in quick strides to the door. Horrified, I see Tony's face peering in through the crack. When Rodney swings the door fully open, Tony stands there, his eyes on his brother.

"What's the matter with you, Victor?" Tony's clear voice pipes into the squalid room. I feel myself straining to be gone from here, to breathe the air outdoors. But Rodney thrusts his thick, muscled arm across the doorway, and now I see the knife blade gleaming in his hand, like an extension of it. He lowers the blade slowly, tauntingly, until it rests against Tony's throat. His eyes dart to me.

"You don't want to report this house, do you?" he asks. He grins and glances at Tony, then slides the knife back and forth against my child's throat, so close that Tony's head rears back and away by reflex. "You really don't want to report this house, do you?" Rodney shakes his head from side to side, laughing softly. Suddenly, like a knife thrust, his expression changes. He lunges at me, snarling, "Get the hell away from here."

When the three of us are back on the sidewalk, I try to keep hold of Victor's arm, but he shakes me off.

"You don't look so good, Victor."

There is a gray, almost greenish cast to his dark caramel skin. He trudges ahead of me and Tony and then slows down.

"I just want to go home and sleep," he calls back.

"You can sleep in the car."

"In the *car*?"

"We're getting out of here, Victor. I don't know where we'll end up, but we're going to your Grandma Ada's." I feel my body tighten. Like a windup toy. If I'm wound up tight enough, I won't keep seeing the knife.

"Huh," Victor says.

27

"What?" I brace myself for the outpouring of objections, for refusal.

"I didn't say anything. Just leave me alone, will you?"

He isn't going to resist. Something loosens deep inside me, and I begin to breathe. I feel the sun warming us and the wonder of being here, alive and together. Things could be a lot worse! The thought makes me smile. Tony seizes my hand and does a little skip step. He feels it, too, the release, the tension easing away.

"We'll have hot dogs before we go," I say. "I've got some in the house, mustard and pickles too."

"Ugh." Victor doubles over, groaning.

I laugh. "You can sip a 7-Up. And have a cracker. Like when I was pregnant. I remember that's all I could get down."

He looks at me over his shoulder. "You felt like this?"

"Yeah, I felt about the way you do now. All green at the edges and kinda fragile." No need to add that I felt almost as bad when I woke up this morning. It seems a long way off. "We'll make a bed for you in the backseat, okay? Would you like that?"

"Why are you being nice to me, Mom? Rodney said ..." Victor stops, looking as if he's said something he hadn't meant to say.

"What did Rodney say?"

He jerks his head away and looks at the ground.

"Something about me, right?" I see that I'm right by the listening tilt of his head. "Rodney doesn't know me, Victor. He just knows people who are trying to escape—"

He whirls on me. "What the hell is so great about you, Mom? That guy comes over and you get drunk and he beats you up. Do you think I don't know what it means when you wear sunglasses in the house? Do you think I'm a stupid little kid?"

The will to keep going oozes out of me with a suddenness that leaves me dazed. I am tempted to lie down on the sidewalk, to quit right here and now. I don't know what to say in answer to Victor. Flashes of me and Red pass through my mind and I squeeze my eyes shut against them. I've been fooling myself, believing I was making a life for my boys here. The neighborhood appears to me now like a minefield. Which houses are crack houses? Tony lets go of my hand. I feel my arms hang at my sides as I force myself to put one foot in front of the other and keep walking.

"Victor, I know I'm the mother. I don't always act like it, but I'm trying." Why is it so damned hard to get the words out? "I make a lot of mistakes, I know. I ..." I start to say I'm not that old myself, but I stop. To him thirty-two is old. We are at our house now. It looks unfamiliar, as though in our absence it has lost whatever made it seem like home. I turn my back on it and sit on the porch step.

"He was here last night, Victor, and I sent him away. I know I've done that before. What's different ..." For one thing, the plot of dirt in front of me. The daffodils have bloomed again, from the bulbs I put in when we first moved here, with Larry. The yellow petals mock me with the hope I had when planting them.

"What's different is we're getting out of here. When he calls, we won't be here. And the only good thing we'll miss out on is those daffodils."

Victor opens his mouth. I cut him off. "We're going home."

His eyes, sullen and questioning, fasten on me. "You told me she never would accept Dad 'cause he was black. You said you'd never go back there."

I take time to breathe in and out slowly, until more words can come. "I've been away too long, Victor. Maybe ... maybe I need to give it another chance." I see grudging understanding in his eyes. Once in a long while, Victor lets his intelligence show, and now it shines out of the gold-flecked brown eyes.

"Come to me, baby," I plead. "Don't let's hurt each other all the time. Sometimes let's rest and let ourselves love." Both boys move into my arms. We huddle together there on the front steps. I feel warmth coming from the boys and from myself, flowing among us and merging us into one. Victor's head, with its soft, nappy-textured hair growing out evenly all around the crown, nestles in my lap and I lay a hand on it, awed that God, or the tree spirit, has brought us to this point.

chapter 7

Deep-drawn lioness energy buoys me up as I move through the steps of feeding my cubs. I've changed from tennis shoes to moccasins—my one lone pair, worn thin at the soles—the better to feel the earth under my feet as I prepare for flight. Fourteen years old, these moccasins; as old as my older son, counting his time inside; as old as my absence from my mother. A voice taunts me, skittering around my mind like the drops of water that crackle on the oil in the pan where the hot dogs fry. *Rodney is the lion, not you,* the skittering voice taunts. *He lurks in that den he defied you to disclose, warning you with his claw at your baby's throat. It can't be this easy, can it, to get away from a lion?*

Why do my thoughts fly to the library book in my desk drawer at work? A symbol of things undone. But escapes don't work unless you cast aside your belongings as you run. I remember a movie, a French family of Jews fleeing the Nazis, dropping their suitcases as they ran toward a fence, a border that meant safety. Allen, a Jew, should understand that.

The three of us have gravitated to our small living room, I drawn by Victor and his silence I don't know how to interpret, Tony drawn by me and Victor.

Tony stands in the doorway and swallows his last bite of hot dog. He looks like a puzzled little angel. "Mama, why did Red call you bitch last night?" There is mustard on his upper lip. "Why did you let him?"

Victor, sprawled out on the couch, lowers the *Rolling Stone* magazine he has been using to cover his face, enough to watch my reaction.

I twist a strand of hair around my finger, thinking that reprieves never last long. I have been sitting in the armchair just to be near Victor, not trusting the miracle yet, afraid to have him out of my sight.

"There's no answer I can give to that, is there?"

"Did you mean it when you said we won't be here next time he calls?"

"No!" Victor's voice cuts in. "She never means anything she says. She's the queen of broken New Year's resolutions."

I feel my body stiffen. He's afraid to believe in me. That's why he socks it to me, knocks the wind out of me. What I have to do is keep throwing the ball back.

"I told you. Just now in the kitchen. We're not going to be here to find out if he calls or comes over or what. We're going to be at my mother's."

"Are we going to live there, Mama?"

Victor regards us over the top of his magazine. "Huh! What makes you think she'll go for that?"

"If we just show up at her door, it'll be fine. We'll take it from there." I wonder if this could possibly turn out to be true.

"Get your black ass outa here, that's what she'll say."

I am up and across the space between us and in his face like a bullet. "Did she ever talk to you that way? Tell me that! Did she?"

He leans away from me. "She's never even seen me, Mom." His eyes tell me how crazy I look. "It's what you said she told Dad."

With an effort, I don't let my gaze waver. "Get some clothes together, Victor. Enough changes for a week, that ought to hold us."

"A week?"

"Mom hangs everything outside to dry. And I'm sure she hasn't changed. Ada's a stubborn lady." I feel the same stubbornness rise in myself. "Get going, both of you! We're outa here in an hour."

"Is the car workin'? Did what's-his-face, your boyfriend, fix it?"

"If it's not, we can take a bus." That way it'd be harder for Ada to send us away. But the car is working. The last time I tried it, the engine started, for no reason I could figure out. A self-cure. I go into the kitchen and wash the hot dog pan and the dishes from Tony's breakfast. There is one pickle left. I put the pickle jar and the mustard in the nearly empty refrigerator and wipe the counters clean. Passing through the hall on my way to pack, I hear them in Tony's room, talking.

"She lives on a *reservation?*"

"She sure as hell does. So wear your feathers, kiddo."

Amazingly, Victor sounds cheerful. If I move fast enough, maybe I really can get him away in time. Later I can figure out what to do next. If only I didn't feel like a woman groping her way out of a dark cave.

Tony pops his head around the doorway. "Does she live alone, Mama?"

"I'm not sure. When I left, your uncle was there."

"Who's that? Who's my uncle?"

"Ronny. He's my brother."

The skittering voice in my head scratches on, taunting. It isn't going to be easy to run away from trouble. I feel a headache gathering behind my right eye. Ronny had been drinking back then. If luck is with us, he will have moved on. That's more likely than him stopping drinking. My brother Harry was the steady one. Not brilliant, like Ronny, but steady. Where is Harry now? Is he still steady?

Victor's head appears above Tony's. "What about your job?"

"I'll call when I get there."

How much more will Allen take? There has to be a limit to how many absences he will excuse just because I'm the best secretary he's ever had. But do I want to be a secretary forever? I once dreamed of being an actress or a poet, and something in me still yearns to vent the mass of feelings dammed up inside. To not be surrounded by piles of other people's paperwork. I go to the bathroom medicine cabinet and take three aspirin from the bottle, then gulp them down with a handful of water from the tap.

chapter 8

"Mom."

"What?" I've been looking at the road so long I've stopped seeing it, and am focusing only on my thoughts. Victor's voice jolts me out of a replay of the one time Larry and my mother met.

"You're running away, you know."

"Of course I'm running away." I feel Victor's eyes on me, studying my face. At the last minute he insisted on sitting in front. It is Tony who is asleep in the nest of blankets in the backseat.

"So long as you know that, I guess it's okay." His voice is full of doubt.

"Victor, we've never gone anywhere. Do you realize what that means?" What does it mean? Why were those the words that came out? Probably they rose straight from the exhilarated rebellion I feel, out here on the open road with a huge pale shimmering sky above us, and our three suitcases packed full and stored in the trunk.

"Well, where's there to go?"

"People move. They make changes."

"We moved. It was hardly even two years ago."

"We moved eleven blocks, Victor."

"Yeah, and it's nicer there. Sorta."

"Sorta. Sorta *was* nicer there. Like, past tense might be more true?"

"Gosh, Mom, what's with you?"

"I'm young, Victor. Me! I'm a person. I want a life for you and Tony that's more than shooting up and killing yourself, but I want a life, too. I even want to have fun."

"Yeah. So what's fun for you, Mom? Having affairs with guys who beat you up?"

He won't let up. He goes right for the jugular. Do all kids know how to do that?

"Look, I've known Red since ... since before your father died. He was your father's friend."

"Oh, great. Oh, yeah. That makes it okay?"

I grip the steering wheel, both hands near the bottom where I like to hold it, wanting to regain the sense of peaceful control I felt earlier, driving in silence.

"There are things I'm not going to talk to you about, Victor."

"Secrets." He loads his voice with sarcasm.

"There are things I keep to myself, yes. So I'll *have* a self!" I throw a defiant look in his direction, but he has turned his head away.

We pass a group of scruffy, two-toned cows, black and white, and then a white farmhouse, set back from the highway in a thick cluster of trees. We are traveling northeast and are approaching the more heavily forested area I grew up in, that I haven't seen since the crazy, angry day when Larry and I took off down this same road, headed the other way, toward the city. For fourteen years I've held onto the anger and refused to drive this road. Gosh, holding onto anger that long I'll get bitter lines! I allow my face muscles to soften. I roll my head in circles to relax my neck and glance at Victor. For the first hour or so he slept, his head slumped toward his left shoulder, his right arm resting on the duffel bag in his lap, his long fingers separate and relaxed. I found comfort in the calm that spread over his features. Now his chin juts out in the familiar angle of wariness.

"What about school?" he asks.

"You can finish on the rez. You've only got two more weeks till summer."

"So this is our vacation, or what? I mean like, I'd like to know what's going on in my life."

"What's going on is you're not going to do drugs. If I have to drag you away, I will."

"I'm done with that, Mom. And don't try to turn it around so you get the credit."

I wait, not quite breathing, afraid of drawing too much hope from his words.

"Do you think last night wasn't enough for me to see what a shit Rodney is? He just gets everybody strung out so he can use 'em." Victor raises his voice. "Look at me, Mom."

I turn my head and for a long moment the intensity in Victor's eyes holds my gaze.

"I'm not a guy you can use. Or fool that easy. Rodney's out for Rodney. I thought he was such a big deal, but he's just a bully, suckering people in." I turn my eyes, full of triumph, back to the road. "Without drugs and weapons, he's nothin'." Scorn punctuates his words.

"So you figured all this out in one wild night. I guess you've got your dad's smarts." It feels good to let myself smile. "Your dad would have seen through Rodney. He'd be proud of you, Victor."

But somehow I have said the wrong thing again. Glancing sideways, I see Victor's full lips tighten, and the familiar puckering of his chin.

"Why is my dad dead? If he was so smart, why is he dead?"

Why is he dead? Why was I in bed with Red? The road looms up through questions that swirl in front of me like leaves gusting in the wind, and suddenly tiredness hits, wiping out the need to do anything but get where I'm going.

"Just let me drive, Victor. I don't have any answers." I reach deep into my jeans pocket and pull out the pack of cigarettes I've been trying not to smoke.

chapter 9

I hadn't known it would feel so much like coming home. That startles me, deep down in the pit of my stomach. It is almost dark when I pull off the highway onto the side road that leads to my mother's house. Nothing has changed. The brown sign that marks the reservation boundary sits slightly askew on its post. A drunk teenager grazed it fifteen years ago on the night of the senior prom none of us went to. Tires and washing machines sit in front yards, and rusted cars fill the spaces between the houses. It's hard to tell which are the ones people are still depending on and which ones they have junked. They drive their cars till the cars die. It is life itself. It is beautiful. In spite of my doubts, I feel my heart surge in my breast. I laugh, a low, satisfied sound.

"What's funny?" Victor asks.

"It all makes so much sense here," I say. "Do you see how everything is used right up until it's gone and yet how nothing's really ever gone? It's all still right here, so you know where you came from and where you've been. How could you forget, with the remnants of your life scattered around you like this?" Victor looks at me, his eyes wide and dark and somber, the pupils dilated, then turns to stare out the window again. Tony, when I checked a minute ago, was asleep with his mouth open, at peace, trusting wherever I take him to be the right place. But Victor leans forward, alert, his hands on his thighs.

We reach a bumpy part of the road and I slow down. Kids, out playing late, drop back into littered yards and observe us with black-eyed stares. I feel older eyes watching from the squat houses behind the kids, from lighted, uncurtained windows that seem somehow askew, under roofs carpeted with moss. I am aware of sitting up straighter, my chest and back tightening. We belong and yet we don't. To shut out the scene, I click on the radio, hear commercials blaring, and turn it off. I reach up through the thickness of my hair and rub my head with my left hand. Suddenly I am hot and uncomfortable and not ready to face my mother. We are entering the row of HUD houses where Ada lives, houses built just twenty years ago. It is the best neighborhood on the rez. Looking at the well-kept houses, I feel a surge of pride, and at the same moment am tempted to turn my old Chevy around and leave. The yards were all mud last time I was here. Now flowers and flowering bushes border the road on both sides. I pull up in front of Number Eight and switch off the engine, then listen to my heart go right on pounding. Somebody peeks out Number Eight's front window and then pulls the drapes together.

"Come on, Victor." I sigh aloud. "We'll let Tony go on sleeping." I get out and go around to Victor's side of the car and wait for him to step out. He finally emerges, but then hangs back and dawdles so that when I am at my mother's front door he is only halfway up the walk. I wait till he comes a little closer, then reach out and knock firmly three times.

The door opens slowly and Ada peers out through the crack. Then it closes abruptly. But after a moment, a moment during which I feel my hopes sink, my mother throws the door wide open and regards us with opaque eyes, taking in everything and giving away nothing. She was always good at that.

"You come home," she murmurs.

I cannot find the words I have been practicing in my head during the hours of driving.

"Yes," I say. "We've come home."

"Where's the little one?" My mother is not smiling. Her eyes have become older, she seems shorter even than I remembered, and the set, closed line of her mouth has been pulled downward.

"Tony's in the car. He's asleep."

"You bring him in, put him on my bed." Ada's small, round figure turns and disappears into the gloom of the house. No lights are on anywhere.

I run to the car and wake Tony, jostling him gently and whispering, "We're here, Tony. We're at Grandma Ada's."

"Huh?" He looks at me, his eyes full of wonder left over from sleep.

"At Grandma's. Come on, honey. We'll let you go lie on Grandma's bed."

I take him by the elbow and lead him up the walk. My mother is back at the door, waiting, ignoring Victor. As he hunches awkwardly in the shadows, a dark shadow himself, I see what my mother must see, a slightly smaller and younger Larry. Ada holds out her arms to Tony.

chapter 10

I lie quiet in the bed, warming to the gentle sounds of morning, of the household's awakening, while some part of me squeezes inward, frightened. Can we stay here? Is this peace anything we can expect to share?

The twig is bent and bent until it snaps, brittle to risk as a life or a heart. Instantly, as the lines form in my mind, I add a response. It snaps back into place. It goes on beating. I don't give up.

A bird chirps outside the screen window. I tilt my head toward the cheerful, insistent chirps and am startled to see the bird, plain as day, sitting on a branch with one bright eye cocked in my direction. I laugh aloud, delighted at this chorus. I wiggle my toes and stretch, arms flung overhead on the pillows, ankles flexing downward, and sink deeper into the comfort of the bed. This is the room I slept in as a teenager, when I was finally able to have a room of my own. The quilt over me is one my mother made. Seen through half-closed lashes, the blue and green and red pattern blurs into a rainbow of color.

How long can I lie like this? Distinctive noises emerge from the kitchen: the clink of metal coffeepot on metal stove-burner and then Ada's ancient refrigerator door banging shut. Finally the smell of strong, fresh-brewed coffee wafts through the partly open bedroom door. It is the coffee that brings me to my feet. I pull on the familiar, threadbare chenille robe, "the color of Woodbury soap," Larry once said, and tread down the hall on silent, shoeless feet. The door to my mother's room is open and I see, with a jolt, that the bed is neatly made already, a bright orange and yellow afghan folded at the foot of it.

No sign or sound of the boys yet. I have no idea where Tony is sleeping. My mother saw to him herself. I take cautious steps into the living room. Victor is a long lump of blanket on the couch. I imagine Tony, wherever he is, sleeping his deep, trusting slumber, angel lashes long on his cheeks. Victor's face cannot be seen, just his nappy head. I venture on to the kitchen doorway, and pause. If only I had a hat to throw in! The thought starts a twitch of a smile.

Instead of a hat I throw a statement, a cheerful peace offering. "The coffee smells wonderful!"

Ada doesn't reply, but pads over to the stove in her moccasins and pours coffee into a big mug she has waiting there. I start to move toward her, but she pivots and sets the mug on the table. With a thrust of her arm, she indicates I should take a seat. Then she pulls out a chair and sits across from me and comes out with it straight, like an arrow to the heart.

"Why did you take so long to come back?" There is a yearning sadness behind the bite in Ada's voice. It almost pierces the resistance I have sustained for fourteen years, and I steel myself against the impulse to yield so easily.

"You said hateful things about Larry."

Ada spreads her smooth, brown hands, with their fine, intricate web of lines, flat on the table. "Ah, we say words and then we don't know where those words will go, who will think what because of them." It comes out like a sigh, this speech from my mother.

I hear the pain. Involuntarily, I reach out a hand. It comes to rest a few inches from my mother's hands. I can't bring myself to make the contact. Ada's eyes are turned downward.

"It's a terrible thing to be as alone as I've been," she says. "You sent me a picture once, just once. I don't know why. That has kept me going and it has almost killed me."

I remember. When Tony was about one and a half, just starting to look like himself, like a boy instead of a baby, Larry took a roll of film. One of the pictures came out showing so much of my father in Tony, the coloring was only part of it, it was also the nose, the strong lean nose and chin, and then, above all, the eyes that looked out at the world so hopefully. My father never

40

lost that. The hope got clouded over sometimes, by worry or pain, but it never went away. An old memory strikes, my father at the door, with that hope in his eyes, and his hat in his hand, or am I imagining that, and my mother shutting the door on him? But it was a dream maybe. He never came back, did he, after he left us? Have I blocked that out, the way I do with all that might break through into me? Did he ever stand at the door hoping to be let back in? Like me just now! And Ada, a sphinx, yields no answers.

The photo of Tony lay on the table for weeks. Then, a few days before Christmas, I stabbed it into an envelope and sent it off. I did it recklessly, almost coldly. No. I just did it, not allowing myself time to think, knowing it belonged to Ada.

Now Ada raises her brown eyes and looks at me, and though there is just a table between us, it seems a great, unbridgeable distance. "Thank you, Katherine, for bringin' him to me. I'll try not to say more about the years."

Words boil up on a geyser of anger. "What about Victor? That's his name, you know. Not that you've asked. What about *him*?" But my mother is up from her chair and stumbling from the room and I see she stumbles because tears are blinding her. I push the mug away and let my head fall onto my fisted-up hand. Do wounds stay open forever, barely under the surface, vulnerable to a scratch? My mind records footsteps echoing down the hall and then silence, to which I listen, unable to stop hoping. For what? Returning steps? A throbbing ache circles my head. I reach into the pocket of my robe for the Pall Malls I stashed there in my hurried packing, planning for just such an emergency, as Larry did with harder stuff.

Tony's warm, soft touch alights on my arm. Where has he come from?

"Mama," he whispers. "Grandma Ada's sitting on her bed. She's crying." I take him in my arms and squeeze him close to my chest, not wanting to see his troubled face. I can feel the steady beat of his heart.

"She's glad we're here," I reassure him.

"Then why is she crying?" Tony pulls back to look at me.

I breathe in and let out a sharp burst of air. "Sometimes we hide our feelings. Sometimes they even hide from us, not letting us feel them or know they're there." His listening eyes are full of worry. "Oh, Tony!" I hug him again, hard. "Maybe it won't be like that for you."

"It's been like that for you?" I hear in his voice the effort to understand.

"Yes, since before you were born. We're gonna change all that!" I realize suddenly that it is true. We have taken the crucial steps and now we are here, the hardest part of the journey in a sense behind us. Except that ... my mother has not spoken to Victor; she has looked past him, through him, beyond him.

Tony lays a warm hand up against my cheek. "What's the matter, Mama?"

"It's all right, Tony, we've started on a good journey, here to Grandma's house. We just need ..." What? What do we need? "We need to keep going on this path."

"I don't want to keep going! I want to stay right here! I want to sleep in the nest Grandma made for me on the floor, next to her window!"

"We're not going anywhere," I say, my mouth easing into a smile. "Not right now, anyway." I place a hand on each side of him, around the small ribs.

"I'll go see if Grandma wants me there with her." Tony squirms out of my grasp and I stare after him, stunned by the pure goodness of his nine years.

chapter 11

I stretch my arms and legs under the light bedcovers and look down at the bumps my breasts make beneath the sheet and thin blanket. A warm breeze floats in from the window I left wide open all night. No one locks doors or windows on the rez! The thought nestles in my mind, tickling some deep satisfied part of myself. The child in me feels safe here, with the sun streaming in, making patterns on the wall. Already we've established a routine, or at least Ada and Tony have. Earlier I heard sounds from the kitchen, Ada getting pots and pans out, banging them around even more than seemed necessary, then plodding down the short hallway in her tennis shoes to waken Tony and finally, after murmurings of conversation while they ate, the door softly closing behind them. Not so softly, a firm, closing sound, leaving me and Victor behind. Then I heard them on the front walk, and next their footsteps crunching on the gravel, off to the tribal center again. Yesterday I dragged out of Ada the information that she recently retired from her job in tribal accounting and now goes in every morning as a volunteer and helps cook lunch for the elders. Tony has become her assistant.

I push down the nagging thought that sooner or later I have to have a conversation with Allen. Two days ago I left a message on his machine that I would be out for a week or two, maybe more, because something—and here I hesitated—something important had come up. "How can you call your boss on a Sunday, you have his home number?" Ada eyed me with her look that questions the very core of me, and I let it pass, but then she pushed too far. "School is out already for kids here," she said. "I'll sign Tony up for the tribe's summer program." "If anybody signs my two boys up for anything, it'll be me!" I blurted out the words and glared at her until she said, "Suit yourself." The phrase resounds in my mind, louder than a small victory.

I stir under the covers, the sheet warm against my skin, and suddenly I spring from the bed and out into the hallway, darting naked into the bathroom. My cosmetic bag sits on the toilet tank. I draw out the bottle of red polish and plant my foot on the toilet seat, then carefully paint each toenail. I haven't done this since the early years with Larry.

The red polish on my ten toenails gives me a finished, complete feeling. Back in my room I stand in front of the mirrored maple vanity my father brought home when I was about to turn thirteen. He mended the broken legs and made it look almost new. I put on a black net bra and a scoop-necked sleeveless top, my favorite green one, and panties and white shorts, then grab my book and go out in search of a lawn chair. Ada must have one somewhere. The weather has turned hot overnight and I feel myself opening up to its influence. Yesterday was cool and cloudy and I sat in the backyard under a tree, wrapped in a sweater, and read and snoozed the day away.

My eye had been caught by my father's worn volumes, lining the two shelves he built on one of the living room walls, high, so as not to take up valuable space. I had to stand on a chair to read the titles. It was philosophers and the Victorians who interested him, with Charles Dickens consuming half a shelf. My feet steady on the chair, I lifted out *Pride and Prejudice* and quickly absorbed the last three pages. No real surprises at the end. Just a typically moral, Victorian, happy wrap-up. Then I pulled from the shelf Jane Austen's *Emma*, its pages yellow and parchment-fragile as an old white woman's skin. It is in my hand now. A mental image of the unreturned library copy of *Pride and Prejudice* in my drawer at work flickers past. Am I going to think about that damned book every day? It is hard to imagine my father leaving his books behind. Did he think he was coming back? Wanting to escape from too much thinking, I run lightly on bare feet past Victor asleep on the couch, then through the

44

kitchen and out the back door, desperately eager to be outside and let the sun burn away worry and thought. On the back porch, I sort through layers of junk and find a long folding chair stacked behind a pile of old windows. Why on earth is Ada storing old windows? They look like they might be from the rickety house we lived in before this one, with its two tiny bedrooms. The five of us moved out of it when I was twelve, way too old to be sleeping with my brothers. It surprises me to see that Ada does have a dryer, after all. Its cord passes through a small hole leading to the kitchen. The dryer somehow lends reality to the fourteen years that have passed. On top of it sits a portable television with its screen smashed, as if by a fist pounded into it. Ronny's? Ada has not seen fit to replace it. There is no television in the house.

Back in the kitchen, the chair tucked under my arm and *Emma* in hand, I see that Ada left a stack of pancakes on a plate, with a napkin over them. I peel a pancake off the top and munch on it hungrily. It tastes good and crunchy, full of nuts and chopped apples. Standing barefoot on the cool linoleum, I eat another one and another, then draw the line. I won't look good in shorts if I keep this up. But there is a hunger in me that is driving, insatiable. I carry the chair out to the front yard, set it up next to Ada's patch of tomato plants, and stretch myself in the chair full-length, flexing my toes and fingers, loving the growing warmth of the sun on my face. I could stay here forever.

I awaken to clinking sounds nearby, but I keep my eyes closed, not wanting to lose the bliss of dozing with sun on my face. Somewhere in the back of my mind is worry over Victor. Does he sleep later and later to escape this new unknown I have hurled us into? It dawns on me that I am doing the same thing. When my eyes drift open, I see a tall, strongly built young man bent over a rake, doing something to the rows of daisies Ada has planted near the house. He is wearing a shirt, but the muscles of his arms and shoulders are clearly visible under it. As I watch, he slowly undoes the buttons and throws the shirt onto the grass. Only then do I see his eyes glint sideways and know he is doing this for me.

I sit up and put my feet on the grass, in the prickly softness of it. That is his cue.

"You been havin' a nice nap?" His tone surprises me. It is confident, assertively male, and in some way suggestive. I press my lips together and look steadily at him, trying to keep my eyes on his face and not on the smooth brown chest. He comes closer and stabs the rake into the ground, resting one hand on it. The hand is large and smooth and well formed. It doesn't look like he does this kind of work often.

"You must be Katherine."

I don't know what to say. Nothing seems quite right about this encounter. Instead of the solitude I expected, suddenly there is a man in my face. Again. Already. I glance toward the house, to see if Victor is watching, if he is anywhere in sight. The man has longish black hair, styled. That surprises me, too. He is almost too handsome, which is one reason I can think of nothing to say.

"Well, it's gonna be a treat havin' you around," he says. "I'm Mark. I help your mother sometimes."

I find my voice. "I'm glad to hear she has help. She works all the time."

"And you like to play." He grins, twisting his mouth in a way that fascinates me. "Am I right? Mind if I sit here, too?" And then he laughs. "On the grass, I mean." I had thought he meant next to me on the chair, and moved over. The blush starts in my cheeks and travels down to my chest. He looks away and I see the long swallow go down his neck, I can almost hear it in his throat.

"You're from the city."

"Yes," I say. "But I thought I'd been away too long. I'm from here really. What about you?"

"I'm a rambler. I'm from Montana but I headed west and now I can't go much farther in that direction, can I, so here I am." He smiles, and I feel warmed and charmed by the smile but something in me flashes a warning, like a red flag at the edge of my consciousness. I run my hand through my hair, a habit to gain time, but his watching makes my hand come to a stop and rest on my neck.

"I hope you'll stay awhile," he says. "Maybe you and I can get to know each other, compare notes." His eyes crinkle up. I can tell he is used to getting his way with that smile.

My eyes are drawn back to the house by something that appears first as a confused blur of red; then my vision clears. The sun had blinded me, and when I looked into the darkness of the open doorway I hadn't realized that Victor was standing there. He is wearing jeans and a red plaid shirt I don't recognize. It must have been left behind by one of my brothers. His face is sullen.

"Mom, all the clothes are dirty! You haven't done any washing." It is an accusation and I want to fling it back at him and tell him he was supposed to bring clothes for a week, but my tongue is stopped, inhibited by this man, Mark. Victor steps out into the sunshine and makes an ugly face when the sun hits him full in the eyes.

"Well, are you going to?" he asks. "Do a washing?"

"Victor, come and meet Mark," I say. "He helps your grandma around the yard and things."

Victor eyes the man suspiciously. "Hi," he finally says, giving the impression that someone is dragging the word out of him.

Mark looks at him with curiosity, the way they all do, figuring it out. "Hi, there," he says. There is distance in his tone.

"That's my oldest son." I say it defiantly, proudly, as Victor goes back in the house and bangs the screen door behind him.

"How old is he?"

"He's thirteen."

"Big kid. You must've started young, didn't you?" He doesn't ask about a daddy. Probably the word is out on that.

"Well, lady, are you gonna go in and do a washing?" There is mischief in Mark's eyes. "Or would you like to offer me a cool drink of tea? Your mama usually does."

"The tea sounds like a much better idea," I say. I feel his eyes hot on my skin as I lean forward, raise myself with my hands from the lounge chair, and walk toward the house. My whole body is burning up, and I stumble over the doorstep. It has been a long time since a man made me this awkward.

When Ada and Tony come crunching along on the gravel and turn in at the front walk, Mark is seated in the grass at my feet. He has just told me he is not only a rambler but a gambler, and we are both laughing. We stop when we catch a glimpse of Ada's face. Ada walks past us into the house, throwing a brief, disgusted look at me.

"Kitchen is for tea," she says. "What are you doin' with a chair in the front yard anyway?" She doesn't wait for an answer.

After she and Tony disappear into the house, Mark lets out a deep laugh. "She never sits in the front yard," he says. "Most people here don't." He laughs again. "Afraid somebody'll think they're lazy!"

For me, the good feelings have shriveled up. I had not meant to cause any problem. I try to fold up the chair, but can't make it come together right and Mark has to help me. I pick up the two half-full glasses of cold tea and the unopened copy of *Emma*. Mark looks at me closely. He must sense something of what I am feeling.

"Don't worry. I'll put this chair around in the back," he says. "I have to be goin' now, but I'll be seein' you." He leans into my space as he murmurs the last words, and I feel the air being sucked out of me. We have plunged right through the barricades of polite nothings people use to keep a safe distance.

I go into the house without a word. He has turned and walked away anyway, not needing or expecting another word from me. Ada glances my way as I enter the kitchen and I see her gaze fix on my red toenails and glitter with rage. I rinse out the drinking glasses, keeping an eye on her as she sits at the table with her arms resting on its scarred wood, her open palms facing each other, her back erect. Under her short, dark halo of permed hair, Ada's wide face is creased by deep lines that etch the insides of her full cheeks. I hadn't noticed the lines before.

"People will think you're drinking beer," Ada says roughly. "How do they know it's tea?" She throws the question across the room.

"Ronny drank beer." I speak without thinking. "You never said anything to him about it that I can remember." I am aware of Tony standing in the doorway.

"You are a woman." My mother fires the words, one by one. "Already they have reasons to think you are a whore, and then you paint yourself and go showin' your bare skin out in the yard."

48

It takes me a moment to grasp hold of what is most wrong about what she has said. I feel dirty and ashamed, and am bothered more by the familiarity of the feelings than by the feelings themselves. I have the sense of wading into impossibly high waves that beat me back, slapping me in the face.

"What do you mean?" I ask. "What reasons do they have already to think such a thing?"

"Huh! You know!" My mother spits the words at me, then pushes her chair back, stands, and leaves the kitchen. Tony turns pleading eyes toward me before he hurries after her. I hear the slam of my mother's bedroom door and only then realize I am trembling. "Everyone will think you are a whore, going with him." It is as though my mother has spit the words at me again, that made me take Larry's arm, all those years ago, and yell back, "Let's get out of here."

My hands clench and I feel them wanting to squeeze remorse out of her. But I know I can't. The thought intrudes and my chest thrusts out against it. My bare foot lifts off the floor, rebellious, ready to fling me down the hall to yell at Ada's door and wrench Tony away from her. I grasp the floor with my feet and inhale deep, desperate breaths. It is beyond bearing that my mother withholds love from me but extends it to Tony, to pull him away from me and bind him to her. It enters my mind to go looking for Mark, even before he comes looking for me. And at that moment Tony emerges from my mother's room and trudges down the hall. He doesn't meet my eyes. He's been sent, to relay a question.

"Can you bring Grandma Ada a glass of that iced tea? Please," he adds.

I bite hard on my lower lip to keep words from flying out. There's no point in venting on Tony my bitter thoughts. Why would Grandma want a whore to serve her tea? Why can't she make her own apologies? For that's what it is, probably. It's the closest Ada will get to one. I close my eyes and let my options, or lack of them, wash over me. I could turn tail and go back, run off again. Funny how clear I am on that one. There's no way I'm ready to give up what is here for me and my boys, in terms of sheer safety, and reenter that maelstrom. I could go search out Mark and prove my mother right on the very day she has called me a whore. No. I know myself better than that. That day will come, but at least I'll have the pride to let him chase after me and not the other way around. I sigh, turn, and stomp into the kitchen, with Tony close behind.

Tony chooses the moment I am pouring tea to grasp my arm. I steady the pitcher with my free hand.

"Mama," he says, "Grandma feels bad she talked to you that way."

"Well, it would be nice if she'd tell me that herself. Here. Take this to her."

"Aren't you going to come?"

"Tony, I've got to be by myself for a while." I'll just sit here and sulk, I almost add, and realize I am feeling better. He goes off with the tea sloshing out of the glass and I flop down into the biggest, oldest chair, the one my dad used to sit in. I could just stay here in this chair forever until she takes pity, I am thinking, when Tony appears again, in his soundless way.

"Mama?"

"What?"

"She wants to tell you something."

What could that be? I stare at him and my pity shifts from myself finally, to notice the pain on his face. He doesn't like being pulled in two directions, between people he loves.

"Okay. I'm coming." I heave myself out of the chair, feeling stubborn, weary, beaten down, all at the same time, and follow him to the door of my mother's room. Ada is sitting on the bed, the glass of tea in her hand. The double bed with its wooden frame and headboard and a small bedside table are the only furniture. There isn't room for anything else.

"The summer program already started," Ada says, in an un-accustomed tone. It takes me a moment to identify it. "I told Robert, the teacher, you'd maybe bring both boys over t'check it out in the morning." It is humility, grudgingly offered.

"Okay, Mom, I'll do that." My voice is heavy with irony, but my mother's face relaxes. Ada knows she has gone too far and is backing off. Why? I see her glance rest on Tony, her eyes full of emotion that for once she is unable to hide. She's afraid of losing him!

"You can go back and do whatever you were doin'," Ada says, dismissing me.

"I'll just do that." As I turn to leave the room, I watch Ada pause between sips of tea to warn Tony not to bounce on the bed. He has been transported into little-boy heaven. I sigh. Maybe there wasn't anything else Ada or I could have said to each other.

chapter 12

"I love that smell. It goes right deep into me." I breathe in and a fit of coughing seizes me. "Damn cigarettes."

"What is it, Mama? What's the smell?" Tony dances rings around me and Victor. He is so happy to be out in the morning with us that he can hardly contain himself.

I laugh, shaking my head. "City boy, you don't know country smells!"

"I want to be a country boy. Grandma Ada says I can stay here forever."

"Oh, she does, huh?" Victor's voice and look turn fierce. The light in Tony's eyes flickers and I put an arm around his shoulders. The warmth of the sun absorbed in his tee shirt filters into the skin of my bare forearm.

"That smell is newly cut grass and manure," I say. "That's the fresh, earthy smell. Great, isn't it?"

"I see the grass!" Tony yells. We are rounding the corner of the tribal longhouse, and a big pile of cut grass comes into view. Tony hurtles into the middle of the soft heap, landing on his stomach. He scrambles to his feet with a dazed grin. I hold him tightly by one arm and brush off blades of grass that cling to him. About fifty yards ahead, a small group is sitting in a circle at the edge of the lawn, where trimmed grass yields to wild, wheat-like growth and scrub trees.

A lithe young man rises to his feet in one smooth, graceful motion and moves toward us. His smile is contagious. It draws me to him, and I see that even Victor responds to this man. He has the fine-cut features common to many of our tribe, and his long, black hair is done up in two thin braids. He wears a white shirt and jean cutoffs and is clean and fresh-looking, as if he just stepped out from under a waterfall.

I feel the light in his deep-brown eyes pass into mine, and then something in him registers alarm, checks itself. What was that about?

"You're here to learn to survive?" He smiles so broadly that I laugh aloud. But he is hiding behind the smile, using it as a cover.

"They are, anyway," I say. "I'm the mother, I'm too old."

Suddenly he is serious. "You're not, you know. You're welcome to join in whenever you want."

"Thank you." I can tell he means it.

"I was wondering," I say, "if the boys can get credit for this class at their regular schools."

"Sure. You're the first to ask. Most kids here don't care about getting credit. But sure. They can." He grins. "I'll write a letter, tell the school how rigorous it was."

"I had to pull them out of school without warning, about two weeks before the end of the term. Victor's an eighth-grader and I want to be sure he gets into ninth next year."

The man holds out a slim, brown hand to Victor, whose hand, I notice, is bigger. "Glad to have you, Victor. I'm Sky. I go by that."

"They told me your name was Robert," I say.

"I needed a bigger name. Little guys need big names!" He is probably five feet seven, wonderfully compact. I recognize his litheness as like my own.

He switches the intensity of his attention onto Tony. "You must be Tony?" Tony extends a hand to Robert and looks away, suddenly shy. Robert's eyes come back to me and rest on my face, taking it in. I can feel he is attracted to me, I see it in his eyes, but there is resistance. Why?

"Do you want to stay a few minutes ... uh, what's your name?"

"Katherine." I smile, wanting to win him over, and wonder why it feels important to have him on my side. "Just that one name, all the time."

"I like that. Okay, come on over and meet the class. Kids, this here's Victor and his brother Tony and their mom, Katherine."

"Wow, you're a mom?" A gangly kid with red hair looks me over.

"She's a mom. Right! Don't forget it. Katherine, this here smart-aleck redhaired one is Steve. We don't know quite what to do with him. We like havin' him around though." I am impressed by the easy camaraderie Robert has with the kids, as he introduces them one by one. "Here's Angel, she's a terror. Watch out." Angel smiles a beautiful, shy smile. "And Tina, nobody puts much over on Tina." Tina, a heavyset girl with straight black hair hanging to her waist, giggles and covers her mouth with her hand. "And Jimbo, Jimbo's our main man." Jimbo stands up and dwarfs everyone with his sheer size. He is a full-blood, with a high forehead and strong nose and chin. Kindness penetrates his gruff expression. I can tell from his awkward stance that he has grown a foot or so in the last year and isn't at all used to it yet. Then Robert points to a dark, brooding, handsome boy who does not stand. "And this is Kirk. Nobody gives any nicknames to Kirk, he won't allow it!" Kirk's black eyes flick over us and linger on Victor, sizing him up. I'm not sure how to read the hardness in his expression.

"Where was I?" Robert asks. In one swift movement he is again seated cross-legged among the kids. "Let's wrap it up. This is a survival class, right? You've all heard it ends with us goin' out alone, each of us by ourselves, for three days on our own land here that belongs to all of us together. It belongs to the animals, too, and the trees. The trees have been there all these years, planted right in the earth, so it belongs to them most." His voice is mesmerizing. I thrill to his sense of belief in the words he is saying. "We'll start with survival skills you might not have thought of as such. We'll have carpentry, a lot of carpentry." He glances up at me. "They all know about your dad's carving. A master carver, he was." Robert's eyes cloud with emotion and I am struck by the depths of feeling his eyes reflect. Probably a lot of women have lost themselves in those eyes. He isn't the type I fall for, luckily. He is too much like me, I realize with surprise. He isn't a type, either. He's pretty much one of a kind, so why like me? Then his words recapture my attention. "We'll learn dancing, too, because if we forget how to dance we

54

forget how to live and we forget our ancestors' secrets. I'll have some of you fancy dancin' by the end of summer." He smiles, teeth very white, soft light glinting in his eyes. "Angel here, she can jingle dance." A blush creeps over Angel's tan skin, but she looks pleased. Robert turns toward Victor. "You ever seen jingle dancin'?" Victor smiles and shakes his head. Robert's face changes, becomes serious. "Angel learned how from her mother. She's a lucky girl to have a mother who holds to the old ways and teaches her to go on a good path." The girl lowers her eyes; I notice how pretty she is and see Victor noticing, too.

With an agile spring, Robert leaps to his feet. "Okay! Enough for today. Let's eat!"

He walks next to me up the gentle slope toward the building. "Try to get them here on time tomorrow," he says. "One thing I want them to unlearn is Indian time." He ducks his head toward me with a comical grimace.

"Sorry," I say. "I had a late night."

"Already? Thought you just got here."

Now I am blushing. Though it was only sleeplessness that kept me up. I read late into the night, disappearing into Jane Austen's world, where a woman could fall back on etiquette when all else failed.

"I'll get them here. What do I call you, anyway? Robert? Sky?"

"Which do I look like?" He stops walking and stares full into my eyes.

"Sky," I say, trying not to laugh.

"It's okay. Laugh if you want to. But I'm Sky, right? That's what I am."

He looks boyish and acts even more so, but I examine the lines of his face and detect a hardness. He's probably older than I am, maybe thirty-six.

"When did you change your name?" I ask.

"Yesterday."

"You're full of surprises, aren't you?"

"I hope so. And are you going to join the class, or did I scare you off?"

"No. I think the boys would prefer me not to."

"You're probably right. But we'll be seein' each other. I drop in on the kids and help 'em with their work at home. This kind of stuff is too hard to learn in ten lessons. Or twenty. Or whatever. Our ancestors spent their whole lives learning it."

"Robert. Sky. This will sound off the wall. I only just thought of it, but I'd like to go on the three-day thing—if I could." To be alone in the wild might be a way to reconnect with a part of myself that has been missing for a long time. I am so absorbed in the thought that for a moment I don't notice that my outpouring is greeted with silence. I lay a hand lightly on Sky's arm. "Could I do it without being in the class? What do I need to know?"

Coldness replaces the warmth in his eyes. He glances away and at the same time moves his arm from my touch. "I'm not sure you're the type to hang in there. Can you cut out the cigarettes and booze?"

Has he heard stories, or can he see telltale signs? Anger rises in me, making the muscles of my back and face rigid. "For how long?" I say the words tightly.

He looks at me with surprise and a hint of respect but still with the underlay of resentment. "At least six months," he says. "Sometimes I'm easy. Hey, you eatin' with us?"

I throw a challenging look at him. "No, I'm in training. I don't eat that fatty stuff my mother serves up when I can help it."

"Have I made you mad?"

"Not exactly. You just pressed a button for a minute."

"I know what that's like. Sorry. I guess you remind me of somebody. It's never fair but that's how it is."

"Who?"

"Maybe someday I'll tell you." His eyes avoid mine. "See you around." He turns and passes through the open door where the kids, including my own, have gone. I see Ada helping serve up plates of fried chicken and potato salad and fry bread. I wish I hadn't spoken so fast. I walk home alone, toward cottage cheese and fruit, yearning for fry bread. This Sky guy, what makes him tick? I felt we were vibrating on the same wavelength, but he showed flashes of downright antagonism. Well, of course! Ada said he's an alcohol counselor. Some nerve he's got. Mostly though, I liked him. Who could I remind him of?

chapter 13

"I need a job, Mom." I say it with my eyes fastened on Ada, to catch her reaction.

"Wally TwoDogsRunning on tribal council needs a secretary. I heard him say so."

I swallow. With that, my trial balloon went soaring skyward. I'd been afraid she might ask coldly if I didn't plan to go back to my job in the city. I'm not ready to answer that.

"Just part-time is all it would be," Ada says, as she continues putting away dishes from the rack, giving them swift swipes with the dish towel. Why doesn't she just leave them there to dry? I get up and go to help her. Why is she always working? She never sits still. It makes me feel guilty about my own love of sitting and reading and dreaming, drinking tea, just being. There's never enough time for all the dreaming I'd like to do. Lately my night dreams flow into daydreams and sometimes a poem emerges, like this morning when I awoke and reached for the pen and notebook under my bed and wrote about the woman caught in a web. The woman spins the web to protect herself, but then she sees a beautiful meadow not far away and wants to go there, only she has spun the web so tight there is no way out.

"Put those smaller bowls in the big ones," Ada instructs. "That gives me more cupboard space."

We finally get everything put away and I sit down again at the table. "That name, TwoDogsRunning—he doesn't sound like he's from around here."

"His father was from Montana, one of those tribes back there. His mother's from here. And Wally married into the Williams family." Ada is wiping out the crevices of her dish-drying rack.

She screws her mouth to one side and glances at me.

"No wonder then he's on council." It's like a comic strip. You go away for years, then come back and the characters and plot have hardly changed.

"That's about it. The Williams girl he married was in politics like her family always has been. Then she set herself up in jewelry, and now Wally represents the Williamses on council."

"What kind of man is he?"

"Oh, he can't do too much harm. He's a namby-pamby kind of fellow. Sorta soft-lookin'. Probably a little soft in the head."

"What does council pay, Mom, for clerical help?"

"Two dollars more than minimum wage. An hour!"

"That's too bad."

"What do you mean, that's too bad?" Ada's head jerks up. "It's good pay and the work's not that hard. Council's only a half-time job and sometimes they're away on tribal business. You wouldn't have much to do."

"I'd make more cocktailing. A lot more."

Ada turns her back to me and begins scrubbing away at the stainless steel sink. "No you wouldn't. Your expenses would eat it up."

"You mean clothes? Sometimes they provide the outfit, Mom."

"I've heard about those outfits. No, I mean food and rent." Ada's voice is tight. I brace myself for what I feel coming. "I ain't havin' no cocktailin' daughter live here." My mother's fists clench at her sides. One hand squeezes the sponge so hard that water runs out onto the floor. Her plump back is straight and angry.

I sigh. "When's a good time to go see this Two Dogs Running?"

* * *

I wait until Ada sets off with jars of homemade jelly she is taking to a neighbor whose husband fixed her roof last fall. Then I pick up the phone receiver and stare at it. Of course, not a push button. Lucky I'm not calling some bureaucracy but just good old Allen. I dial the number slowly, wondering if he'll answer the way I do: "Allen Schuster's legal office, may I help you?" No, he comes on with a curt, abstracted "Hello." He sounds like he's a couple of feet from the receiver. Probably he's going nuts without me there to keep things sorted out.

"Hello, Allen?"

"Katherine!" Suddenly his voice is loud in my ear, and I hear the relief, even joy, in it. I feel worse about what's running through my mind to say to him.

"Allen, I'm still here. At my mom's."

"Oh." I hear the letdown. Had he thought I was on my way over? To relieve him of these duties he's no good at?

I plunge ahead. "Allen, I don't know how to ask you this."

He cuts in: "Just go ahead and ask." I'd forgotten how he can be when he feels threatened or at a disadvantage. He likes to meet things head-on. It must have been a real challenge for him, doing little conversational dances with me these past four years. Once he told me: "You know, you're not as torn away from your culture as you think, Katherine. You have this maddening way of never telling me anything directly, especially if you think it's something I don't want to hear."

I take a breath and let it out. "See, it's this way, Allen. My mom didn't throw us out when we showed up on her doorstep. And she could have, I wouldn't have been all that surprised. And anyway, it's summer here, and—"

He sighs, and I pause.

"Go on, Katherine. I want to hear this." There is patience in his tone now.

"Well, it's safer here for the boys. Victor got into some trouble and that's why I took off." I correct myself. "That's part of why I took off. And it wasn't trouble really, well, it was, but—it's more that I knew things would get worse, though now ..." I stare out the window at a neighbor trudging down the road, pushing a wheelbarrow full of her smallest kids. Blue gardenias. For a moment I think that's what I'm looking at, in the flower bed Ada put in by the road. But that can't be. They must be bluebells. I can almost smell the gardenias, though. There's romance here, something to do with the pace, with having time to notice flowers ...

"Katherine? Are you still there?"

"Yes, I'm sorry, Allen. I guess I just need to stay here longer. That's what I need to say to you. And there's no way I can expect you to hold my job for me, because it's probably a whole summer we're talking about." I want him to know I don't expect any favors. That's only fair.

Now he is the one who is quiet on the other end. I can picture him taking off his glasses and wiping his eyes, then putting the glasses back on, having reached his decision through some process known only to him. Or maybe even he doesn't understand it.

Right on cue he says, "Look, Katherine, this is what I'll do. I'll hire some temp help for the summer. Who knows." He actually chuckles. "I may save some money. I just hope I'll get somebody with half a brain. We'll make it, though, till you get back. For one thing, there's my vacation—"

"Allen."

"What?"

"You've never taken a vacation. In four years you've never taken a day of vacation."

"Maybe you're not the only one coming to some realizations, Katherine. Anne gave me the old ultimatum. Unless I take her to Tahiti or Mexico, or Hawaii at the very least, she's walking."

"And you're going to?"

"Hard to picture a pale intellectual lying on the golden sands?"

I giggle, mostly with relief. "It's a nice picture, Allen. Just take lots of sunscreen."

"Or I'll look like a lobster with no brain?"

"I'm just so happy, Allen, the way you're reacting. I've dreaded making this call. I mean, it's not that I don't know how lucky I am to work for you, and you've put up with—"

"Cut the crap, Katherine. We'll talk when we're both a little clearer about where we're going. And meanwhile ..." I hear the slight hesitation. "Don't do anything I wouldn't do."

"You know that's asking the impossible." I say it quietly.

"Just don't go off the deep end. You're too good for that."

"I'll try to keep my head above water." As I say the words, I wonder what they mean. He's right. It's time to cut the crap.

"Keep in touch," Allen says. "Hey, what's your number there? I don't even know how to get hold of you."

I read it off the phone. It's not a number I've ever called. How odd that is. I hope it's the right number. Ada might have borrowed or bought somebody else's phone. When I say goodbye, finally, and lay the receiver in its cradle, I, too, feel the need for cradling. But there's nobody to do it. So I lie on the couch and pull a cushion, the one my mother's sister embroidered, up under my cheek. I barely remember Ada's gentle sister, who died when I was no more than three or four.

Flowered teacups line the small rack below the two long shelves of my father's books. I hadn't noticed the teacups before. My eyes always go right to the books, drawn there as if by Dad's spirit. Lying curled up on the couch, I feel as small and solemn as when I used to watch him carve. I'd sit on a little stool and try to figure out how he was turning a piece of wood into a horse, or into a totem with each face of it different and having a meaning. He used to tell me the meanings. Everything had a meaning. I'd forgotten that. "And what was the meaning of you going off and leaving us, Dad?" I murmur the words into the pillow. But as soon as they're said, the untruth of them hits me. "Mom pushed you out." I say those words aloud, too. Are they true? There is probably no way I can ever ask Ada, or expect to get a straight answer. Probably Ada herself doesn't know. And again comes the memory of my father standing at the back door, with his hat in his hand, asking with his eyes to be let back in. Or do I just wish that to be so?

chapter 14

"Katherine."

I look up from the letters I am sorting, not startled, though he expects me to be. I smelled him standing there, the leathery maleness of him, before he said anything. My eyes move up the long length of him, liking the leanness, liking the slow smile on his face, but something is nagging in my mind, a memory of a dream maybe, like a warning, though I've lost the sense of it.

"Katherine."

He has a low, stirring tone to his voice when he says my name, laying claim to me with it. I let myself go, sucked under by it, and smile.

"Oh, let's get away, Katherine. C'mon! I'll show you a place nobody knows."

"Really?" My heart skips and I do go with him, drawn by that lure of a place nobody knows, though that doesn't make sense because he'll know and then it won't be a place I can go and find solace—I'll need to find my own. But he doesn't see any of that.

"You don't need a sweater." He takes it from me and hangs it on the coat tree, laughing. "It's eighty degrees outside. High noon. Are you hungry?" He looks at me, his eyes searching deep into me.

"No," I whisper. This isn't fair. He's stealing me piece by piece, my appetite even.

He takes me by the arm, above the elbow, and I feel lightheaded in his grasp. We stroll together out of the building and as the old men sitting on the steps nod at us and smile, Mark lifts his worn Stetson an inch or two in acknowledgment.

"You're done workin' for the day, right?"

"How do you know that? I am, but how do you know?"

"I make it my business to know about you, especially about when you're free and I can have you to myself." His smile is wide and beautiful in his dark face, but still his words jar me, probing some sore spot deep within.

"How can I be free when you have me to yourself?" I manage that much aloud, but he has sucked my voice away, too, and the rest of the thought continues in my mind. How can I be free if you're making me your business? Your free and my free aren't the same free.

"You're a deep one, Katherine, you know that?" His fingers press into my arm, always claiming me, and the heat, the sun's heat and the heat rising from my flesh into his make me want to be claimed by him. I feel it rush all through me, that wanting to be claimed, and I stumble, my legs suddenly weak underneath me. He catches me, holds me up, laughs. His bent arm presses against the side of my breast. "We'll be there soon."

He knows. I feel a blush surge through my whole body.

"Where are we going?" I try to curb the runaway wildness that took hold the minute he stood, too close, leaning in, the male scent of him like an animal closing in, and myself an animal responding, rising up to follow him. It is so familiar, this feeling, since the first boy when I was fifteen, since I saw my dad ... and the click comes, shutting off thought. Rocks along the roadside pierce into the thin soles of my sandals, and the grass growing high around my legs, tickling them, makes me want to get there quickly, wherever it is we're going.

"So where are you taking me?" My voice comes out husky and he laughs, the same laugh as before.

"Do you care?"

Climbing out of a hole is what it's like. Again familiar. To pull myself out I use talk, tossing it out by the spoonful.

"Tell me about yourself, Mark. What do you do around here besides rake my mother's flower bed?"

"Whoa!" He pauses in his long stride, looks down at me, then, persuaded by my smile, responds.

"I'm just killin' time really, with jobs like that."

"So what's the big one you're waiting for?"

"Too big." He says it with smugness creeping into the edges of his mouth.

"Tell me about the something big." I say it softly, knowing he'll lean his head down close to hear.

"When it comes, you'll be the first, baby, the first one I'll tell. We'll know it when it comes, eh?"

"You from Canada?" I ask it to throw him off balance.

"Canada? Whaddaya mean?"

He can't move quickly, his mind can't. Sky would know I'm playing games. I am surprised to think of Sky when I am feeling merged into this man beside me, warmed by him right down to my toes. Go slow. Who said that? God, now I'm hearing Larry's voice. A warning from the dead, from the one man who knew how to satisfy the emotions behind my body's urgings. Before the heroin ate his mind away, he held me as steady as I'd ever been.

"Tell me about us, Mark, where it is you think we're headed." I glance up at him and he's watching me, all of me. I'm glad I left the top button of my blouse undone. I really wouldn't need to say another word, would I? But then I know what the ending would be and how quickly it would come. So when he takes hold of my upper arm again, squeezing it, claiming me, I draw a deep breath and try to claim myself back. He steers me off to the right and I see the shimmering pond, a golden haze of sun hovering over it. I must have been seven when I first started coming here with my brothers. I laugh, remembering boys from high school who brought me here, and marvel at how far gone I must be not to have known where Mark was leading me.

"What's funny, Katherine?"

"I feel good! Good to be out of that office, getting to know you, taking our time."

He senses the barrier I've thrown between us, and I hear the breath he takes, getting hold of himself, readjusting. We are alike that way. I try to distance myself.

"Do you read much?"

"Read? Me?" He grins at me.

"Yeah. Stories, newspapers, dirty books. Comics?"

"You makin' fun of me?"

"Sure, I'm making fun of you. No, Mark. I really want to know. What do you like to read? When you're by yourself and nobody's looking."

"I mostly drop off and sleep." He crinkles his eyes in the way he is so dangerously effective in using, to pull me back into the mood. "How 'bout you?"

"Toni Morrison is my favorite. But lately I've gone back to the Victorians, maybe for contrast. I'm reading Jane Austen. And I write poetry." I speak out of stubbornness, wanting him to know what he's taking on.

"Poetry, huh? Rhymes?"

"Hell's bells fell in the well. Anyone can do rhymes. Poetry's more than rhyme."

We are at the edge of the pond and he pulls me down next to him with practiced ease. "Make a poem about this," he says. "This place where we are right now." He removes his hat and lays it on the ground.

"I came here a child who ran and flew and bounced like a skipping stone."

"That's pretty." He squints out over the water and puts an arm around me, then lies back, drawing me with him. "Bet the fishing's good."

"My brothers fished here. There probably aren't any fish now."

"Why's that?"

"The dam upstream from here. Timber people built it." I don't want to think of that and have anger drive away the warm, melting sensation in my stomach.

"That's progress," Mark says. I glance over to see his expression and he is serious.

"There haven't been any fish in this pond since I was fifteen," I say.

His eyes are vulnerable, close to mine, revealing how much he wants me. "Oh? I'm sorry to hear that."

"You don't look sorry." What else changed when you were fifteen, I want him to ask.

Instead he glows brown-black eyes at me and whispers, "Katherine, you're enough of a poem for me."

I edge away from him, some self-preservation instinct flaring into life, or maybe Larry's voice calling again from the dead. "The novel I'm reading now," I say carefully, "is called *Emma*. It's about a woman trying to find her destiny as a person."

He makes his move then, and it is more subtle than I expected. He rolls over onto his side and lets his arm fall across my chest. I wait, feeling the heavy warmth of his hand on my breasts, the slight moving pressure of his fingers, and nothing happens except the pulling together inside me, the craving and wanting him to fondle me, and I wait until I can't stand it, then unbutton the rest of my blouse. His hand strays as I get up onto my knees. I stand and strip down to bra and panties in an instant, then leave my skirt, sandals, and blouse lying on the bank and walk into the pond, making soft, splashing noises.

Mark rises up to watch, his head propped on his hand, his elbow planted on the ground. I wave to him from the middle of the pond. I feel cool and in control of myself, scissoring my legs to stay afloat. Maybe for once it won't happen on the first date. But he is up like a whip and out of his leather belt and jeans, flinging his shirt into a bush and clambering in, as noisy and naked as a buffalo. I swim away but he is on me in seconds, pulling me up against him and rubbing himself into me, and then the two of us swim back to shore and take just enough time to retrieve his shirt and spread it out to lie on. Much later, hurrying home alone, I can't remember which one of us did that and all I think about is how it felt to have him enter me, how it felt to have him big inside me, exploring, moving and warm, driving thought away.

It doesn't stay away. In the night I awaken and stare at shadow patterns on the ceiling and fear creeps into every part of me because I forgot about condoms. Again. Victor's face comes into my mind, more accusing even than Ada's when I rushed in late for dinner, my clothes damp from wet underwear. We ate in silence, Victor and I, while Ada made conversation only with Tony, and I left the table with Mark's warmth already swept out of me and shame spreading in to take its place. I will myself to let go of worry and drift back to sleep.

When my eyes open in the morning it takes awhile to remember the dream. I dreamed of the dog, dead now for three years, the dog Larry named Spook. In the dream I had forgotten that Spook was in the basement, and by the time I remembered it had been weeks or months, and all that time I had neglected to feed him. I was afraid to go down and see what had become of him, but I made myself do it and found him lying there thin and pitiful, trying to wag his tail and greet me.

chapter 15

The smell of dust being burned by hot sun pierces my nostrils and I let my feet stop walking and dig my toes into the dirt, stretching the muscles of my feet. This is it. Just this. Me walking barefoot along this dirt road on my own reservation, the same land my people have walked forever. Why did I fall in love with a boy who could dance and love and laugh and make my heart sing when he looked at me with that gleam in his eyes, and stop my heart completely when he kissed me, and then start it up with a jolt he felt in his chest pressed into mine, we both felt it. I could have died then and there and been happy forever, and it happened over and over, every time he loved me, till the drugs started and he'd shut himself in the bathroom and lock me out and I'd knock on the door and beg for a word to tell me he was still alive but he wasn't really, not the man I fell so in love with. I'd drop like this into a bed of dry grass by the road just to dream about the way his hair grew out of his head, bursting out and frisky and alive. How can he be dead? The boys have that same hair, Victor does, with a life all its own that can't be squelched, hair that springs out and sends secret messages. Soft cotton rising up to meet my palm. My legs tingle from the prickle of grass under them and ants crawl up into my clothes and onto my skin, but I don't get up and shake myself until my head starts itching, and then in the distance I see an old man walking toward me, wearing a hat, turning the brim to cool his head, and it hits me like a powerful rush of icy water that Larry is a memory, not in the world, and I have to go on being in it.

At that moment the plan comes to me, and I don't know

why, but the plan forms anyway, taking shape. I scrunch the sides of my heels back and forth in the dirt, the next best thing to digging them in. I laugh and turn and run back to my mother's house, not wanting to meet another person on the road and have to greet that person and give away something of myself. I want to keep hold of every piece of myself.

Ada is at her small worktable in the living room. She looks up from the rows of colored beads. I stare at her, unable to put the plan into words.

She sighs, reading my face. "You're goin' on a trip. Where?"

"You know, Mom, it doesn't even surprise me. That you know that."

"You been here a month, right?" Her cheeks and mouth pucker and her eyes stare warily at me. "You're not takin' the boys, are you?"

I hear the quiver behind the words. "Yes, Mom. Just for a week or so."

"Why?"

"They have to go with me. I'm going to see their father's mother." And why would I abandon Victor here for you to ignore and wound? I wonder why I can't say it aloud.

"Hmmph." My mother sounds more surprised than displeased. "And when did their father's mother last see them?" I was wrong. Her voice has turned to steel.

"She lives down in Louisiana," I answer. "So she hasn't seen them all that much."

"But it hasn't been fourteen years, right? Has it?"

"No, it hasn't been fourteen years. Let it be, okay? I'm tired, Mom." I flop down on the couch and stretch out on my back and shut my eyes, feeling the stiff silence of my mother's unspoken questions. She will have to find out from somebody else that Wally TwoDogsRunning gave me a one-week vacation, after my working only a month, because the tribe is sending him to Washington, D.C. Something about selling trees.

Ada's voice jerks me up off the couch.

"You don't care a damn thing about those boys!"

I can't speak. Fury holds me, shaking, on my feet.

"You just run off like you always did, messin' up your family's life. What d'you care who you hurt?"

Something twists inside me. I want to race from the room but my body won't go.

"Run! Go ahead! Run off!" Ada dares me with her eyes and her voice. "Like you always do."

The dare pulls a yell out of me. "All you think about is you! You don't care if the boys see their other grandma or if anybody loves Victor. You just want Tony here! You want to control me!"

Ada sits very still at her worktable. Her arms hang at her sides. "No," she says. "It's the boys I care about, but you don't think about anything but what foolish thing you want to run off and do next. They're just startin' to fit in and have a place here and now you want to yank them up. They'll never take root." I feel the words like blows, driving me from the room.

* * *

So why am I here on the road to the south alone, in my beat-up green Chevy, trying to ignore an intermittent thump from under the hood? To drown it out, I switch on the radio and hear Dwight Yoakam bawling a tribute to a woman he can't ever have. It soothes my nerves to feel the rhythm and the words of it wash through my mind and body. I'll stop soon and run barefoot in the grass. The next rest area. And not worry what all the old, white retired couples think. Why do they look alike? Were they different before they got old? From one another? Or were they always cut from the same pasty dough, with the same unforgiving cookie cutters that don't leave them a shred of grace or sexiness?

I know why I am alone here, thinking mean thoughts, my bottom sticking to the hot car seat. My mother's reasons make sense. The boys are into the camp program, winning friends, getting ready for the powwow. They'd lose the places they are weaving in the mesh of reservation life if they went off with me now, so soon. I left mad, though, slammed the door to my room and tossed things into a suitcase and was off before the boys even got home. Another mistake. They love Grandma Arethea; they won't forgive me, will they, for rushing off like this without telling or asking or explaining? It's times like this I hate being a mother, having to ask myself such questions, always being accountable to someone else for every hour of my day, every act. I feel better, admitting the heresy. It's as if I have dragged a

70

dried-up, dead mouse from under the car's floormat and laid it in plain view on the dusty dashboard.

I breathe more deeply: long, slow pressures and releases that cool my brain and ease my spirit and swell it with freedom, the car a machine under my hand and naked foot's control, erasing distance between me and the only woman I have ever thought of as a possible friend. Why is that? Ferntree was gentle. And made me laugh. But gone too soon, when I needed her most. Ferntree passed the gift for laughter on to her son, but he, too, was gone too soon, leaving his daughter in a drunken wake of disillusionment. There was a teacher once, but I was too in awe to get close enough for friendship. And Ada's mother was religious. I still see the disapproving downward curve of her mouth, the eyes shutting me out, even before I turned wild and boy-crazy, as if with grandmother cunning she sensed it coming. The clarity of vision cuts too deep, too sharp, and I turn up the volume on the radio and tilt my head back into the hot wind whipping through my hair. With the windows open I can stay awake for twenty hours maybe, and only have to stop at a motel once. I rest my hand on the carton of Pall Malls on the seat beside me.

chapter 16

I see her in my heart's eye and feel the strong, fine bones in the grip of my own hands on the steering wheel as I drive this last stretch of road without consciousness, lost in past trips, Larry and I alone, like kids on a date, the fire inside us fusing us close together, and then later with Victor yearning forward from the backseat, his head thrust happily between us. The humid, sultry air invades my throat and chokes me with longing. One time the river air got into my lungs and filled them and I was unable to talk during the whole visit, but Larry squeezed me and held me up on his powerful arm and supported me proudly, his mute wife. It seemed he liked me even better that way, that he'd never loved me so much as when I couldn't speak and had to rely on him for everything.

I am still running on strength from sleeping round-the-clock in the Colorado motel, while the bearded mechanic across the highway replaced the broken fan belt for twenty dollars and a smile. If he thought he was going to get more, he found out he was wrong. I awakened once to insistent knocking and then, deliberately, dropped deeper into sleep. I crush out my last cigarette in the ashtray and flick the stub out the open window. No way will I smoke around Arethea.

It is almost dark, but I am already drawing up to the house. Distances have gotten shorter. The town always seemed a long way off from this house set back a bit from the road, the paint worn away a generation ago and its bare-boarded porch sagging off the front of it. But I'm hardly out of town and still caught up in the sense of eternity in the Louisiana twilight, of dusk closing imperceptibly around people drawn by its magic to sit outside on porches and steps, faces becoming darker as houses turn shabbier, and here I am, arrived before I know it. Larry's mother is there on the porch swing, strong and tall as she has been in my vision of her all the weary length of the road, and her black skin, like the road, is dusted over with time and wear, but her eyes beam out strong and shining. They lead her forward, out of the swing and to the edge of the porch; and a big, slow smile, Larry's heartbreaker smile, reaches over her face and claims it, settling there.

Something catches in my throat, and I know I won't be able to speak until the swelling love goes down and gives me space to breathe. I am in Arethea's arms now, safe in those bony arms that wrap around me and hold me close, making me feel as small and frail as a child. She holds me away to look in my face, and the emotion that glows from deep down behind her eyes goes right into me. My spine would melt if Arethea were not holding it firm with one strong hand.

"You've come all this way, haven't you, just to see me?" The voice is rich, but I can tell it hasn't spoken for a while, not to someone who answers back. It has the resonance of one who talks to the dead or to the core inside herself.

"I've come ..." It's all I can say, and Arethea, with hands that are firm and gentle on my shoulders, sets me down in the swing and caresses me along the sides of my arms, sending chills through me.

"I bet you're hungry."

I quickly shake my head to hold her near. "I ate just a while ago. I had a cheeseburger and fries and a root beer milkshake."

"Just like the two of you used to, and then you were always still hungry when you got here!" Arethea twists her head back and forth, pressing her lips together, as if relishing the memory.

"Arethea, you look beautiful. Your hair's different, isn't it?"

"You mean, did I finally have sense to stop colorin' it and straightenin' the life out of it? You bet I did!"

"I love the way it grows out so lively-like. Victor's got hair like that, all crackling with its own energy. Makes you feel good just to see it in the morning."

"Katherine, you're still a poet!"

73

"Is that poetry?"

"Maybe it's Victor who's the poetry, and you put the words on it." The large brown eyes cloud over, but she doesn't ask.

So I tell her. "I left them back with my mom."

Why? the eyes ask, and I see the hurt, like Larry's, that would never vent itself out loud.

"I needed to see you by myself. It was real selfish, I guess. Was it?"

"It must be somethin' you had to do." Arethea lifts her head to the last violet-blue streamers of light that shimmer in the sky as if reluctant to leave. "I do crazy things here sometimes, alone. Just 'cause I can't help myself." A smile edges into her eyes, lighting them from the inside. "See that tree over yonder?" I squint to make out the gnarled, low-lying branches of the ancient oak off to the side of the house. "I got myself up there on that highest branch the other day. See? The highest one of those that spread out so inviting-like, almost like stairs? Stairs to heaven. I got me up there and stayed I don't know how long, Katherine. The postman came by and left the mail and never did even suspect I was up there. So I can understand when you just have to do somethin' and you go and do it. If you didn't—I wouldn't understand that as good." Arethea cocks her head, listening. "Hear that train whistle? Makes me want to be on it. How 'bout you? Oh, you just come on a trip, I forgot!" Her smile reaches out and touches me.

"No, it makes me want to be on it, too, Mama. Every time I hear one of those trains whistle." I study her face. "Do you see very many people, out here? Ones to talk to?"

"Oh, seems like they all died or went off somewhere. Or just got busy. Why is folks so busy these days? All these labor-savin' machines, you'd think they'd have some free time now." But she's keeping something back. I see that in the shift of her mouth and eyes over to the side. What could it be? With her arms behind her, Arethea hoists herself up onto the wooden porch railing. "I made this dress myself, out of feedsacks. Is that what you're lookin' at?"

"I'm lookin' at you, how strong and lean and lovely you are, able to get up in a tree and stay there resting and enjoying yourself! Where on earth do you get feedsacks?"

"I have 'em in a drawer. They were my mama's. Every once in a while I get some out and make me somethin'. You like this print?" She tucks her chin in and looks down admiringly at the blue-and-yellow-flowered design.

I settle deeper into the porch swing. "I love it."

"Well, I'll make you one like it."

I remember then how Arethea is. In the morning I'll find her stitching away, the dress almost finished.

"I'm glad in a way, Katherine, you wanted to see me all to myself, just the two of us. Kids are the most wonderful thing the Lord makes, but they do get underfoot and in the way and make conversation next to impossible, don't they, sometimes?"

"Arethea." I decide to come right out with the idea that took shape as I drove almost nonstop to get here. It was probably the reason for my coming, though I didn't know that till I got on the road and the miles of driving left me free to consider it. "I thought you might go back with me," I say.

"Back with you? Where?"

"I'm living on the reservation, with my mother, right now. Victor was having a hard time staying out of trouble in the city. You know how that can be."

"I know how that can be." A film settles over Arethea's eyes and she slips into that place inside herself where she sometimes goes. I remember. You just have to wait till she comes back. Her head holds as still as a deer, listening. Finally she asks, "Did y'get him out soon enough?"

"I hope so. I think I did. That's another reason I didn't bring them. Tony's practicing to be in the dance competition and Victor's helping out with carpentry. He's learning how to work."

"That's a fine thing for a man to learn." She lets out a snort. "Not too many of 'em get it right, though. Can't blame 'em, I s'pose. Now I never had trouble findin' work. It don't skeer folks when I show up at their door!" She is on her feet suddenly, pulling me up, too. "Come inside, honey, afore it gets so dark out here we can't see each other. I'll feed you, don't you worry, I didn't forget."

She turns on a light as we go in and I glance around the neat, sparsely furnished room. There is a brown, upholstered

75

recliner chair under a reading lamp. A red and blue afghan is thrown over the chairback, and two stacks of books, each about three feet high, stand on the floor next to the chair. Most of the books have markers sticking out of their pages.

I chuckle, my gaze traveling around the room. Arethea frowns. "You laughin' at me, girl?"

"Yes, I am! Your housekeeping style hasn't changed, has it?"

"Now what would you mean, I wonder?"

I smile and lay a fingertip on the sideboard, lifting a thin layer of dust. "Preventive housework, you called it once. Keep everything neat and the dishes washed up, but don't bother dusting or sweeping till you hear tell company's coming."

Arethea's eyes widen and her mouth juts forward in a pout. "I didn't know you were comin', Katherine."

"Oh, Arethea!" I wrap her in a hug, swaying her around in a circle. "I use it myself, your system. I love it! How else would we get all those books read? I wanted you all to myself, Arethea."

"You already said that!"

I feel myself warmed by the gleaming glance of affection she throws my way so easily as we go together into the kitchen. She sets out a slice of ham, a jar of mustard and half a loaf of rye bread. She opens a jar of homemade applesauce and spoons it into a cornflower-blue bowl. Then she slices a cucumber into another blue bowl and adds a shake of pepper and vinegar. Finally she sits across from me at the table and pours hot tea from a thermos into two chipped blue cups.

"You know, Katherine, I'm afraid ..." She picks up her cup, then stops.

"Of what?"

"Oh, I don't know if I oughta say. I could be wrong, too. There's that to think of."

"Just say it, Arethea. Whatever you're thinking, I want to hear."

"It's that I get this funny feelin' you're runnin' away from something—somethin' else than you've said."

I concentrate on spreading mustard on bread and layering it with ham and cucumber rings. When I raise my eyes I try to keep them expressionless, knowing all the while that it's hopeless to expect to hide anything from an old witch like Arethea.

76

"I didn't mean to suggest you're runnin' in the wrong direction," she says, "but it do seem to me you act like somethin's after you." She pauses. "It ain't a man, is it? You can tell me if it is. I know you're a warm, pretty woman and Larry's been dead over two years —wouldn't be natural if there weren't a man in your life by now."

"No." I sigh. "I'm not running from a man. I seem to run right into them more than away from them."

"I know what you mean."

I look at her sharply. "You do?"

"Oh, yeah. I do."

I want to burrow into Arethea's wisdom and save myself the pain of learning everything the slow, hard way. That, too, is why I have made the long trip to Louisiana, but now that I'm here I don't know how to ask for what I need. I'm not sure even what it is. "Could you tell me, Arethea ...?" I hesitate. "Could you tell me how it's been for you?"

She gazes through the window over her kitchen sink. She has hung no curtains to shut out the world. The first stars glimmer, and I sense that they are old friends. "I been alone a long time, Katherine. So long I've lost track. Right after he died, I hardly could stand it in the evenin'. I was used to being alone days, you know. Days went fine. But evenin's, when the sun goes down, it's like that old Ray Charles song."

"Your husband." I say it low, wanting to be very sure, and not imagine anything into what she is saying that isn't really there. "You mean when your husband died?"

She glances at me, surprised. "Yes. I mean Donald. You thought Larry? You be always thinkin' about him, don't you?"

I want to ask if there were ever any other men for Arethea besides her husband, when he was alive, but seeing the pleasure that comes over her face from thinking my mind is full of Larry, I can't. I pick up a spoon and stir more sugar into my tea.

Memories sit in the dark pools of Arethea's eyes. "He was a charmer, all right. Like a slinky panther he was, leadin' you on!" She erupts in a burst of laughter and again I'm not sure which man she's thinking of.

"Larry?"

"Well, both of 'em! They got a long way on it, too; Donald did anyways. But Larry, he seemed doomed somehow. Like the charm would work against him in the end. I knew that, y'know? I always feared that."

"It was real charm, Arethea, sincere, it was the way he was."

"When you were in the room with him it was magic, yes! The smartest woman in the world coulda fallen for it. Well, you did!"

I am thrown off balance. I hadn't known his mother saw him so clearly, maybe more clearly than I did.

"When he weren't in the room, you began to wonder, right?"

"I did wonder," I admit. "When he wasn't there I'd start worrying about bills to pay, all that stuff he made seem so trivial."

"But it weren't so trivial when they didn't get paid, isn't that it, and you'd get your phone cut off or some such thing?"

"How do you know, Arethea?"

"Oh, Donald and I went through that for a while, but he settled down, Donald did." She rises from her chair and goes to the kitchen counter and rests her hands on it, leaning forward to stare into the night. "There weren't no drugs close by to tempt him. Donald, he was lucky. And he couldn't drink at all. He never could. And he had sense enough not to try."

She turns, settling her hands on her slim hips. "I want you to know, Katherine, as my friend, I'm not all alone all the time. You know what I mean?"

I nod, not sure I know, but hoping she will continue.

"I don't want anybody here with me all the time, man or woman. I'm used to myself. I hardly ever get so lonely I can't stand it. Only sometimes. Maybe you know that feelin'?"

"I do," I say, with memories rushing through me so vividly I fear Arethea can read them in my eyes.

"Well, I've got me a friend. Had him a long time." She darts a quick look at me. "I lets him know when he's welcome t'come over. Now if I was to up and leave with you, I wouldn't wanta be gone more than a few weeks at most."

I am on my feet and around the table in a rush of joy. "You'd come with me, Arethea? You really would?"

"Well, it's probably foolish of both of us, but to tell the truth I'd love it, hittin' the road with you for company and then gettin' to see the boys. And I'd meet your mama, too, wouldn't I?"

I allow myself to think for the first time of the meeting of the two grandmothers. I have managed to keep that scene out of my imaginings and now here it is, exposed and troublesome.

Arethea is cackling. "Two grandmothers in one house! How long would we last, I wonder? Oh, Katherine honey, if you kin run out on a limb on an impulse, so kin I! And you'd be amazed how nice I kin be if I try."

"No, Arethea, it isn't that." I try to find words for the pain I lived with during all the years of loving Larry. "They're worse than white people, sometimes, about color. It doesn't make sense but—"

"Are you sayin' I wouldn't be welcome in your mother's home?"

"No, I'm not. It's more that she'd keep a distance from you. She'd be jealous of you, too, because we're closer, you and I, than I am with her. You're a friend to me, and with her I'm the daughter who's made her life miserable and I'm her child who never does anything right and—"

"Wait a minute." Arethea lays her long index finger softly against my lips. "Didn't I hear you say you want me to come with you?"

"Yes, of course. I'm just worrying, though, how it will be for you. I'm wondering if I spoke too soon, asking you. It's what I want, but I don't want you to get hurt." I plead with my eyes. "It's not just Mom, it's a whole lot of folks there. Not all of them, but a lot. And they don't necessarily say anything—"

Arethea raises her right hand. "Katherine, I accept your invitation."

"You do?"

A smile slides over her face. "Sometimes our yens just pop out afore our mind has time to say stop."

"What's that supposed to mean?"

"Just that your heart is thinkin' of your boys, and Victor especially." She locks eyes with me, pulling me closer in. "If he kin take it, so kin his gramma."

79

I swallow down tears. "I can't control anything! I want the world safe and good for them—I wanted that for Larry—"

"It's all right, honey. It's all we ever want, but it's more than we get. We keep goin' anyway. You were there for him. That's what counts. He needed to be able to count on his woman and you gave him that."

I bury my face in her shoulder. There are things I can't tell her, after all, and a sick heaviness weighs down my whole body. She reaches past me for a worn, flowered cloth napkin from the table and tucks it into my hand.

"I think I need to go to bed now." I turn away, blowing my nose.

"Of course! Here you are, tired out from drivin' and I don't even think to let you wash up or rest. You know where the bathroom is and you kin sleep where you always slept. The bed's made up."

"Thanks, Arethea. I'll just go straight to bed. I'll wash up in the morning."

"Are you all right, honey?"

"Yes." I am unable to say more, so I go into the spare bedroom, drop my clothes to the floor, and climb under the thin quilt. Gradually numbness eases away. I am on the side that was always mine, and it feels like Larry is here next to me. I resist the urge to reach out for him, so I can go on feeling him close to my body, almost touching.

chapter 17

The next morning we are on the road by eleven o'clock. I am wearing the dress I awoke to find Arethea hemming. I lay in bed listening to the murmur of the sewing machine, reluctant to extricate myself from the embrace of Larry's memory—something stronger than memory, a presence really. Arethea's creation is a surprisingly chic sundress, with spaghetti straps, cut low over the tops of my breasts. So here we are in matching print dresses, "fresh as daisies after a shower," to quote Arethea. She brought just one piece of luggage, a battered, black suitcase. So far in her life it's been enough, she remarked. I wonder how much traveling she has done. I suspect this may be her first trip, judging from the fact that she's acting as excited as a young girl. At breakfast, she said it was a good thing she had had that dress to work on, and a suitcase to pack, because she couldn't have slept a wink anyway.

"Honey."

Her voice yanks me from my thoughts.

"I need to go back."

Oh, no, she's changed her mind. My chest tightens, and involuntarily I speed up, not wanting to hear this.

"I forgot to leave my man friend a note. It'll take me only a few minutes. Lucky we haven't gone far, isn't it?"

I sigh in relief. "It is, Arethea! It's real lucky to forget something and remember it this soon."

She glances sideways at me and I know she sees the smile twitching at the corners of my mouth. "You look pretty as a picture, Katherine, in that dress. And now all the town folks will get to see us go by agin."

"Well, I guess they're the lucky ones then."

"You know, I was gettin' too lonely, there by myself as much as I am, and I didn't even know it."

"Yes, I imagine that can happen. Loneliness isn't something I've had a lot of."

She looks at me with witch-like probing eyes and I respond. "Well, let me take that back. The kids are always there but some part of me is out there alone, screaming in the wind. Does that count?"

"Tell me about the man in your life," Arethea responds.

"We're almost there. I'll wait till you go in and get your note written." We ride in silence and then I pull up at the house we left half an hour earlier. "I'll wait here."

"Sure. This won't take long." She strides up the walk and turns her key in the lock, then disappears inside. In two minutes she is back with a piece of pink notepaper she tapes to the front door.

"That doesn't look like it has much on it," I say, as she settles herself back in the car. "What did you say?"

"Gone travelin'. Be back before you know it."

"Well, that'll mystify him!"

Arethea has a sly look on her face. "Be good for him," she says. "He was startin' to take me for granted."

"Amazing, isn't it. They can do that even when you're not living together."

"So tell me about your man." She rubs her back into the seat as though making herself comfortable for a good, long story. She's like a child, a wise old child.

"How do you know I have a man? Maybe I don't need one."

"A woman like you always has a man." She says it softly, not judging.

Then, as I struggle to find the words to explain, she speaks again, still in a soft, neutral voice. "It must have been hell for you those last months, when he was so heavy into the drugs. How long did that part go on?"

"About two years. And you're right. It was hell." I drive without thinking about driving, all my thoughts focused on that crazy time. "In some ways it was like he was already gone. Do you know what I mean?"

"Like sex?"

"Well ... yes." I can't say more, even with this invitation. I am too surprised.

"I figured that. You need to talk about that, Katherine. You haven't, have you? I kin tell."

She really is a witch. She's going to drag this thing right out of me. The realization brings a slow surge of relief, like the gradual swell of a giant wave forming and breaking into surf. "I've been carrying it inside so long. I don't know if Victor knows. I think he does." I say the last words so low Arethea leans toward me to hear.

"That must worry you. What you're carryin' inside."

"It drives me crazy."

"Well, don't let it do that. Nothin's worth that. Why don't you just tell me what happened. I pretty much know anyway."

"It was the night he overdosed. I mean, that wasn't the first time but it's the night that still presses on my mind." Suddenly I am sobbing. "I loved him so much. How could I be with someone else when he was dying? Maybe I could have saved him."

"Pull over, honey."

I slow onto the side of the road, but my vision blurs. The car tilts wildly, then shudders to a stop. I grasp Arethea by the shoulders. "Did you hear what I said? I could have saved him if I'd been there. Your son. Victor and Tony's– "

"Stop it, Katherine. And let go of me. We're stuck in the ditch, dammit. I didn't mean for you to drive into a ditch."

"Now I've messed this up, too!"

"Just calm down. We'll be here awhile probably, so let's act sensible."

"Arethea, you think I'm a monster. Do you? Tell me."

"I think *you* are not thinking very clearly and all this time you haven't been and I know why, too."

"Why?"

"Gosh, you want me to tell you the answers to all life's problems, don't you? Well, it's simple. To me anyway. You loved him too much. You still do. Too much to see anything."

"See what? What don't I see?"

"Katherine. My son, your Larry, was a drug addict. If he hadn't died that night it woulda been some other night." The edges of her eyes brim with tears. "Now, I could spend the rest of my days," she says, "berating myself for every time I hit him, every time I didn't listen when he wanted to talk, every time I put his father first and him second, every time he saw me get hit. Do you want me to do that?" Her whole body is shaking. I hesitate to intrude by reaching out and touching her but I can't bear the separation. I take hold of her hands.

"No, Arethea. I don't." We move then into each other's arms. "He was a good son and a good man." I speak with my face pressed into her shoulder. "That's what makes it so hard for me. He never once hurt us, not at any time, ever."

She pulls away. "Yes he did, Katherine. I'll be damned, havin' a daughter like you. You can't see it, can you? The goddamned drugs hurt you. And they hurt Victor and they hurt Tony. He's the one took the drugs. The drugs didn't take him. And he left those two half-breed boys without a father and they need one, especially 'cause of who they are."

"I know that."

"Well, thank God you see one thing at least. Can we just go on now with all these lives that are still here on earth and lay my son to rest? Please?"

"Thank you, Arethea."

"Thank me! I feel I've been wrestlin' with the devil. And he's me, as usual. You know, I'm not sure we can get outa this car. Not on my side anyway."

I laugh. "I need to learn from you! How to deal with what's right in front of me."

"It's all anybody can handle—and more!"

"God, Arethea. You're all squished into your corner."

"Are you tryin' to make me laugh? Just cut it out, girl. Maybe if you climb out your side I could get unsquished."

I try my door, but it is too heavy for me on the first try, at the angle the car has wedged itself into the ditch.

"I can't believe this," Arethea says. "Here I am on the first car trip of my life and we're already stuck in a ditch? We've hardly left home!"

"Well, we can talk about guilt some more," I venture. I feel mischievous and giddy with relief.

"You just talk about it with yourself till you get it outa your system. I'll lean back and get some rest."

We settle in to wait. An occasional car passes. Motorists slow down enough to look in at us, but no one stops. The first black people to come along are a middle-aged man and his wife, wearing white straw hats, identical but for clusters of cherries decorating the woman's hat brim. They slow to a stop beside us.

The woman rolls down her window. "You folks need help?"

Her husband doesn't wait for an answer. Why am I so sure they're husband and wife? He pulls in ahead of us, takes his time getting out, stops to open the trunk of his old gray Ford, and pulls out a heavy length of rope. He has a grin on his broad face as he saunters toward us in his white shirt and brown trousers, the coil of rope held firmly in his hand. Sweat glistens on his forehead.

"I reckon you need a pull outa there. Or were y'all fixin' to stay in this here ditch all day?"

I speak to him through the open window. "Can you do it alone? Won't you need help?"

He throws back his head to laugh, showing a mixture of white and gold teeth. "Honey, I'm strong as an ox, and so's this here vehicle o' mine. You two just sit tight. Good mornin', ma'am." He leans in toward Arethea. As he does, he lifts the straw hat an inch above his head.

"A good mornin' to you, sir. It's right nice o' you to help us out."

chapter 18

We have been riding in silence for some time when I suddenly notice the shiny maroon pickup tailgating behind us. I speed up. The needle climbs past seventy-five and the distance between us and the pickup lengthens a bit. I check to see if Arethea is awake. Last time I looked, she was napping peacefully, her head tilted back. Catching up on missed sleep! Now she sits erect and motionless, her head turned slightly toward the window. To gaze at the oil wells? They have replaced the wavy rows of corn.

"Arethea, are you hungry? We've been on the road for hours."

"Oh, I could eat pretty soon, I 'spect."

"How about stopping at the next town? We'll find a restaurant."

"Honey, it be best just to keep goin'. You ain't traveled in the South all that much. It's best just to keep on the move. You get there sooner."

"I'm hungry though, Arethea. I'll drive better if I have something to eat."

"I brought us a little somethin'," she says. "Ham and cheese sandwiches and a thermos of iced tea. Some apples, too."

"Sounds great! No wonder you don't want to stop at a restaurant. We'll be there sooner, too, as you said. So you've traveled in the South, have you? I thought you said you hadn't."

"Oh, we hear tell." She shifts her head slightly and grows silent again.

"Well, I can hardly wait any longer. Are you going to bring those sandwiches out or what?"

"This isn't the time, Katherine. Just hold steady on your speed, or maybe pick it up a little, just a little though, and gradual."

"I'm not going fast enough for you? We're quite a bit over the speed limit!"

"There's other things to worry about than speedin' tickets." Arethea barely moves her lips, and I realize in one quick instant that she is watching the side mirror, eyeing the truck, and the truck is tailgating again, closer this time.

"Dammit. There's hardly anybody on this road. Why don't they pass me?"

"Just hold steady. Are you at seventy-five?"

"A little over. But this doesn't make sense, Arethea. I'd slow down, make it easy for them to pass, if they'd give me half a chance."

"Honey, I forget what a northerner you are."

I glance again from the road to the rearview mirror. Three white men are in the front seat of the pickup.

"They've got a shotgun in the back," Arethea mutters. "At least it's still up there in its rack. That's some comfort."

My palms begin to sweat and I remove them one at a time from the steering wheel and wipe them on my new dress.

"No tellin' what they might do," she says in a low voice. "Police would just laugh." She mumbles so low I barely make out the words. "And if we take out across these fields, they'll have a lot better vehicle for it than we do."

"Arethea, they're just horsing around. They'll get tired of it, right?" I wish I believed myself. "I certainly don't want to overreact."

"No, honey, you sure don't." The dead seriousness of her tone frightens me. "Are we near any big city?"

I had been thinking the same thing. "Oklahoma City," I say. "Less than sixty miles. I saw a sign back there."

"That's our best bet then. Just go for it."

"What about the towns we'll go through on the way? We'll have to slow down, won't we?"

"Yeah, but not much."

"Look! They've dropped back." I notice the line of her mouth tighten, and then I see why. The truck is now accelerating and angling toward the center line. It edges up and around until it pulls steady alongside us. I roll up my window at the same time Arethea does.

"Just don't look," she says, through tight lips. "Keep goin' at the speed you're at—you're doin' just fine."

After what feels like several minutes, the pickup fades back behind us again.

"Katherine, you got a sweater or anything to cover up with?"

"Cover up? Are you kidding? I'm sweating! Can't you tell?"

"They're lookin' down your dress—that's why they pulled up like that. One reason anyway."

"I've got a cardigan in the backseat. Hand it to me, will you?"

She reaches back for the sweater, then holds the sleeves out one at a time so I can put my arms in.

"I'm glad they're not tailgating right now," I say. "I sure couldn't do this at eighty or whatever I was up to."

"You were eighty-five there for a while."

"So, have they given up?" I button the sweater at the top, with one hand. "God, I feel like a pig roasting."

"Here they come!" Arethea warns, as the truck swings up alongside again. The driver lays a heavy hand on the horn. I flinch but don't look over at them. I keep my eyes on the road, push the accelerator to the floor, and pull ahead of the truck.

"Hey, how fast kin this thing go before it pops?"

"I don't know," I say. "I remember how Larry used to plan our trips so carefully. He'd fill up the tank real often to make sure we didn't run out of gas and—"

"How are you on gas?"

"We'll make it to Oklahoma City. We'll need to fill it when we get there."

"They'll be gone by then," she says. "If we just keep on like this, I think they'll maybe find somethin' better to do. We kin hope."

"He used to have me lie down and sleep in the backseat, with something over me. Larry never needed sleep himself, re-member that? We'd drive straight through. One or two naps, that was enough for him."

"Katherine, you pick a hell of a time to reminisce."

I tighten my grip on the wheel. "I remember he always had me wait in the car with the doors locked if he had to go in and buy something or ask anything. Usually he didn't even do that. Go in anywhere, I mean. If he could help it. Except that one spot where we always got the burgers and milkshakes. Black folks work there."

"Katherine, I think they're losin' interest. Don't want to crow too soon though. What speed are we at?"

"Seventy-five."

"That's good. Just hold it."

"But we're coming to a town."

"Well then, slow down!"

I ease up on the pedal as we approach a sign. It says Population 2,336. I see that, but not the name of the town. Suddenly my body tenses. The pickup draws alongside and I can feel Arethea's eyes focused straight ahead. I keep my own eyes fixed on the road as the pickup slowly passes. When it is directly in front, the man on the far right leans out his window and thrusts his middle finger back at us. He mouths the words, "Fuck you," his little piggy eyes buried in the contorted folds of his cheek flesh.

"Hard to understand, isn't it," says Arethea, "where that kind of energy comes from. All bottled up like that inside him, you'd think he'd poison himself with it."

Arethea is talking us through, trying to get past the anger she too must feel. I feel stifled and choked by the heat that has built up inside the car, and my eyes are blurred with sweat. I wipe them on the sleeve of my sweater. When I try to speak, my voice is raspy. "I feel shaky, Arethea. I want to stop the car. I have to—"

"Keep goin', Katherine. You been doin' fine. You've got to keep doin' it till they drop off somewhere. I know they will, too, now I've seen the face on that one. They're cowards. Underneath all that bluster, they're a bunch o' cowards."

"I've got to take this sweater off. I can't stand it."

"Not yet. Just hold steady."

I press on, willed by the firmness of her voice, not thinking anymore. At the other end of town, the truck swerves wildly, crunching into a gravel lot outside a small cafe.

"Okay," Arethea breathes. "Pick up your speed real gradual. When we're down the road a ways, I'll open up our thermos of tea. You kin take that sweater off now too. You must be dyin'.

Unbutton it, honey. I'll pull it off you." She peels the sweater off a bit at a time. It is stuck wetly to my body, like an unwanted layer of skin.

"Open your window, too," she adds, as she rolls down her own window. "There!" She leans over to get the thermos jar from her bag, unscrews the lid, and hands me the jar. I take one long swallow, then another.

"Finish it if you want," she urges.

I turn to look at her and for the first time see the sweat soaking her face and neck and arms. Her gray hair is plastered to her head in tight ringlets.

"You were as scared as me," I say.

"And almost as hot!" She wrinkles up her nose.

I hand her the jar, eyeing her.

"Do you ever get tired of being black?"

She tips her head back and drinks steadily from the jar. She hands it back almost empty. "No. I get tired of them bein' white."

"That's what I mean though." I drain the last drops.

"There's a difference."

"You know what the worst of it is?"

"What?" She looks at me.

"I feel like we got off easy."

"And that's right. We did."

"But I feel like we'll pay for it, d'you know what I mean? Like something worse is bound to happen to us now?"

She laughs and settles back against her seat. "That's the curse we live under, honey. Anyway, no need to go lookin' for trouble, it comes sure enough on its own."

I drink in deeply the fresh air breezing through the open windows. The wet cotton of my dress clings to my breasts and thighs and back, molding them, stuck there by my own sweat.

"It feels good to breathe again," Arethea smiles.

chapter 19

"I've never seen it rain this hard." The muscles in the back of my neck feel so tense they could snap. Coming over Stevens Pass was a nightmare. I lean forward over the steering wheel, peering through the windshield, trying to make out the road ahead through the sheets of rain.

"You haven't, huh?" Arethea falls silent again and I continue to peer out. I can tell where the road is only by the landmarks on either side of it. Not the best way to drive, but so far it's working.

"Arethea, you've grown awful quiet. Ever since we entered Washington state." I ease up on the pedal. If we go ten miles an hour, not much can happen.

"It's the first time I've been through here. I'm lookin' around."

I laugh and feel my neck muscles ease. "I can't imagine what you can see, with this rain."

"I been thinkin' what it was like for Larry, livin' up here in the North. Maybe he never got used to it."

I hadn't looked at it that way before. Being with Arethea hurts sometimes, but it feels like being on track, being headed somewhere. The thought reminds me to concentrate. "I'd know that tree we just passed even if only the top of it was sticking out of a snowbank. Could be though it's the bend in the road I know, as much as the tree."

"Lucky for us you even *saw* the bend in the road. You been doin' a fine job of drivin'." She chuckles. "That practice we got gettin' through Oklahoma helped some."

"You seem more like yourself now. I'm glad. I was wondering were you sorry you came."

"No. Nothin' quite like that. Just a little nervous is all. I ain't traveled much, you know."

"I know. Well, I'm delighted and honored you came with me."

"Oh, now, don't go on about it." She reaches over and gives me a push.

"Don't do that!" I grin. "We'll be in the ditch again."

"Now that would be somethin'! You think they'd ever find us way out here in the middle of nowhere?"

I glance at her in surprise. "We're in the middle of my hometown, Arethea. I know it's not much of a town, but it's what we've got."

She sits up straighter. "We are? How do I look, Katherine?"

"You look beautiful."

"Oh, what's the sense askin' you, of all people!" She giggles. She must really be nervous. It's not like her to giggle, or to worry about how she looks, either. It's usually the last thing on her mind, and she always looks wonderful and like nobody else in the world. Now she gets out a little pocket comb and fluffs up her hair, and I slow down to five miles an hour to give her an extra minute. With a swishing noise, the car slows, slides into a puddle, and comes to rest.

"We're here," I say, feeling the fatigue. All I want is to crawl into a warm bed. Where will Arethea sleep? I hadn't thought of that before and now I wonder if she has been concerned about it. Then my mind clicks back on and I know where Arethea will sleep. The question is, where will I myself end up?

"Let's run for it, okay? Too bad we've got no umbrella!"

"I'll look like an old, soaked rat," Arethea objects.

"They'll just be glad we made it. They'll know it wasn't easy, in this weather. Come on, let's go!" I don't give her time to protest. I step out into a puddle, then slosh around the car to open her door. "Watch out for this river!"

In the short dash up the front walk, we get drenched. I pound on the door. No one answers.

"We might as well go on in. It's never locked."

"No!" Arethea grabs my arm. "Wait, Katherine. I think I hear somebody."

92

The door creaks open. Ada's face, usually so unreadable, looks as if it might crack from the strain of trying to remain composed. Maybe I should have warned her. I was afraid of being told "No" if I phoned and asked, but I have never known my mother to turn away anyone who showed up at her door. I know Arethea assumed Ada knew she was coming. Now I begin to see how unfair I may have been to both of them.

"Mom, this is Larry's mother, Arethea Washington. I was able to talk her into a visit. Isn't that wonderful?" It doesn't seem at all wonderful, judging from Ada's expression. I press on. "Arethea, this is my mother, Ada Jack."

"I'm very pleased to meet you, ma'am." Arethea speaks through a cascade of raindrops dripping down her face from the top of her water-soaked head. "I have had the pleasure of ridin' with your daughter on the longest trip I've ever taken, and I realize from what she has to say about you how mighty a woman you are, Ada."

Ada looks as if she just swallowed something she isn't sure whether she's going to spit back up or let go down. Finally she turns and leads the way in.

"You picked a real rainy day for your travels." She walks right on out of the room and into the hall.

"Didn't she know I was comin'?"

I avoid Arethea's eyes and shake my head.

"I shouldn't—" Arethea begins, but I clap a hand over her mouth to prevent her saying more.

"Don't! Wait, please!"

And then Ada comes back, hurrying, carrying two towels. She hands one to each of us. "You'll catch pneumonia," she says. "Now you get your coat off, Mrs. Washington, and sit here in this armchair. Here, let me help." Ada reaches up to assist as Arethea, who is by far the taller, sheds her wet coat, and I see in my mother's movements the deeply ingrained respect an Indian woman has toward someone she recognizes as older than herself. I breathe a long sigh of relief and sink into a chair.

"Katherine!" My mother's voice is sharp. "You get in there and make hot coffee! Right now! Mrs. Washington could use a cup. And stir up that stew. I put a fire under it."

How can she know? I marvel. Arethea is five years older than my mother and doesn't show it except for letting her hair go gray. How can my mother possibly know? If only Larry had been an old man. I smile as I get up and go to the kitchen. Ada is on my heels, telling me to pare a couple of potatoes and cut them up small to add to the stew. She pulls out a bunch of carrots from the vegetable bin and twists off the tops and prepares to scrape them, pausing to put bread in the toaster, and I remember you start bringing out food when a guest arrives, even if it is the middle of the night. And the kids wake up and come to join in the eating. I remember that part even before I hear Victor run into the living room from wherever he's been sleeping. He is clasped tight in Arethea's arms and Tony is clinging to his back when I glance out the doorway.

chapter 20

The next morning I am at my desk early, before the rest of the administration staff, and before the waves of preschoolers, parents, elders, and folks who drop in just to see what's happening. I like to be here already when people arrive. It helps me feel connected. I am aware I don't quite look like I belong. My hair has grown only a couple of inches below my shoulders, and the blunt-edged cut still gives it a stylish shape. Most of the girls and young women like me have hair halfway down their backs. Either they've permed it or it hangs like a blanket around their shoulders and bodies.

And yet I do belong. Everyone knows who I am. They know I am the daughter of Big Jim Jack from an Indian band in British Columbia, and that Jim was raised here on the reservation by an aunt who married into the tribe. They also know Jim learned carving from his uncle, the aunt's husband, and that he had it in his blood already, because his grandfather up in Canada was a carver. Also known is that Ada Jamison's family are all from around here and have lived here forever, though most of them have passed on. Folks my age and older remember me as the girl who turned wild and ran off with a black man. And now I've got two half-breed kids and am back home with my mom after not talking to her for ten or fifteen years. I doubt there's anyone who doesn't know at least that much. And I know they wonder if I'm back to stay. Suddenly I chuckle, as my gaze flits around the room. It certainly looks like I intend to stay! I made most of the changes my first week on the job. My office is an entry room from the side porch, where weathered wooden chairs invite sitting and smoking. Some people use the side porch as an entrance to the tribal office wing, instead of coming in by the front door in the middle of the longhouse. When I first began work, I mentioned at home how bare my office looked; the next morning Ada presented me with a row of potted green plants, brought over by Tillie Turnipseed, who stood nearby looking pleased and commenting Ada had more plants than places to put them and won't it be nice to set them out where more folks can see them. Some were too tall to fit in the car. Victor and Tony made two trips, helping me carry them the short distance to the tribal center. We placed the ivy plants on the metal four-drawer filing cabinet, where the dark-green leafy vines could trail down the sides almost to the floor. Ferns and avocado plants spread sheltering fronds and drooping leaves in the corners of the room, and I love the tropical feel they give. But my favorite is the prayer plant, scrolling and unscrolling its delicate leaves from the top of the bookcase.

I stand and hike up my narrow black skirt, then reach under it to pull my blouse down tighter, liking the feel of silk against my skin. Then I finger the earrings carved in the shape of bears, made from elephant tusks, which match the ivory sheen of the silk. Nobody else dresses up, but maybe they take it for granted I'd be different in this way, too. Tomorrow I'll go casual and wear my red-and-white-striped tee shirt with the pucker at the V-neck.

Aunt Betsy's braided rugs enliven the stained, threadbare gray office carpet with swirls of green and blue. I discovered the rugs rolled up along the baseboard of Ada's storage room. "My sister didn't live long enough to put any wear on anything," Ada had said, with a strange, tormented look. I run both hands slowly through my hair, still wondering at that look. A pile of accumulated mail topples over on my desk, reminding me of what has to be done. I begin opening and sorting. A good amount of it is from the Bureau of Indian Affairs. A few brochures advertise equipment the tribe can't afford and I toss them into the woven recycling basket. My mind drifts homeward. Last night was the best sleep of my life and I awakened rested and renewed. It seemed a good idea to get out of the house quickly and leave the two grandmothers alone to get acquainted. Or was I taking the easy way? I sense eyes watching me and turn my head quickly. Sky winks at me from the doorway.

"Good to see you back. This was kind of a dreary old place without you. Even your plants got lonesome, so I threw some water on 'em."

"Well, thanks. You surprised me! I thought I was the first one here."

"You gotta get here early to beat me and Whit." He saunters around the desk and sits on the one corner that doesn't have letters piled on it. "She's doing an intervention today. Her first solo."

"And you're here to give moral support?"

"Yeah, you could say. She's gonna meet the guy's family down at the store and they're all going out to the town where he lives."

"Here I am!" Whitney zooms in from the hall. She is wearing red lipstick and thick black mascara, and her frizzy, reddish brown hair stands out around her face like a halo gone wild.

"This little character is makin' me go out there to honkyland on my own. The first off-rez intervention and Sky sends me!"

I respond to her broad smile. "You look ready for anything."

"I'm wearin' my power suit. The Sunday paper said a woman in black exudes power."

Sky buries his forehead in his hands. "I doubt whoever wrote that thought some alcohol counselor would turn up at work in black leather pants and a black leather shirt and jacket."

"I feel powerful!" Whitney grins. "It's workin'!"

From her jacket pocket, she draws out a case made of shiny aluminum. She uses a long, red-painted thumbnail to undo the catch and lift the lid. An eagle feather rests on a brown velvet lining.

"I'm takin' this," she says. "To use for the talking circle."

"What's a talking circle?" I've learned I can ask Whitney such questions and get a straight answer, without feeling put down.

"It's when we sit around in a circle and if you're holdin' the sacred object, the feather or whatever, it's your turn to talk. And when you're done, you pass it on."

"You got sage with you?" Sky asks.

"Out in my carrier bag." This time I don't ask why. There's a limit to how much cultural ignorance I'm willing to show. Anyway, I half-remember that sage is burned for purification. The half-memory connects to a very small girl entering a dark and steamy sweat lodge with grandmother Ferntree, while another old woman keeps a fire blazing outside and heats stones. Sky is watching me thoughtfully, running a forefinger across his lips.

"The alcohol program's gotten more traditional the last few years," he explains. "Burning sage, for smudging. Things like that. We're goin' back to the old ways. A lotta people out there drinkin', they don't just need to dry out, they need a new way to live. What's new for us is to relearn what we've known for thousands of years."

"It's the same at Turtle Mountain, where I come from," Whitney adds with her usual forthright smile. "They're not usin' the white man's way anymore. Those charts and slide shows they give us? They don't go over all that great. I mean, my dad knows his liver is pickled. Don't need to watch a movie to find that out."

"That's in Montana, isn't it?" I ask. "Do you know Mark Whittington? Is he from your tribe?"

"Mark's adopted," says Whitney. "He grew up with white folks." She looks at me sharply and with a tinge of something like sympathy. "He hasn't told you that, huh?"

I feel my face grow hot. Mark and I haven't done much talking.

"Funny, isn't it," Whitney muses, looking at Sky, "how Mark hung around here, talkin' to Wally when Katherine was gone."

"Yeah," Sky says dryly. "Seems like old Mark's suddenly developed an interest in timber." There is more that they aren't telling me. Why?

"When did Wally get back from Washington?" I keep my tone casual.

"A couple days earlier than he thought he would," Sky replies.

Whitney shakes her head, catching her lower lip under her front teeth, smiling. "When Mark first came here, he was askin' for help to get his adoption records opened, so he could find out what tribe he is and get enrolled. Remember that, Sky? He thought some tribe out there had a whole big bunch o' money waitin' to hand over to him."

"Yeah, and I remember how mad he got when nobody could help him."

"Well, he's calmed down some," Whitney says. "Must be tough. Bein' close to full-blood Indian and not knowin' what tribe you are. Or even what your real name is." She clicks the lid shut on the eagle feather and returns the aluminum case to her pocket. "All set for the talking circle." Whitney's expressive face is serene, as if the feather protects her.

Sky grins. "If you get that far."

"You're right, what in the hell do I do if he's shit-faced when we show up?"

"What did you tell me once?" Sky's straight black hair hangs loose today, and he runs the slim brown fingers of his right hand through it. He pretends to look puzzled. "Never try to talk to a drunk? Was that it?"

Whitney nods. "They'll never remember one thing about it," she says. "So if he's totally wasted, we'll just pack it in and try another day."

"Good thinkin', Whit."

"Cut the crap, Sky."

Whitney reaches out both her hands and Sky takes hold of them and a look, like a current of strength, passes between them. I feel rather than see it, and then Whitney frees her left hand and reaches out for my right hand and scrunches our fingers together in the same embrace she shares with Sky, and Sky reaches for my left hand and I feel the strength surge around the circle. Whitney gives a final squeeze and lets go, abruptly. She strides to the front door. "I hope I make it back for lunch, it's Indian tacos!" The door bangs shut behind her. Moments later we hear the Harley revving up.

"She makes me grin," I say. "Even the first time I saw her."

"Yeah, I remember that, too."

"You weren't there, silly."

"No, but I had a first time with Whitney too." Reacting to my glance, he backs off with his hands lifted in the air. "Nothin' like that! She's too much for me, Whitney is, when it comes to woman."

"When it comes to woman." I narrow my eyes at him.

"But when it comes to friend, I'll put my money on her. So tell me about the first time."

I slit an envelope and glance at the contents. "It was my first day working here, that freak morning when the fog was so thick? I couldn't see the building till I almost walked into it. I don't think I'd have driven that day even for an emergency."

"Got it! Real foggy. And then comes ...?"

"Whitney, roaring up full speed on her Harley! She was inside before the roar died away. In purple leather and a purple helmet! 'Do you mind?' she asks, and she lays the jacket and helmet on my desk with those bright eyes of hers sending out darts. Her eyes are almond-shaped, don't you think?"

"You're the almond-eyed beauty, Katherine. Whitney's a big bouncing Tigger straight out of *Winnie-the-Pooh*."

"Hey! Didn't know you'd read that."

"Go on. Don't stop."

"Well, she took hold of this big lavender tee shirt she was wearing, with a gold dragon across the front, and lifted out the sides and shook it to give herself air and then she let out that holler of a laugh. She had on pink knit gloves with no fingers, and pink leather boots."

"And her chest stickin' out to here?" Sky struts around, jutting out his own chest. I laugh.

"Yes, I did notice that about her, too. I guess I'd never seen anybody so ... just kind of all hanging out there, putting herself on the line."

"She does that, doesn't she? She doesn't hold back. Once I sprained my ankle at soccer. I'm lyin' there and everybody's standin' around, and old Whit comes barrelin' up and grabs me under the arms and yanks me up. Then she lets go and drops me on the ground, like a dead weight. 'Whoops! Gotta check if he's in shock!' I tell her, 'I just need help gettin' home, Whit.' And she pretty much carries me over to her bike. She's not really that big, you know? It's all that adrenaline keeps her so pumped up."

"You know what I think though, Sky, it's the stuff she's been through. She's trying somehow to outride it and make herself strong so no matter what hits her she won't fall. Has she told you about any of that?"

"Yeah, I've heard all that. And more."

I pause in mid-slice with my letter opener, surprised at the wave of bitterness that distorts Sky's face. "Don't you think that explains a lot?" I ask.

"Like what, for instance?"

"Like," I try to pass over the hardness in his voice, "like why she's so understanding. Of anybody else's pain. And such a good counselor. Because of the parents she had. Did you know her father used to make her dance at the tavern while he passed the hat for money to buy drinks? And her mother—"

"Listen, Katherine, evidently some people open up and confide in you—well, good for you, but I don't want to hear this."

"Sky, what's wrong? You should see your face. It's all closed in on itself." I don't tell him the rest of my thought, that the liquid beauty of his eyes is smoldered over as if with ashes. "What's wrong?" I repeat.

"I'll just say this, okay? We're not what we are because of our parents. Some of us know that. Maybe some of us don't even have parents." His voice tightens. "Some of us have been our own goddamned parents and we've managed to become a person on our own and it has nothin' to do with parents!"

I fold my lips together. "I'm really sorry. I ... I pushed a button or something, I guess." I can't think of right words to say, and it makes me wish to be free of him.

"One of these days you'll meet my so-called parent. And I just want you to know, any parenting I got was not from her." He turns on the heel of his boot and leaves the room, my wish coming true, yet when I am alone I find I want him back. Someday I'll make him tell me, I think. All that bottled-up feeling. I'll bring it out. I lay my head down on the desk, cradling my face in my hands and feeling my hair cascade over my hands as if to comfort them. I had wanted someone to talk to and I had thought Sky could be that person.

I look up to see him in the doorway. He steps in with the hesitant, halting, almost comic gait he uses when he wants attention. Already I know that about him.

"You were right," he says, and his eyes are open to me again. "You pushed a button. That's what *I* want to escape—the rawness that comes from having those buttons out there exposed."

"Not so exposed. I never saw a button. I just wanted to get closer to you, and that's hard for me. But you didn't make it easy."

"Look, let's try again. But parents, except for your dad, are off-limits."

"Did you even know my dad? I don't remember you from back in those days."

"The year your dad was livin' off by himself? That was the year I came in from the city and stayed with my grandmother. Your dad used to let me watch when he carved, and we'd talk. He never mixed drinkin' and carvin'. To me the man was a saint."

"I'm not ready to hear my dad made into a saint." I say it like a warning, but he misses it.

"Katherine, you know why he was a saint? Because he was so human, and at the same time—"

"What do you know about how human he was?"

"Uh-oh. Now I pushed a button. Sorry about that." His expression, like a small boy's wanting back into favor, touches me. "Katherine." He reaches over and takes my hand. "No parents, okay? We won't talk about a one of 'em. We'll just believe Whitney was fathered, or mothered, by a Harley Davidson and I had a circus clown raisin' me and you ... you were born of a rose."

I blush at his look. "And now we're all blowing in the wind. Pollen drifting around. Funny. Your saying that makes me feel like a rose."

"And look like one."

"Sir, you're too gallant."

He executes a pirouette and lands with his arms out, feet planted in a vaudeville pose. "Does our friendship have a chance, tell me that, Miss Jack?"

I stand and walk around the desk. "Let's go over to the clinic for coffee. Theirs is better than ours."

It would be nice to have a man for a friend, especially Sky. Just a friend, no sex complicating things. Then, out of the corner of my eye, I catch him staring at my legs. Unable to stop myself, I straighten the tight, short skirt, adjust it from the waistband so it fits my hips more smoothly, knowing his eyes are still on me.

"You ready?" I ask, and I can't resist the feeling of triumph at what I see flash in his eyes. But then it is gone and we are safe again, scampering through the doorway like children let out of school.

chapter 21

"How was your trip, anyway?" Sky asks, his mouth full of chocolate doughnut, as we walk back across the courtyard, sipping hot coffee from foam cups.

"My dead husband's mother wants to meet you."

"She does, huh? Why's that?"

"I talked about you on the ride home. Had to stay awake somehow. I must have managed to make you sound interesting."

"I'd like to meet her. After you went to all that work."

"Don't go getting a big head. She loves anybody who's good to her grandsons."

"Did you tell her Victor's turning into a first-class carpenter?"

"Yeah, I did. I've never thanked you, Sky."

"Well don't start now! Don't you know we're not a thank-you culture?"

"Come for dinner, okay? I'll call Mom. And I'll peel an extra dozen potatoes when I get home."

"Hmm, you haven't noticed what a skinny old rail I'm gettin' to be."

With my free hand, I grip his upper arm between my thumb and fingers. "Hey, those are muscles!"

"I'm gettin' in shape for the wilds. The kids do it by bein' young."

"I still wish I could go, but everything's getting so complicated. Why is my life like that?"

"You're making excuses. Wally'd give you time off."

"It isn't just that."

"Oh, the hot romance!" He holds the door open for me and catches my look of surprise. "The word's out on that, you know.

You two were seen at the pond lookin' pretty chummy." Sky waves briefly as he passes through the doorway that connects to the rest of the building. "See ya tonight."

I sit unmoving, wondering just what anybody saw and who it was who saw it and who all is talking about it. Wally Two DogsRunning appears in front of me, light and soundless on his feet despite his heavy bulk, a shy smile on his earnest round face.

"Welcome back, Katherine." He has a stiff way of speaking, and he always gazes at a point somewhere below my chin. Either it's pure bashfulness or he intends someday to get fresh, I haven't figured out which.

"Could you type this letter up for me? I wrote it out longhand."

"Sure, Wally. And I'll bring your mail in after I finish sorting it. Here's one from the BIA, forestry, marked urgent." Wally gives a slight start and his placid features crease into a frown. He adjusts his glasses to peer at the envelope and walks out with his shoulders hunched. My mind drifts to worries about Mark. How can I get him to come to the house to meet Arethea? He won't want to. I dread following the thought where it leads. Do I know this man at all? And why would he be talking to Wally? He doesn't care about trees, I know that much. Sky missed me. I could tell by the way his glance lingered on my face. I take out my compact and raise the mirror to study my eyes. They are definitely almond-shaped.

Behind the compact, suddenly there is Wally. I run my fingers through my hair, embarrassed to be caught admiring myself.

"Uh, Katherine, we need you to take minutes at council this morning. Rosie has to go into the city for a funeral."

"I'll be glad to, Wally." I slip the compact into the middle drawer. "I'm sorry about Rosie. Whose funeral is it?"

"One of her nephews got shot comin' out of school last week."

I am silent for a beat. "That's why I wanted to get my boys out of the city."

"Is that right?" Wally's eyes grow thoughtful behind his glasses. "Rosie lost her own boy last year. Just two miles from here."

I watch his face and wait.

"You know that railroad track runs down along the lower end of the reservation? He lived over there in one of those fallin'-apart shacks. Most of the folks who drink heavy end up there."

"I know. It's where my dad ended up. What happened to him?"

"Train got him."

"He was in a car accident with a train?"

"If you call it an accident to get so drunk that sleepin' it off parked on a railroad track seems like a good idea."

Why is he telling me this? To warn me, remind me you can't escape trouble? I feel a rush of anger. Then, minutes later, awe washes it away as I walk into the council room with its beamed dome and natural wood paneling and windows reaching from floor to ceiling on three sides. It is my first time in this room. The long oak table is surrounded by tall armchairs with dark-brown leather upholstery on the seats and backs. I slip into one of them, feeling small. My short skirt leaves my lower thighs bare against the leather. Wally sits down silently beside me. My guess is that he is even more intimidated than I am. It takes awhile for the other six council members, who are standing near the coffee-maker, to fill their cups, finish their conversations, and gather at the table. No sooner is the last one seated than we all rise and Tom Matthews offers a prayer, speaking in Lushootseed. I learned the word from Victor, who learned it from Sky. I get chills, hearing the depth of emotion in the man's voice. I hear it like a plea, repeated over and over, higher and stronger with each repetition, and though I don't know what the strange words mean, the musical cadence strikes a near-forgotten chord. My eyes have tears in them when he comes to the end and says, in English, "All my relations," and looks around the table at each of us. My father admired Tom Matthews as a spiritual leader and interpreter of dreams, and it startles me to see how vigorous and healthy the man looks. He was considerably older than my father, and Big Jim has been dead for fifteen years. Gray-black strands of hair frame the strong features of Tom Matthews's weathered brown face, and thin braids hang down over his vest, ending in buckskin ties.

"Thank you, Tom." Virginia Kelly, as tribal chair, opens the meeting. She calls our attention to the two items on the agenda: vote on gaming commission and vote on fish hatchery.

Virginia is camouflaged by comfortable rolls of fat and looks like she ought to have two or three grandchildren settled in her lap, but I know there is a cutting-edge business mind beneath the soft facade. Ada spoke proudly of the "woman chairman" who gave up her job in middle management at Boeing to come home and help out her tribe. She has a bad heart condition, too, Ada admitted, when I pressed her to explain what kind of altruism would prompt such a move. The only other woman on council, Diane John, is about thirty, with long, straight black hair and a trusting demeanor. Who is it she trusts? I don't have to wait long to find out. And from the looks that pass around the council table during the charged discussion, I can tell they have been over this ground many times before. As I take notes on the different opinions, I sense a certain respect for the position of the traditionals, tempered by determination to go where the money is. When the vote is called for, Diane John votes with Tom Matthews against establishing a gaming commission. Theirs are the only "no" votes, even though most of the arguments against legalized gambling were raised by Richard Dillon, a lean, angular man with an honest face and the air of an intellectual.

Dillon stands to summarize the reasons for his abstention. I study his features, noticing again the black ancestry apparent in the texture of his hair, the set of his eye sockets, the cast of his skin color, which is exactly like Victor's. "I can't countenance an activity linked in the white world to organized crime and drinking," he says. "But I won't vote against it because tribal members so desperately need the jobs a casino will bring." He slouches back into his seat, looking resigned and depressed.

"Why didn't he just say that in the first place and save us some time?" Stan Moss, Jr., flashes a look across the table at me as he mutters these words to Frank Vitello, who sits next to him. I decide I was right in my initial distrust and dislike of the man. I felt it the first day, when Wally took me around for introductions; Stan Moss, Jr., managed to look over every inch of me as I stood briefly in his doorway. He has been eyeing me from the start of the meeting. He is easily the biggest man in the room, with massive shoulders and heavy jowls and meanness behind the irony in his eyes. He wears his black hair longer than Dillon, Vitello, and Wally. He looks like a handsome pig. I'd hate to be caught alone with him. A slight shudder passes through me, and his mocking smile deepens. He's watching every move I make! The realization brings out my stubbornness, and I look up from my notepad to stare right back at him. It is pure pleasure to see the confusion that comes into his eyes, and then they shift away from me.

Richard Dillon introduces the topic of the fish hatchery, then steps out in the hall to summon the tribe's biologist, who has been waiting there to make a presentation. The mood eases while Dillon is gone. Little Frank Vitello leans forward to grin down the table at Tom Matthews.

"Had any visions lately, Tom?"

Tom smiles good-naturedly.

"Well, let us know if you do. We're not choosy where we get help from."

The biologist and Richard Dillon appear, carrying an easel and a stack of charts and posters. The biologist is introduced as Rudy Vitello.

Frank's grin widens. "See? I said we're not choosy. Now my kid brother is an expert!"

I am fascinated by the biologist's projections for restoring the fish runs to 1950 levels. Virginia Kelly asks if the projections take into account that the state may continue to overlicense commercial fishing.

Rudy Vitello runs a hand through his styled mass of black hair. Like all the other men in the room, he is wearing jeans, but his look better because he is slim and graceful. He has on a fitted pink dress shirt.

"There are signs the state is catching on to the folly of that," he says. "We've been pointing it out to 'em ever since we started having joint meetings, after the Boldt decision. Now they're comin' up with it like it's their own idea."

"Call for the vote," Stan Moss, Jr., says. Ever since I stared him down, he has moved uncomfortably in his chair, as if eager to get out of the meeting.

I feel satisfaction as I write the last sentence of the minutes: the vote was unanimous to allocate funds for construction of a fish hatchery. Behind me, the low voice of Stan Moss, Jr., intrudes on my complacency.

"Don't look so worried, Wally," he says. "We've got the votes."

I must remember to ask Ada what she knows about Stan Moss, Jr. Or Stan Moss, Sr., for that matter. Why is the name familiar? And what votes is he talking about? Junior looks to be about fifty, but he's probably younger. I can tell from his eyes that he drinks.

chapter 22

The soft poignancy of a rain-cleared, midsummer evening envelops me as I step outside and start homeward. I wore my ivory silk blouse with the heart-shaped neckline because I more than half expected Mark to come by, or to be waiting when I got off work, but for a change no one at all is on the porch. It took awhile to get away from the office. After the meeting, Wally came in with a list of words for me to look up and write out definitions for him. Most I was able to do without bothering to use the dictionary, but it was a long list and took more than an hour. He's in over his head on the job that council gave him to regulate forestry. Two weeks ago he had me contact the Bureau of Indian Affairs and the contractor to request copies of "any and all documents" relating to the tribe's ten-year-long negotiations for the sale of its north-end trees. That was smart. But now he's buried in fine print, poring over paragraphs of legalese and making lists of words. When I suggested we go over the documents together, so I could understand better and be of more help, Wally shook his head like a bear warding off bugs. Did I imagine the desperate look in his eyes? Or maybe he suspects me, rightly, of wanting to call a halt to the whole deal. Cutting down trees isn't my idea of progress.

My walk home is short. I wish it were longer. I feel safe here on the rez, with no need to be on guard against gangs or muggers. No rednecks either. Only the BIA lurking out there, ready to ambush. Old-growth forest means nothing to them but dollar signs. Probably you have to be born in this forested area to have the love of trees in your bones. Fish, too. When Tom Matthews ended his prayer with the words "all my relations," I remembered my dad telling me, with a kind of wonder, that each animal and fish he carved was one of our relations, and so was the wood itself. Mark was indifferent when I spoke of dams that helped loggers and killed fish runs, but he was born on the plains.

A row of maple trees lines each side of this road that leads from the tribal center into the cluster of old HUD houses where Ada lives. Behind the old are the new HUD houses, twenty of them, almost ready for occupancy. I've been out to look at them more than once. A creek runs alongside four of the houses, and they are the two-bedroom size, the ones I will be eligible for if I put my name on the list. I've found that if I follow the creek one way it flows into the river, and if I go the other way it feeds into the pond. I draw a deep breath and my eyes take in patterns of green leaves flirting with delicate blue sky. Muted sunlight wraps me in images of Mark and a sense of his nearness, and I step onto the dull-red rectangular paving stones of Ada's front walk still submerged in the remembered smoothness and hardness of his body and the warmth of his breath in my ear. The smell of fried onions intrudes, confusing my senses, and hits full force when I open the front door.

"Hi, Mom. Sorry I'm late." Ada stands at the stove, sturdy and compact, wearing brown trousers and a red powwow tee shirt with "USA Is Indian Country" written in broad letters across her back. Her feet, clad in tennis shoes, are firmly planted on the cracked linoleum as if rooted there. "What can I do to help?"

"I set the table already. Six of us, countin' the teacher. I've just got one pan goin', so I can't use another fry cook."

"Fry bread!" I resist the urge to hug her, I don't want to risk having her stiffen and pull away. Would she be soft, I wonder, to touch? I dance a little twirl around the table.

"Watch out, you'll knock the soup off the stove." Ada frowns into the sizzling pan, her head held slightly back from it.

I dip a spoon in the soup pot and blow to cool off the creamy liquid before sliding it into my mouth. "I love your clam chowder," I say. From the corner of my eye I observe Ada's face settle into satisfied lines as she wields her tongs and retrieves plump crisps of fried dough from the hot oil.

"Mrs. Washington peeled the potatoes. A whole big pile of 'em. She's pretty fast." I hear admiration in my mother's tone. "She and the kids and their teacher are out there in back, all of 'em. You're the last one."

I push open the screen door and see Arethea about to pitch a softball to Tony, who is leaning into practice swings with a thrust he must have picked up from television. Sky is behind him, crouched down, and when he catches sight of me he unleashes a series of elaborate hand signals to Arethea. Victor weaves back and forward in the outfield.

"Do we look like pros or what?" Sky calls out. Arethea pitches, and Tony hits and connects. Victor is too far in, has to run for it, and then throws the ball to Sky as Tony dashes from second to third base.

"That's my cosmetic bag!" I yell, as I recognize second base.

"We couldn't find anything else," Victor yells back. "We dumped your stuff on your bed."

"Gee, thanks a lot." I sit on the steps and watch Sky pick up the bat. Tony squats behind him, with the mitt held down at the ground. Arethea pitches true and steady right over the plate, a tin pie pan.

From the open screen door behind me, Ada calls out, "That's somethin', Mrs. Washington, how you can pitch that ball right smack over my pie tin."

Arethea's white teeth flash in a smile. "I was on a team when I was a girl." She waves briefly to me. "Remind me to tell you somethin' later," she says, and goes into her windup. Her tone resonates in me like a warning bell, a caution not to get too happy, and I see now the tiredness in the heft of her arm, something unseen that weighs it down, and Arethea pushes against it, gives her best effort, and lets the ball fly. The pitch is almost perfect and Sky wallops it.

"It's outa the yard!" Victor yells.

"I've got it!" we hear from two yards down, and as Sky rounds the bases, exaggeratedly touching his toe to my flowered bag, Floyd Bill puffs into view. "Here's your ball. I caught it. Sky, you're out."

"Well, heck, Floyd, you're not even in the game."

112

"I am now. I'm on this here team." Floyd winks at Victor.

Arethea asks, "Can you pitch?"

"Yes, ma'am. I was pitcher in high school." He raises his voice. "Remember that, Ada?"

Ada calls back, "Yeah, and you always hogged the ball then, too."

Arethea smiles, handing him the softball. "I've done wore myself out," she says. "Here, you and my grandson there can handle it on your own."

From behind the screen, Ada mutters, "That mound Tony built up is gonna cave in under you, Floyd, you big old ox."

Wiping perspiration off her forehead with one arm, Arethea deposits herself with easy grace next to me on the steps.

"Remind you to tell me what?"

Arethea meets the question with eyes that caution silence, and a motion of her head back toward the screen door. She sits with her hands folded loosely in her lap, and a sense of stillness and heaviness settling over her.

Victor yells, "Come on back in, Grandma! I need you in the outfield. I can't cover it all alone."

"You're doin' just fine, hon." Arethea's low, hoarse tone doesn't even need to be raised for him to hear.

"You all right, Arethea? You look tired out." I search her face.

"You're the one I'd think would be tired. All that drivin', then off you go to work." Is there a reproach in the words, or am I imagining it?

"How was it here, your first day?"

"I just stayed to home."

It isn't until we hear Ada banging lids and pans that Arethea speaks again. "I almost had a visitor. I thought you might want to know that." I see a muscle quiver in the strong jawline.

"Who was it?"

"Katherine, if I tell you this ... it's just because it happened and ... you probably ought to know." Arethea speaks with effort, bringing the words out haltingly.

"What? What happened?"

"That fellow you told me about in the car comin' here? Mark? The one does yardwork for your mama. He came by today to get his money for work he did."

"Mark was here? You met him?"

"I think that's what your mama had in mind." Arethea's face is grim. "She offered him some iced tea and sent him into the kitchen where I was. She said she'd be right in."

"In the kitchen? Yes, he does that, stays for iced tea."

"Well, today he didn't. I guess he didn't like the company."

I stare into Arethea's face, a microcosm where so much is going on and yet there is so much stillness. I see worry for me layered over whatever she herself is feeling. I cup my hands around the worn, black knuckles, folded over each other in the skirt of her cotton dress.

"He didn't stay for the iced tea?" All my questions sound foolish, but I ask them anyway.

"No, honey, he didn't stay. And he just about run your mama down gettin' outa here."

"Getting out?" I watch Arethea stare at the ground, looking like Tony or Victor when they hold onto something painful they can't put into words, and I begin to understand. "Did you have a chance to say anything?" I hear the fear in my voice and despise myself for it because what I fear is having to choose, having to give him up. Don't let him have done anything too bad, is the thought I can't silence.

"I had time to introduce myself as Victor and Tony's grandmother." Arethea draws herself up. Her eyes go back inside themselves. Slowly I take my hands from hers.

"Did he say anything?"

"Did he say anything?" Arethea turns to face me. "You mean, such as 'I am pleased to meet you'? Did he say anything like that, that most people would say? No, Katherine, this man of yours just wheeled around and shot himself right out of this black lady's presence."

Can't anything be simple? I feel a flash of anger. Then shame bears down. "I don't know him all that well," I say finally, and a blush creeps over my cheeks as Arethea gazes at me, unblinking.

"No," Arethea says. "I don't think you do. But *I* know 'im."

I keep silent and feel the distance lengthen between us.

Sky is up at bat, a worry line between his eyes, trying to watch me and the ball at the same time. He swings and misses.

Arethea lets out a slow sigh. "Let's not talk on it no more," she says. She sees into my mind. She sees me wanting to find excuses for him. But will I even be able to ask him about it? What could he possibly tell me?

"Strike three!" Victor yells. Victor is pitching now. I hadn't noticed. I hadn't known he could. Tony comes to bat and I concentrate on watching Victor pitch, wanting to block out thought, but what I see is Larry's grace in the ripple of Victor's upper arm muscles and in the tautness of his leg as he slides one foot back and pauses. Mark has the same tall, muscled leanness I loved in Larry. Is that the magnetism?

"Arethea," I say. "My head aches. I'm going inside to take some aspirin and lie down." She turns wide-open eyes to me and again I see the microcosm, everything there, so much that nothing is clear or simple but the love. And inside me is the sick, sinking feeling that again I am a disappointment to myself and those who love me.

chapter 23

I look up from Austen's *Emma*, which has come to feel like a friend I am beginning to know and trust. At first it all seemed too much, too impossible, and that was what kept me drawn in, that anybody could have a life like Emma Woodhouse's and make no apologies for it. As if it were the most natural thing to be handsome, rich, and clever and have every advantage. Over and over, I turn back to the beginning and read that first sentence. And Jane Austen, who wrote it, never married, never did much of anything. Did she ever fuck anybody? I giggle, squirming deeper into the pillows I have piled up to surround myself. Probably not. Probably Jane Austen's whole life went by watching other people go to the edge, draw back and make their calculations, then jump into the fray.

I haven't really been reading this evening, rather communing with the book itself, as if it were a living thing. My eyes travel around the room, studying its contents. Only the pillows and the flowered teacups and the books are accessories that might have been found in Emma's house. Everything else — the colorful beadwork on Ada's table, the wood totems Big Jim carved, the wool blankets with vivid designs, even the paintings and photographs on the wall — are specifically Indian, each of them meaning something. I don't know what, that's the catch. The pages of the book fall together. Another time. This isn't the time. Mark is in my thoughts now, and in my senses, an itch that won't go away. He hasn't called or come by to see me and I've been back two days. I haven't wanted to ask anyone at work. Especially not Sky or Whitney.

"Mom?" Victor looms in the doorway. I wouldn't be surprised if he's grown an inch while I was away in Louisiana.

"What?

"I don't have any clean underwear."

"I'll go do a washing. Right now."

"Are you serious?"

I yawn. "Where's your Grandma Arethea?"

"She's out in the backyard."

"Doing what?

"Looking up at the sky." He sits down in my dad's old leather armchair and turns his baseball cap around to the front. "She knows the names of all the stars," he says, "all the important ones. Some of 'em are in groups and she can spot 'em and put names to 'em."

"Constellations," I smile.

"Yeah, I know. She called 'em that, too."

"So what've you been doing?" I can't resist. "Going around with no underwear on?"

"Cut it out, Mom."

"How are things at the center, at your camp thing?"

"It's not a camp thing, it's like culture and survival. You know that."

"I'd know more if you'd talk to me about it."

The front door opens and Arethea appears, her face darker than the darkness around it, her eyes wide and still excited.

"I love it here at night," she says. "I've just been out there walkin' all around the yard, lookin' up till my neck is sore. Y'all have more stars here than we do in Louisiana, did y'know that?" She speaks to Victor. She hasn't been addressing herself to me directly. Not since last night. It's not noticeable to anyone else probably, and even Arethea and I pretend it's not happening. It'll pass. I'm counting on it passing. I long to be welcome in her arms again, as who I am, even if I'm not what either of us wants me to be.

"How do you know their names then, Grandma?" Victor asks. "If you don't have 'em at home."

Arethea winks at him. "Books. I've got me a big old star book I brought along in my suitcase. Come on. I'll show you."

It isn't until the clothes, the second load, are in the dryer and I am on the couch again, not even trying to read, that I hear

117

a faint sound and realize I've been waiting all evening to hear a knock at the door. There's no way a man could be this much on my mind and not show up. I know it's not just me who remembers, in every pulse of my body, the one time we were together. It's not enough. I don't let myself think beyond that, beyond it not being enough. And there he is at the window, knocking, so softly it could be a branch rapping. Everyone else is bedded down. He must have waited, and watched, till lights came on in the bedrooms and went out. Except Arethea's light. She'll still be reading. I can see in my mind how her whole body settles into her reading, absorbed into ideas springing off the page, a live connection between her eyes and the written word, between her mind and the author's mind. I remember my own inability to make that connection throughout this long evening of waiting, and know it for what it is. It is a refusal to think, my body refusing to let me think. It has happened before and I should be forewarned, be cautious, but instead I feel my mouth twitch into a smile as I tiptoe to the door, open it, look out, and see him there waiting, off to one side. The steady chirp of crickets rises to meet me, and I breathe in the sharp, clear tang of the night air.

"Come on out, Katherine. I'll buy you a drink." Mark's voice has an edge of command. Is the courting to end so soon? What did I expect? Reading Jane Austen is like leading a double life. If I were to express my mental comparison of him with Knightley or Elton, Mark would be on guard, thinking he had rivals, somebody to punch out. The smile deepens and spreads inside me, and excitement rises, the excitement of going out late, when the rest of my world is sleeping, unknowing.

"Wait till I get a jacket."

"No. You'll wake somebody. I've got one in the truck. Somewhere."

I shut the door quietly, whispering, "What makes you think I want a drink?"

"Oh, come on, Katherine. Get movin'." He is on his way down the walk, halfway to the pickup already. He strides around to the driver's side. I pull the heavy door open and step up, a high reach, and lift myself in.

"I'm not going to one of the taverns around here," I say. My bluntness gets his attention. He looks at me.

"Why not?"

"I'm not having folks tell Ada they saw me out drinking." I sit silent and still, and both of us know I'm taking a stand on this, instead of talking about his walking out on Arethea. Doesn't he know you don't treat grandmothers like that? Maybe that's how I can bring it up.

"Okay." He is reluctant. I see it in the deliberate way he turns the key in the ignition, then pauses, his hands gripping the sides of the steering wheel. "Where do you want to go?" There is a stubborn set to his jaw I haven't seen before.

"Anywhere there aren't Indians."

He shifts from first to second quickly, then into third, accelerating fast. "There's a place fifteen miles out. I've never been there."

"That'll be fine."

He drives without speaking. I should have known he'd deal with it this way and I would be the one to do all the work.

"Mark, I've been wondering about your life, growing up. Did you get to see your grandmothers, ever?" This is too sudden. I should have led into it better.

"I've got no grandparents." His hands clench on the wheel.

I wet my upper lip with my tongue, thinking how to get him to talk. I taste the lipstick I put on earlier that evening, in the hope he would come. "What was it like where you grew up, there in Montana?"

"Do you really wanta know?" He turns toward me, and the look in his eyes arouses a long-forgotten memory. I was very small, watching my brothers corner and torture a stray cat.

"Yes," I say softly, remembering I wanted to rescue the cat and was afraid of the fierce terror in its eyes.

"It was like being a big, dark-skinned kid in a swarm of Scandinavians and Germans and everybody thinkin' it was funny to call the big dark kid 'chief.'" His hands open and flex on the wheel. "It was like overhearin' my puny white adoptive father tell his wife, 'He doesn't have the brains to come into the business with me, and anyway people don't take to him.'" Mark looks over at me and I see the cat's eyes, betrayal transformed into self-preservation, hard and opaque. "It was like sitting in class and never bein' able to concentrate because I was always tryin' to figure out who the hell I was."

No point in talking about grandmothers. I wait.

"As if I wanted to be an overworked asshole pharmacist. I couldn't even breathe in that place where they live." He glances at me. "It's in Iowa, not Montana."

I let my eyes ask the question, and he answers. "I'm pretty sure I'm from a Montana tribe. That's all the adoption agency would tell me. They wouldn't say which one."

"Wow."

"Yeah, wow. That's what I say. Let's forget it, okay, Katherine? The only way I've been able to put a life together is to leave it behind. I try to pretend it happened to some other guy." He can't let go, though, I see that he can't stop speaking now that he has started. "Gettin' rescued by a good white Christian couple who gave him the advantages his own no-good mother couldn't give 'im. They called her that, y'know?" I watch his mouth twitch, the muscles out of control. "I listened outside the kitchen door, and I heard him call her a no-good Indian slut."

I picture the boy growing up, tall and dark and more like a brooding, handsome Indian every day, the outsider, and some-how untrustworthy. In that Iowa town. I slide closer to him until my hip touches his.

"Let's go dancing," I say. But he doesn't loosen up or relax. I lay a hand on his thigh and feel the muscles, hard as rods. Lights ahead illuminate the words "Teeter-In." A sign featuring a neon-outlined Indian chief's head hangs over the tavern door. Tension creeps into me, a gathering, unbidden awareness. I try to shake it off. My body wants to move and forget.

"Do you like to dance?"

"Sure. Sometimes." His mouth is grim as we walk toward the entrance. A muffled din of voices and rowdy laughter reaches our ears. He hesitates a split second, then pushes the door open and stands motionless, as if he expects someone with a gun to be waiting on the other side.

And all noise ceases as we enter.

What I had wanted was a place to drink and dance and be anonymous. Instead, here we are, faced in an instant with the impossibility of forgetting ourselves. I don't meet anyone's eye. That would invite trouble for Mark, or for me. I am sorry I don't have a jacket on, something to hide in. The black, scoop-necked leotard is cut too low, and the jeans fit too tight. I move in front of Mark toward one of the two empty tables. Mark is careful not to touch me. We might almost not be together, as we sit down on opposite sides of the table, wanting only to escape more attention. I hate this moment and the memories it brings of other such moments, of entering rooms with Larry and hearing the sudden silence, and then the comments in voices raised just loud enough to hear. I hear the words now and shut them out. I should have known better than to come here. Mark looks diminished in this setting. His jaw is rigid, his features contracted.

"Do you want to stay?" He barely moves his lips to ask.

"Let's have a beer and then go." At least we can make a pretense of doing what we came here to do.

Mark's mouth cracks just short of a grin. "Well, don't expect speedy service."

I smile back and keep my voice low. "You'll be surprised. They'll want us out of here. Sometimes that lights a fire under them."

I'm right. A beefy, middle-aged man in a grease-smeared apron appears.

"Okay, folks. What'll it be?" He is probably the owner. He doesn't want trouble. I see that in his effort to create an air of normalcy. He is carefully polite. After Mark orders two beers, I dare to look around and take in the scene. I notice a medium-height, dark-blond kid in a black cowboy hat, standing with his two buddies at the bar. His booted foot is up on the rail, his leg turned outward, his whole stance insolent. He is staring at me.

The beer arrives and music starts up, a small country western band with a knee-jiggling beat. Couples go to the space cleared in front of the stage and slip into a conventional two-step. Hardly a good dancer out there. I drink as much of my beer as I can in one pull and feel my tension harden into rebellious anger. I yearn to dance. What the hell, we should have just gone to an Indian bar. My body begins to sway in response to the music. I don't see Mark lean slightly toward me, warning me with his eyes, until the blond cowboy is standing next to me.

"How 'bout dancin' this one with me?" The kid's eyes are bloodshot. He's been drinking all evening, I suspect. He barely hides the smirk on his face. His buddies at the bar are watching, intent. I look at Mark. His face is impassive.

"Go ahead," he says. "If you want."

It takes only a second for the alternatives to flash through my mind and be rejected. I had half-hoped Mark would shake his head and tell me no. I get up and follow the kid. He can't be more than twenty. When we reach the edge of the dance area, he whirls around and clutches me up close to him, pressing my stomach and pelvis against his. The sour whiskey smell of him, mixed with a faint stench of vomit, sickens me, and I pull back, trying to free myself.

"Whatsa matter? You don't like our friend?" The two bigger guys move in. I see them glance toward Mark, who is taller than either of them.

"What are you afraid of?" I make my voice bold and loud. "You outnumber him three to one." I look challengingly around the room. "Maybe a hundred to one."

It surprises them. They hadn't expected me to say anything. Nothing sensible. I seize the advantage.

"I've had enough of this place," I say. "Hey Mark! Let's go!"

Mark gets up and walks stiffly toward me. My dance partner's arms hang at his sides. He doesn't reach for me. I start toward the door, willing Mark to follow. He does.

Nobody comes out to watch us leave or to stop us. I begin to breathe easier. It feels like a battle has been won.

Mark's words hit like sharp, separate blows. "Don't ever do that to me again." His voice is compressed, tight. Anger seethes under each syllable. "Ever."

I begin to tremble. I'm not even sure which part of it he means, and I am afraid to ask. Back in the pickup, I stare out the window, hardly breathing. I don't know where he is taking me and still don't when we get back to the rez and he pulls up between two rows of houses. My eyes take in the front yard of a house across the road, the only one with lights still on. My mind notes details, as if to fill itself and leave no room for anything else. The shell of a Ford from the fifties rises from the bare ground. It has no tires, no engine, no seats. Some distance away lies a steering wheel. The seat of the car leans against a tree, with its plastic cover ripped open and springs showing through. Two tires rest near the road, not far from a car radiator. On the porch of the house, a cracked wringer washing machine stands next to a rusted lawn mower.

"We'll just party at home," he says. He saunters around and opens my door. I can tell by this, and by the tone of his voice, that he feels better. My silence was the right thing. He reaches an arm around me and lets out a laugh. "They all wanted you and I'm the one's got you!" His voice is hoarse. He walks me to the door of an unlit house, his arm on my shoulders. He unlocks the door and propels me inside with his hand against my back, his push too strong, making me take a running step to regain my balance.

"How d'you like it?"

"Is this your place?" My quick glance takes in a well-stocked gunrack. Nothing else on the wall. No pictures, no carvings.

"Sure is."

"You've got a whole house?"

"Yep, three rooms." He runs his hands down the sides of my head, smoothing my hair, then reaches into the front of my leotard and squeezes my breasts, too hard, hurting me. "Let's forget about them, okay?"

chapter 24

The next night I glide into Arethea's room, which had been mine, unable to stop myself. It is a few minutes before midnight and rain drums on the roof. This has always been a house where you can hear rain pelting down, drowning out other sounds, shutting people together in a fragile cocoon, reminding them how little lies between shelter and the outside. Arethea is propped up in bed with two pillows behind her back, reading. The title is *Crime and Punishment*. An involuntary smile comes over her face when she sees me, and on seeing the smile, I close the door behind me and move toward the bed.

"Arethea?"

"What, honey?" She leans forward in her pink flannel nightgown, her eyes concerned, gathering worry. "Oh, you do look mournful, child. I hadn't looked at you close till this moment."

"I am mournful. That's as good a word as any."

"Come up here and sit next to me." Arethea scoots sideways, making room. I have my green robe on over a pair of Victor's striped pajamas, rolled up at the sleeves and pant cuffs. Sleeping on the couch now, with Victor relegated to a pile of blankets in the hall, just outside the bathroom door, I don't feel right being naked when I get up to go to the bathroom. And tonight I haven't been able to sleep at all, even though I and the rest of the household have been bedded down since ten. I have lain rigid and anxious, hearing every tick of the clock.

"What's hit you this hard?" Arethea's voice soothes, probes. "You've got little hollows under those big dark eyes of yours." She lays the index and middle fingers of each hand gently under my eyes. I let the lids of my eyes close. I would like to stay like this forever. I don't speak again till she moves her fingers slowly downward on my face, tracing the outer edges of my cheekbones and then, with an even lighter touch, the jawbones.

"I don't feel it now as much, Arethea, having you touch me like that."

"Feel what?"

"Anger, rage—wanting to strike out at the white man, like he's out there, all personified in one man I could wipe out and it'd be gone."

"What, honey? What'd be gone?"

"Racism. What it does to us. To our men." I hate putting the words out into the air, like a pollutant.

"Mmmh-hmm." Arethea breathes out heaviness.

"I hate what it does to the men, I hate what it does to me, but I'm used to it and—I don't know—maybe I'm kidding myself, thinking the slurs don't get to me. Maybe my whole damn life has been acting out that goddamn stereotype of the Indian whore."

I turn my head toward Arethea, who sits silent, her eyes grown bigger and wider, her head nodding ever so slightly.

"He's the way he is because of that, you know." I say it without knowing I was thinking it until the words come out. "That's what's wrong with him."

"That man Mark, you mean? He the one, isn't he?"

I nod, feeling my nod to be a response to Arethea's, creating a tie between us.

"They probably don't even know the harm they send out into the world," Arethea says, "just by steppin' away from us like they do. Little things like that. Crossing the street when they see our men comin' along." Her eyes drift away. "And the dogs barkin'."

"What about dogs barking?" I feel quick fear, as if I have stepped too close to the edge of a steep cliff. Something in Arethea's tone.

"That's how they got my papa's grampa," Arethea says. "Papa told us about it when we teased him once too often 'cause he was skeered of dogs. He hated walkin' into town, Papa did, and when we kids figured out he was skeered to pass by all the places with dogs, we teased him somethin' awful." She stops.

125

"What did he tell you about his grandfather?"

"His grampa was a slave, and one night he ran. It was after he'd been sold away from the plantation he'd been born on, where he married my great-gramma, jumpin' over the broomstick, like they used to do? They didn't get no chance at much of a ceremony. He was tryin' to get back to where she and the kids was, is what we think, or maybe just tryin' to get to freedom. But from where they found him, looks like he was runnin' home to her." Arethea's face closes, as if to shut out some image looming up in front of her.

Finally I ask, "Who told your dad this story? I mean, if his grandfather ran off and they caught him ..." My voice trails off.

"Papa's gramma told him. She heard it through the ground, like the moccasin telegraph you-all have. We have somethin' like that, too. Somethin' to do with drums once upon a time, and sometimes even now, or just a way of lookin' at each other and tellin' a tale and passin' it on. Different ways, you know? Maybe a tappin' of the foot or a shrug o' the shoulder. Ways of getting things known to each other."

"What did she hear?"

"She heard ..." Arethea's eyes close and her mouth draws tight over her teeth. "She heard they tore him up with those dogs. You couldn't even recognize him as a human being."

Her eyelids open. "That's one story the masters helped spread. They fed it right into our pipeline so we'd all hear about it. That's what our papa's gramma told to him."

It startles me when she speaks again, her voice conversational, more like her normal tone. "Papa's gramma got her freedom two years later, along with her kids, when the Civil War ended in 1865. My papa's papa was just four years old then."

Suddenly hungry and restless, I swing my legs over the side of the bed to the floor. "I'll get us the last of those doughnuts in the kitchen and make some coffee."

Arethea stops me with a question. "Did you ever read in the paper 'bout that young black man they lynched in Alabama, in 1982, I think it was? One o' those years Reagan was president."

I turn back to her. "No. I never heard of that."

"He's not the only one," Arethea says. "They just somehow didn't manage to hush that one up. No coffee or nothin' for me, honey. Thank you anyway."

I put my hand up against the closed door, rest it there for balance, wondering if Larry knew, if he would have told me something like that if he knew, and Arethea breaks witch-like into my thoughts.

"Shoot yourself full enough of drugs, I guess you don't have to remember such things when you're tryin' to fall asleep at night," she says. "Hearin' noises and creaks you don't know what they are, or who's roamin' around outside your window. And some noises you do know what they are, like dogs barkin' at a poor critter they've got cornered."

I turn the knob and leave the room quickly, not able to listen anymore. I pause to look at Victor, rolled up in blankets on the hall floor, his face burrowed into a pillow. He is on a small area rug that Ada gave him to lie on. Like a dog.

Arethea's voice floats out from the bedroom, unstoppable. "What those boys of yours don't be needin' is a man cut off at the stem who can't help 'em through the pain gonna come their way." I flee from the words, but the carrying mumble pursues me down the hallway. "There be enough white men out there waitin' with their lynchin' ropes. No need to bring home a stepfather with a rope of his own to yank the spirit out of 'em." I hurry to the kitchen and pick up the only chocolate-covered doughnut left on the plate and eat it in big mouthfuls.

chapter 25

"Arethea, do you want hot chocolate?" I lean against the kitchen doorway, content from doing an extra good cleanup job, with both boys helping, after the Saturday breakfast Ada served. For a brief instant I try to picture Mark in a scene like this, and can't. I am seeking refuge in domesticity, reclaiming my children, and all the while wondering how long it will last. Tony slides under my raised arm. He has a dish towel draped over one shoulder, in imitation of Victor.

"With marshmallows!" he announces to Arethea. She is wrapped like a mummy in an afghan, stretched out on the couch reading the final pages of *Crime and Punishment*. "I want to finish it," she told me at breakfast, "so I can pass it on to you." Because I need it so badly there's no time to waste? Arethea probably heard me when I crept in at dawn, morning before last. Talking in the night we got close, but still I didn't tell her what's going on with Mark. Do I even know? I wonder. And why did Ada's retreat to her room, when Victor picked up a dish towel, feel like a slap in the face?

"Hot chocolate with marshmallows! How could I pass that up?" Arethea gazes out the window at clouds amassing and blowing. "Another storm comin', but I'd say not before four this afternoon." She shifts her weight and sets one foot on the braided rug.

"I'll bring it," I say. "You stay where you are."

When I appear with a steaming mug, Arethea hitches herself up against the pillow propped on the arm of the couch. She is wearing another bright-patterned feedsack dress, with a white yoke. Tony walks in from the kitchen with careful steps, holding a full Snoopy mug and staring at it cross-eyed in his effort to keep it from spilling. Slowly he eases himself onto the floor. I settle down beside him and hand him a spoon and two napkins.

"Tony! You've got one, two, three, four, *five* marshmallows?"

Tony pokes in the mug with his spoon and creates an upheaval onto his plaid shirt and red jeans.

Victor hovers above us. "He's got eight in there, Mom. I watched him."

"I notice, Victor, you're not showin' us how many you've got in that big old cup of yours! Say, you know what I been thinkin', Katherine?"

"What, Arethea?"

"This is the first day off you've had since you got me here. I thought maybe we could go someplace. All of us together."

"Where did you have in mind? I'll take you anywhere you want. We could go to the mountains even."

"Well, that's not exactly what I had in mind. You know, Katherine, what I'd love is to go to the county fair and see these boys shoot some ducks and all of us ride on the ferris wheel."

"Really, Grandma? Mama, could we?" Tony begs.

"We'll do whatever Grandma Arethea wants," I say. "But I don't know about any fair going on." White people go to county fairs. Maybe in the South, black people do, too?

Arethea produces a newspaper. "One of those old papers your mama had out there in the kitchen? It tells about this here fair in your county. Tomorrow's the last day and it's gonna rain all day tomorrow. We better be gettin' there quick if we be goin'. Where's your mama?"

"I'm in here." Ada appears from the hallway. "I suppose I could ride along," she says.

"Well, good! That's just fine!" Arethea's eyes shine as she flashes a wide smile at Ada. I notice Ada can't help herself, she smiles back. Only Tony, and now Arethea, can draw out those rare smiles.

Tony tips his head back to slide the last cocoa-soaked marshmallow into his mouth. Then he is on his feet. "I'll be back in a minute," he says.

I call to him as he flies out the front door, "Where're you going? Didn't you hear?"

"Down to Pete and Adrian's! I'll be right back!"

"He'll probably bring them along." I sigh.

Arethea uncoils herself from the afghan, stands up, and begins folding it. "This is a lovely piece of work, Ada, the way you've joined these pinks and purples into each other, kind of zigzag like. I sure do think it's pretty."

"Well, thank you," Ada replies. "I can teach you that stitch, Mrs. Washington, if you like." Neither I nor Arethea has been able to budge her into calling Arethea anything but "Mrs. Washington." Ada goes to the window and looks out at the blackish-gray clouds scudding past. "It's funny weather out there."

"We should bring a wrap," Arethea says. "You know, I'd love to learn that stitch from you, but my fingers don't have the nimbleness yours do."

She's priming Ada for something. I can only half-guess what trap Arethea is setting, but I know her to have the patience of a prize-winning knitter, an Arachne spinning her web. "It's ten-thirty," I remark. "I wonder if you're right about the storm not coming till four. It'd be fun in a way to get caught in it."

"Yeah," Victor says, "get electrocuted up on top of a ferris wheel when lightning strikes." I glance at him, expecting a look of sarcasm, but he is grinning at Arethea, who winks back at him.

"Maybe I'd better be packin' a lunch." Ada starts toward the kitchen, when Arethea lays a hand on her shoulder.

"No, Ada, don't you trouble yourself. This is my treat to y'all. We'll get ourselves some hot dogs and soda pop and, if they have 'em, those good, tart apples with sweet caramel glopped on. I'm gonna go look for my green button-up sweater."

Ada produces two voluminous, lightweight jackets, fire engine red, and holds them out to me. They barely clear the floor. "You and Tony can use these," she says. "They're kinda big. I got 'em at the end of a sale tribal council had. Tillie Turnipseed didn't tell me till it was almost over." Too bad she told you at all, I think. I knot them around my waist over my jeans.

Tony is running down the road toward us as we emerge from the house. Victor and Ada hunch over in their jackets, his black

and hers shiny red. They look somehow alike in their distrust of
the world. It makes me smile to find something alike about
them.

"Who's that running way behind Tony?" I ask.

Ada squints to see better. "It's Adrian, and way behind him is
his and Pete's big sister."

Victor covers his mouth with his hand and lets out a snort.
"She sure is big, all right."

"Victor, that's mean."

"Well, it's true, Mom. She's as big as—"

"That doesn't mean you can say something, just because it's
true."

"Oh, boy! Let me think that one over."

"She's right, Victor, you know." Arethea wraps an arm around
his waist, and I watch him settle easily into her embrace. "I
wouldn't want you pointin' out how I'm an old, skinny thing like
I am." She gives him a quick squeeze and lets go before Tony
reaches us. A boy about Tony's size, with two thin black braids
flying out behind, is close on Tony's heels.

"Pete can't go," Tony explains to Ada. "He went somewhere
with his dad and won't be back till night. But Adrian can come,
and his sister, Paula."

The sister arrives, panting. She is dressed in layers of black
and brown and it is impossible to guess how old she might be.
Her plump hands are covered with large turquoise and silver
rings.

"Hi, Paula," I smile. "I've seen you helping out with the
preschoolers, but I never got to say hello. This is Mrs. Washington, Tony and Victor's grandma from Louisiana."

Paula's breath comes in short, panting gasps. "Hello," she says.
"I've never been on a ferris wheel."

"Yeah," Tony grins. "I told her where we're going—and that
we've got plenty of room. She can sit in back with me and
Adrian and Victor."

"She's not sittin' on *my* lap," Victor mumbles. I step on his
foot, to hush him. It's lucky the car has four doors, I think, as
Paula squeezes into the backseat. Victor shoves Tony and Adrian
in after her, then slips into the small bit of space that remains.

In my rearview mirror, I watch Paula dart admiring glances at Victor. Next to me on the front seat, Ada sits erect, with an air of expectancy that is close to apprehension. Her small feet, in white socks and black Keds, don't quite reach the floor.

"We haven't gone on an outing in a while," Ada says, and it hits me that never until this day have the boys and I and Ada ever gone anywhere together.

"You sure that rain's gonna hold off, are you, Mrs. Washington?" Ada asks.

"Well, I wouldn't bet money on it, but I'm a-hopin' it will."

As we leave the reservation along the rutted road that passes beside the worst bunch of houses, I slow down. Three small children dash out across the road in pursuit of a dog with hair missing, showing scabby patches like those on the children's arms and legs. This is the area where most of Whitney and Sky's clients live. I asked Whitney once if it didn't discourage her that so many of them miss appointments or show up, if at all, on the wrong days. Whitney's clear eyes rested on me thoughtfully as she answered that she herself had made more false starts than she could count, that one of her relapses lasted six months, a period of which she now had no memory at all. But she did remember a woman from her tribe's social services group who came out to see her when she hadn't been drinking for two months, and that woman had told her how pretty she looked and how she hadn't recognized her at first. When the woman hesitated and Whitney pressed her to say why, she finally told her it was because the last time she'd been out, Whitney's face had been so puffy and her eyes so bloodshot. And Whitney didn't even remember ever seeing the woman before.

We are out on the highway now and I flick on the radio. They are playing country oldies. Dolly Parton belts out "My Coat of Many Colors My Mama Made for Me" and, after a moment, Arethea joins in with low alto harmony.

The air is sultry when we pile out at the fairgrounds' parking lot, a field about three-quarters full of cars. We wait for Paula to extricate herself and then begin a slow circling of the booths and rides. The ferris wheel gleams silver against a gray-white sky. Brightly painted airplanes extend out on spokes and rise and dip as they rotate in a circle. A roller coaster chugs up a modest incline and zooms down the other side. Perhaps a hundred fifty people are at the fair. We're the only dark-skinned people. The thought brushes me like the familiar, unwanted touch of a fly on my skin. But we're probably safe. There are seven of us, and we're all women and children.

We manage to get past a weight-guessing booth without comment from Victor, then pause to watch a woman throw darts. Her fiercely determined face is framed by an orange beehive hairdo. She leans back, takes aim, and hurls a dart at a board covered with red, yellow, and blue balloons. She misses the board, and the man operating the booth has to duck to keep from getting hit.

Adrian stage-whispers to Tony, "Good shot, lady, you almost got 'im!" They leap into an elaborate pantomine, Tony holding his arm back for the throw and jutting his chin out like the woman dart-thrower, and Adrian cowering, with both hands shielding his head. I shoo them along, unknotting the red jacket from my waist and wielding it like a matador's cape. A man stops to look, grinning, and his wife's face clouds jealously. I catch both expressions and subdue the impulse to clown.

"Here, Victor." Arethea thrusts some bills in his hand. "You take these and get us some hot dogs and french fries and pop." She follows Ada to look at a display of colorful, handmade quilts. Paula and I settle in at a picnic table next to the fast-food booth. Soon all seven of us are crowded together on the table's two skinny benches. Tony has only to rear back, with a baboon-like frown on his face and an imaginary dart in his raised hand, to reduce us all to gales of laughter. We wait for Paula to finish a second hot dog and then get up and circle around to the duck-shooting booth. A black-mustached man in a white shirt, his green pants held up over a protruding belly by striped suspenders, greets us with a comically untrustworthy grin.

In two turns, Victor knocks over only one duck. He hands the rifle back to the grinning man and starts to shuffle away. "It's fixed," he mumbles.

"Wait!" Paula whispers. "I see how he's doin' it. The ducks jerk a little and slow down. You have to aim at their tails!"

Purposefully, she strips the rings from her fingers and gives them to her brother Adrian to hold. She pays her money and waits for the man as he finishes fiddling with the rows of yellow wooden ducks, sets them back in motion, and settles himself onto a folding chair. Then she picks up the rifle with an unmistakable air of expertise. She takes her time sighting the target. In an experimental kind of way, she shifts the rifle slightly from side to side. When she finally shoots, a steady line of ducks falls, one by one. The man jumps to his feet as if he's been shot himself. Paula takes aim again.

"Okay," he says. "Tell ya what. I'll give ya the biggest prize I've got if you'll just move on. Okay? We got ourselves a deal?" He reaches up to the top shelf for a gigantic pink bunny with floppy white ears, gets hold of it by one paw, and dangles it in front of Paula. She reluctantly yields the rifle to him. Adrian hands Paula her rings one at a time and she pushes them back into place. Then she embraces the giant rabbit, clutching it to her chest. She turns to Victor.

"I never won anything before," she tells him.

Victor laughs. "That guy's afraid you'll win every prize he's got! Where'd you learn to shoot?"

"Hunting. I go every year with my dad." Paula eyes him shyly. "Do you want to come with us next season?"

"Oh, I don't know what I'll be doin' then." I see that Arethea, too, is watching Victor's effort to act offhand. She also sees that the idea of the dad bothers him.

"I've got me a rifle down home, Victor," she says. "Down in Louisiana. We kin try it out when you come to visit. Skeer those little rabbits and foxes!"

Tension eases from Victor's face. He looks at Arethea with interest. "Do you hunt, Grandma?"

I wait to hear what answer she'll concoct. Arethea hates even the idea of hunting. The dusty rifle hangs up high next to the ceiling and is never touched.

"I bet together we could outsmart those old foxes," she says. "A friend of mine, he raises chickens, and he be out there at that chicken house hidin' in the tall grass every full moon, tryin' to outsmart old sly Freddy fox. We could help him out. I'm not sayin'

134

I'd exactly go out there huntin' with you, but I'd make something to eat for when y'all got home."

"I felt a drop of rain," Ada interrupts.

"Uh-oh. Victor, you an' Tony run and get tickets with this." Arethea hands Victor another twenty. "We'll meet you at the ferris wheel."

"No ferris wheels for me," Ada says. "I'll just get me a cup of coffee and watch."

"Won't you ride on it?" Arethea's face registers surprise.

"I don't like to leave the ground," Ada admits.

"She won't change her mind," I whisper, as Ada goes off to buy coffee.

"I know." Arethea sighs. "I'd just hoped to thaw her out a little. There's something frozen deep inside that woman. Some secret she's got hidden away, eatin' up her insides." A vendor passes with a cartful of candy apples. "Say, I'll take some of those!"

Arethea distributes candy apples and tickets as the line moves forward.

"Two to a seat!" drones the operator. He is small, wrinkled, and watery-eyed. He watches Paula seat herself next to her rabbit. It is obvious there is no room even for a small boy to squeeze in beside them.

"You want me to hold that rabbit for you, Paula?" Ada calls out from the bench where she is about to sit down with her coffee.

"No, thanks," Paula yells back. She has her arm around her rabbit and a firm, excited expression on her face. The operator looks at her glumly. Arethea and I are in the seat behind Paula. Only one empty seat remains. He gives a tired shrug of his shoulders and sets the wheel in motion, lifting Paula and the rabbit into the air. Then he turns to Adrian and Tony and Victor, who stand expectantly near the empty seat, unsure what to do.

"You two little guys," the old man says, "just crowd in with the big fellow and don't make any commotion."

We are stopped at the very top when Arethea again brings up the subject of Ada. Swaying in a seat below us is Paula with her rabbit. I glance back at the boys, whose seat rocks wildly.

"Stop pumping!" Adrian yells.

"She should be up here, Ada should, and feel her heart rise up out of her into this crazy sky. Look at them dark clouds, Katherine, glowering down on us!" Arethea lets out a sudden whoop and brandishes her half-eaten apple at the darkness swelling above us.

I catch the excitement, the thrill of swinging high above the world. "The clouds are coming closer," I say. "Let's reach out and put our hands in them."

"Something's eatin' away at her," Arethea says. "Do you know what it is, Katherine? Has she always been like this?"

"I would say it was Dad did it to her, but you know, now that I think, yes, she has always been this way. As long as I can remember."

"That's a long time." She shakes her head from side to side. "Look around you, Katherine. Isn't this just the best feelin'? Look, we're higher even than those evergreens! Here we go again!"

We revolve downward and Paula angles herself back to roll her eyes and wave the rabbit's ears at us. Then she takes a big bite out of her candy apple.

"She's having fun," I say.

"I know. I'd hoped Ada would join in and act like a kid and cut loose."

We are nearing the top again. I feel a giddy rush of blood. I lean over the seat railing to look down. "In her own way, Ada's having fun. She's drinking coffee and watching us all go in circles while she keeps her feet planted on the ground."

We glide downward and Arethea waves as we scoop past and upward. Ada lifts her white coffee cup in salute.

"You've got to try to find out what's hurtin' her inside, Katherine. It has something to do with you, I think."

"With me?"

"Don't go lookin' guilty and worried. No, I mean if you find out what's been gnawing away at her all these years, I think you'll know why she's acted toward you the way she has. Always so madlike."

And then there is no more chance to talk because Paula's candy apple flies out of her hand and straight into the ferris wheel motor. We are jolted out of our seat and pushed back into it by the restraining bar, in one quick motion.

"Damn!" The operator's hoarse shout rises up from below. "How in the hell did you do that?"

"It's all right!" Paula yells back. "I was almost done with it."

"Well, hell! The damn wheel won't move till I get that stick outa there."

"Oh," Paula says. "I'm sorry!"

I look back in time to see the boys' grinning faces disappear behind their baseball caps. The storm hits just as the wheel lurches back into motion. When each swinging carriage reaches the bottom, the elderly operator lifts the bar to let people out, muttering all the while about it being the dangedest thing he ever saw, first time in over thirty-five years—what'd she do, *throw* it at the motor?

Arethea climbs out and takes a folded-up bill from her dress pocket. She hands it to the old man, interrupting his mumbling. "Here's somethin' extra for your trouble." His mouth falls slack in his whiskered jaw as his eyes fix blearily on the ten-dollar bill.

"He kin go buy himself a drink to warm up," she says to me. "My papa had a low-pay job, too, that he worked at till he was too old to work."

Ada is peeling off her jacket. She thrusts it at Paula. "Here! Put this on that rabbit of yours. It's losin' its fluff!" Paula drapes the jacket over her prize and we all run for the car.

For a minute, a second, I think I am the only one who sees the small blonde girl in the path of the brown van backing out next to our Chevy. The child has run ahead of her mother, who pushes an umbrella-covered stroller with a baby in it. The mother has turned her head to talk to a woman friend walking beside her. Both are wearing sweatsuits, the hoods pulled up to protect them from the rain. The child, maybe three years old, looks down, pulling her pink cardigan with her hands, as if trying to make it reach the hem of her dress. She does not see the van steadily backing toward her, only inches away. The width of the Chevy and obscuring sheets of rain separate me from the little girl. I open my mouth, but no words come. Then, like an avenging angel in black jacket and black jeans, Victor swoops up the child at the last possible instant. He clasps her to him and swings away from the van's path. The little girls shrieks and pushes small fists against Victor's chest, and I see the mother whirl and take in only the dark-skinned stranger with her child fighting in his grip. I see it through the mother's eyes, wondering even as it happens how that could be, how I could be seeing my own son as a stranger, through a stranger's eyes.

"Let go of my daughter!" The woman's voice pierces, shrill, like an alarm whistle. The van swooshes off, spraying water as it goes. Ada is in the way of the woman charging forward to rescue her daughter, and she gets knocked against the rear fender of the Chevy. I feel a sharp pain shoot behind my eyes like a knife slash.

"Shit, lady!" Paula yells. "He just saved your kid's life. She woulda been run over!" The mother shoves Paula aside and reaches past to yank her daughter away from Victor. He tries to hand the child to her gently, but the woman tears her from him in a kind of ripping motion and the little girl screams.

"Mama won't let him hurt you! Mama's got you!" The woman's friend pulls at her arm, to get her to hurry away. Both women shoot looks of angry suspicion back over their shoulders as they push off with the stroller against the driving rain. Victor stands with his arms out awkwardly.

"Rain makes white people plumb crazy," Arethea says, linking arms with him. "Somethin' wrong with 'em, that's for sure. Let's you and me get in the backseat. Paula, you squeeze in, too."

Driving home, I grip the wheel to keep my hands steady. Tony, Adrian, and Ada are lined up next to me.

Arethea mutters, "Freud would have something to say about that woman." Nobody else speaks until we drive past the sign that tells us we are entering reservation land.

Then Adrian asks, "Would that little girl have got run over if Victor didn't save her?"

From the backseat, Paula answers, "She sure would. And in the army he'd get a medal for what he did."

"Well, maybe I should just go join the fuckin' army," Victor says. "Get myself killed."

Ada contributes her enigmatic logic. "Some days a person wonders if he wouldn't be better off stayin' in bed. Or else other people should of."

"Victor does sometimes, Grandma Ada." Tony pipes up, earnest and helpful.

"There must be a moral in here somewhere." I throw out the challenge, wanting help, reassurance, something I can't name.

Ada responds, deadpan. "Don't nobody go out in the rain?" And she twists around and winks at Victor. Or have I imagined the wink? Has Ada ever winked at anybody?

chapter 26

I sit at the kitchen table in my bathrobe, reading a week-old paper, the most recent I could find. Ada brings remnants of newspaper home from the tribal center. She retrieves them from wastebaskets, I have seen her do it. I sip from the mug she plunked down in front of me, savoring the coffee's sharp taste and the hotness of it. A soft humming alerts me and I look up to see Arethea in the doorway, wearing a spotless white cardigan over a crisp pink-and-white housedress. The rest of us live in jeans and tee shirts or, in Ada's case, polyester pants. And I've been too lazy and relaxed this morning even to pull on jeans.

Arethea tips her head sideways into the room. "Mmm, that smells good! Mind if I come in and just breathe in that goodness? Blueberry pancakes, am I right?"

"You can do more than come in and breathe, Mrs. Washington," Ada says, standing at the stove with her spatula in hand. "I'll fix you up with a stack of pancakes and some coffee. Katherine here, she won't eat in the mornin'. Not till she's been up awhile." Her voice fades to a murmur. "Maybe my cookin's not good enough."

"Morning, Arethea," I smile. "How did you sleep?"

"I slept so well I didn't even know I was doin' it. Never in my life have I slept so well outside my own bed as I do here in your mama's house."

Satisfaction settles on Ada's features and she turns to flip the pancakes on the grill. I almost let out a giggle, thinking that Arethea may never have been outside her own bed until this trip, and she slept like a log in the one motel room we shared and awoke rested and clear-eyed from roadside naps.

Arethea is examining the homemade objects hanging on the wall. "Isn't this lovely," she croons.

Ada picks up the cue. "What's that?"

"Why, this spice rack. This is remarkable workmanship! So much care went into it, you can see that!" Arethea runs her index finger along the curved edge. "Must have been your husband made this," she says. "I've heard from Katherine he was a master carver."

What is she up to? She has infused more reverence into her tone than any wooden spice rack could merit.

"No," Ada says. "It's Victor made that for me. He made it while Katherine was on the trip to get you." Her voice, as always when she has to say Victor's name, is distant. Is there less distance in it than usual, or am I only wishing?

"How he must love you! I can see why so much care was taken, if he was makin' it for you. You're that special to him, I've seen that all right." Arethea seats herself at the table and manages to appear lost in thought. "I wonder now ... I wonder where he gets the carving gift. Wouldn't he from our side of the family." She shakes her shoulders, as if to rouse herself. "Why am I sittin' here like a lazybones? What can I do to help? Here, let me set out plates. You'll join me, won't you? I'm not much for eatin' alone." Another lie. Or is Arethea practicing her witchcraft?

In a few moments, Arethea has two places laid and the butter and syrup and jam set out on the table, and the two women sit down across from each other with plates of pancakes in front of them. Ada takes a thoughtful bite and fixes her eyes on the carved spice rack, as though seeing it for the first time.

"Victor did do a good piece of work there," she says. "Maybe today I'll put some spice bottles in it."

I choke on a mouthful of coffee.

* * *

Leaning back against the tree's rough bark, I sit in a blaze of sunlight. It feels good to stretch my legs as far as they will go and wriggle my bare toes in the cool, damp grass. The lawn needs mowing. I love it this way, high enough to hide toes in, and secrets. The sounds from the kitchen are a familiar background, a reminder that Ada's one release is to bang metal against metal, to clang pots and pans and lids with wild abandon. Has she ever done one single other thing in her life with abandon? I lower my chin and regard my breasts swelling out of the white halter top, my slim calves emerging from rolled-up faded jeans. I feel sixteen, or even younger. There is a sense of peace here. Though I may be making it up, believing Ada is beginning to accept Victor, and believing it to be real because I want so much for it to be. I dream it to be a lasting peace we can sink into, Victor and Tony and I, and be borne up and held safe, the way I sink my legs into this grass and the earth bears my weight. Drifting, nothing to do ... how wonderful. How clever of me to escape a stressful city, an abusive man ... no, keep drifting, don't get that specific ... thoughts come, though, when the mind drifts, open and relaxed, thoughts feel the invitation, the space available to creep in and lodge in the brain. Why do I keep so much distance? The thought sails in, tantalizing, disturbing. Why do I keep myself separate, removed, even from myself?

The screen door bangs. It is Ada, come to stand on the back porch. I feel her there, watching. Does she watch in disapproval? Maybe not. Maybe she's glad I'm safe where she can keep an eye on me. Yet I keep the distance. Or is it she who keeps me far from her, even when we stand side by side at the kitchen sink, working on the same task?

I tilt my head back and lift my face to the sky. Wisps of clouds scud by like angels, or missiles. Crazy thinking, let it go. Who are you sitting here under the sky, on land your ancestors walked and hunted? A survivor? Smallpox and wars took their toll and your people bled and failed and died. No, they were killed! Those weren't natural deaths. And all you can say for yourself is you haven't slept with the enemy? Is that enough to build a self on? Where will your own meaning come from? No one will give it to you. You have to claim it.

My body. I have that, slender and lithe here in the grass, brown like the earth and the trees. And I have ancient memories and imagination. But no one expects me to be anything. And nothing will happen if I don't make it happen. Am I trying to keep out of range, beyond the possibility of hurt? Is that why I keep the distance? It's our way to work together, to be part of the same effort, to keep the self strong and inviolate so it can carry its weight. I grew up here. I know these things. But I was sent to school in town, where we became "those Indian kids." Nobody held out any expectation that we would succeed, and we clung together with a new feeling of shame mixed in, because we knew our clinging together now was forced on us. It had been joy and freedom we sprang from before, playing and yelling, a bunch of laughing kids who didn't know fear, and now we were surrounded by white achievers and white mediocres and white trash, all of whom knew they were better than any one of us and made us know it. It was our first experience in separateness, in being kept at a distance. And we felt it in our individual souls.

But I am not unworthy. The thought startles me. My back separates from the tree and I feel the tree's strength in my spine. I am not unworthy. They have made me think I am and even act as if I am, but I am not.

And I smell lilacs! In the city I forgot the fragrance of lilacs. They were overpowered by exhaust fumes. Here they know it is safe to bloom and spread their souls. I turn my head gently and my eyes melt into the softness of the purple whose beauty cries out to be noticed. Alice Walker, a black and Indian woman, heard the purple flowers cry out and wrote it down. That was the first book Arethea ever gave me.

* * *

I have my bare foot on the top step and my hand ready to pull the screen door open when I hear Victor's voice.

"Where's my grandma?"

I stop, knowing he means Arethea, waiting and fearing to hear my mother's answer.

"What do I look like, Victor? Don't I look like a gramma?"

"I ... I'm sorry," he stammers.

"What's there to be sorry about? That I look like a gramma? I've got used to it, can't you?"

"I didn't mean that ..." His voice sinks away.

"What is it you need a gramma for? You look kinda done in, Victor. Why don't you sit down here and I'll fix you a Coke in a glass with ice."

I don't think I'd want to move even if I saw flames coming out the bedroom window. I'd want to know what's going to happen next.

"Somethin' went wrong, didn't it? I see it in the way your mouth is all twisted up." I hear the tinkle of ice cubes. What does Ada see in his face that is changing her into my dream of her? "Here you go. A nice, tall one."

"Thanks," Victor says. He doesn't add the word *grandma*, but I imagine I can feel him wanting to. I hear a chair scrape on the floor. My mother must be sitting down across from him.

"I don't know what good a gramma is, Victor, unless you can tell her your troubles." I begin to breathe again.

"What happened, Victor? It's okay to tell me. Whatever it is." My eyes close, and I wait. "You know somethin' funny? You've got that mouth of yours set just like your Grampa Jim. I could always tell when somebody had hurt 'im. He was a man who got hurt easy. Maybe because he was such a kind person himself. He couldn't handle it at all if somebody talked rude." She sounds now as if she is talking to herself, then she seems to remember where she is. "Who hurt you, Victor? What did they do?"

There is a silence. Into it Victor finally drops reluctant words. "Nobody did nothin'. Just this guy said somethin' is all."

"Did this happen at your rehearsal for that skit you kids are gonna do?" Ada is on the scent, sharp-nosed as a hound dog.

"Yeah. It did."

"Who was it?"

"Just this guy Kirk who doesn't like me. He ... I don't want to talk about it."

"Yes you do, Victor. You'll feel better if you tell me. And I sure don't want nobody sayin' nothing to hurt my first grandson."

"That's why you're asking?"

I wince at the hope that springs out of his voice.

"Do I look like an idle gossip, Victor? Or a nosy busybody?"

"No, Grandma." There! He said it. Tension eases out of my back, and I lean against the wall of the house. "Okay, well, it's just ... This guy ... when Sky was gonna choose me for the part of the young brave who's the chief's son? The one who gets the girl?"

"Yes?" Ada sounds wary, on guard. "That would be a good part for you, Victor."

"Well, this guy Kirk didn't think so. He said, real loud, so all the kids heard ..."

"What, Victor? What did he say?"

In a low tone the words come out. "You can't give that part to a nigger."

Something in me suspends itself, loses consciousness, so that when a chair scrapes again, my head jerks involuntarily and my mother's voice comes from far away.

"Go ahead an' cry, Victor. There's no one here to know but your gramma. Big Jim cried. He cried more than I did. Nobody knows that. Except now you know it." I move soundlessly away and down the steps and back to the tree. If my mother or Victor looks out, they will think I have been there all along. I turn my head aside so my face can't be seen from the house. Tears run from my cheeks into the ground.

chapter 27

Whitney is sunk deep into an armchair with no springs. Her black leather boots rest on a wooden table amid old *Redbooks* and *McCalls* and a few current issues of *People* magazine. I stretch out on the worn, once-beige couch. The lounge is quiet because everybody who can spare the time is in the longhouse working on regalia for the powwow. The walls surround us with photos of kids and elders and long-dead ancestors and dancers in war bonnets. Paula passes through with a carefully balanced load of bone chokers. Six or seven preschoolers trail her, with clumps of braid ties clutched in tiny hands. They look very solemn as they trot along behind Paula, who resembles a mother hen, I can't help thinking. Victor said last night they've scrapped the old play and in the new one Paula gets to be a medicine woman.

It's been a week since the day he talked to Ada in the kitchen. Sky came by the next morning and waited till Victor got up and dressed, then gave him and Tony a ride the quarter-mile to class. Arethea told me. We both know Victor wouldn't have gone otherwise. Sky sat on the floor by the couch where Victor was sleeping, or pretending to sleep, and talked to him in low tones. Arethea couldn't make out the words, and at last Victor got up.

"We're on coffee break," I call out to Paula. "I'd come and help but I have too much work to do—I know it doesn't look like it!" Paula nods her head and scuttles her brood of chicks through the door.

"What did your brother look like before he started drinkin'?"

Whitney's question startles me, and I say the first thing that comes to mind. "He was always tall. It's funny, I remember him as always being the tallest of the three of us, and yet he's the youngest."

"Okay, tall. He's still tall. So what else?"

I take a sip of hot coffee from my foam cup. "My mother had the three of us boom-boom-boom, hardly a year in between, and then she figured out how not to, I guess, because there weren't any more. Do you really want to hear this?" Hearing my own description starts me wondering. Did they sleep together, Mom and Dad, in those years after we kids were born, the years I knew them?

"Yeah, I really want to. I mean, I know Ronny only as this wasted guy who shows up once in a blue moon and your mom throws him out."

"Is that what she does? The last I knew, he was drinking even then, but she acted like it wasn't happening, though there'd never been a drop of alcohol in her house."

"What was he, her favorite?"

"Seems that way, doesn't it? Why are you asking about him?"

"You want to know?"

"Yes, Whitney, if there's something to know."

"I fell in love with him. Even wasted like he's been these last few years, I fell for him and I guess it bothers me how that could happen."

"Did anything come of it?" I ask it gently.

"I don't want to talk about it."

"But you still want to hear about how he was? Before?"

"Yeah. I do."

"What I remember is once, just once, he had a teacher who understood him. In third grade. He was like a willow, you know? A tall, slim, bending, graceful thing that you want to have around just because it's so beautiful. And yet somehow you know it can't stay that way." Something fills my throat, makes it hard to speak. "We all loved him the best, it wasn't just Mom."

"Tell me about the teacher."

I take a small sip of my coffee. "She called Mom in for a conference. She said, 'Ronny's read every book in the school and he's bored. Do you take him to the public library, Mrs. Jack, so he'll have books to read at home?' Mom had never been in a

147

library. She found out where the nearest one was, and she got Mr. Eaglefeather from down the road to come and get the car going—Dad was on a binge—and we went chugging into town, Mom and us three kids."

"And?"

"Mom brought her knitting, and we were there till the darn place closed. They dimmed the lights and made an announcement, if you wanted to check out books you had to do it in the next five minutes. I remember the look on Mom's face. She was sitting there with her knitting trailing down to the floor. It was a red scarf she was making for Dad, hoping to keep him from freezing, I guess, next time he passed out in a snowbank." I bite my lower lip, seeing remembered scenes like loose pieces of a jigsaw puzzle scattered on a table. "She had no idea what checking out a book was about. She just gathered up her knitting and told us to remember what page we were on, we'd be back as soon as she could bring us."

"All three of you were readin'?"

"Ronny and I were. Neither of us could hardly bear to leave. Harry fell asleep propped up in a corner behind some shelves where Mom couldn't see him."

"What were you readin', do you remember?"

"I'll never forget. I read that book over and over. *The Velveteen Rabbit.*"

Whitney chews on a thick, purplish-pink stalk she's pulled out of a deep pocket in her multicolored cotton vest. It looks like rhubarb, and it makes my face pucker just to watch. "Your house has more books than any house on the reservation. I don't get it."

"Those are Dad's books. We never used to think of them as anything we could touch. And they're not really something an eight-year-old could read."

"Huh. All those books and none of you read 'em."

"I started after Dad left, when I was fifteen. Some of them had really good stories. If I stayed with it, I'd get interested and want more. I'd give a book fifty pages, and by then I was sucked in."

Whitney comes to the end of her stalk. She pulls the shredded remains out of her mouth. "All chewed-up, isn't it? Like a

148

book you've eaten up! What about your mom? Does she ever read any of 'em?"

"She's never been a reader. For her, books don't exist. Even though half the time Dad had his nose in one. Mom's a doer. And sometimes what she'll do is go into a kind of trance, sitting in her chair at her bead table, or in the kitchen. It's like—"

"What?"

"I don't know, it's like her head's so full of something she doesn't have room to put any more stuff in."

"Hmm. Not like me—my head's a big, empty bowling ball. It gets lonely not havin' more ideas bouncin' around in it. I'm always lookin' for stuff to fill it up with." Whitney grins and heaves herself up from the depths of the chair and walks a little stiffly over to the coffeemaker. Today she is wearing red satin pants with ironed pleats around the hips and a border of white stars beginning a few inches above the point where the pants disappear into her boots.

"Gosh, I'm only thirty-four and already my joints get stiff from sittin'!" She brings the carafe back and fills both our cups, then returns it to rest in the Mr. Coffee machine. Gingerly, she eases back into the gaping armchair, holding the cup out to the side in case it spills.

"It's like Mom's head is full of memories that keep every-thing else out." I say the words wonderingly, feeling the truth of them.

"She probably never talks about 'em either, does she?"

"She hardly ever talks to me about anything."

"Don't take it personal, Katherine. Most of the stuff that hangs us up is from so far back we don't hardly remember it."

"You think so?"

"I know so. Want one o' these?" Whitney sets her cup on the threadbare arm of the chair and pulls another tough-looking stalk from her pocket. "It's velveteen rabbit food!"

"Velveteen rabbits draw the line at rhubarb."

"Rhubarb's good for the blood." Whitney crunches her teeth into it. "You said your dad left when you were fifteen. What happened?"

"Mom caught on he'd picked up a female drinking partner. She threw him out."

"Not much of a compromiser, is she?"

"You think she should have compromised?"

"Something's eatin' that woman. I don't know what it is. But throwin' your Dad out didn't fix it."

"It sure fixed him," I say. "He froze, you know. About a year later. In that shack where he went to live. I went crazy then, crazier even than I already was."

Whitney stretches out a hand and strokes my head. "It wasn't your fault, or your mom's either. It was the drinkin' did it."

I stare at her. "You know, it just hit me that everything we do is connected? There's nothing that isn't related to something else. It's a big, enormous spiderweb. And as delicate and sticky as one."

"How d'you figure?"

"I don't know, Whitney, but look at it! Ronny drinks like Dad did, and Harry's all closed in like Mom, and I'm—I don't know what I am. But it's connected somehow. It's all connected."

Whitney's listening eyes turn sad. "Probably it is."

I try to hang onto the insight and not let it slip out of my grasp. "I don't see all the connections, Whit, but I know they're there. I feel them pulling on us, sometimes pulling us apart and sometimes together. We're all caught in the web!" In my mind, I see a braid of black hair lying on the floor. The big, redheaded kid grabbed Harry and held him while the blond one took the teacher's scissors and in one clip destroyed years of growth, of Indianness. Harry's eyes turned dull from one moment to the next. My baby brother full of wonder, reaching for life like a toy, was gone. At home that night, Ronny vowed to Ada that she couldn't stop him, he'd find the sons of bitches and cut 'em up. "That won't help!" Ada's voice had been a hoarse bellow from someplace inside her never tapped before. It stopped Ronny, held him safe in the house. But safety didn't last.

"I remember a thing happened when I was a little bitty girl," Whitney says.

"What's that?"

"My mom took me and my brothers and sisters to the city once, I don't even know what city it was. And suddenly she says, 'Hey, there's a colored man on that corner.' All we'd ever seen up to then was Indians, except for white social workers. I was excited. I thought, gee, I'm about to see a man who's all different kinds o' colors! I love color—you've maybe noticed that about me."

I smile. "Yeah. I have noticed that, Whit."

"Well, I look and there he is, and he's just this ordinary, brownish black color. And here I'd been expecting a rainbow!"

"A rainbow wants to connect things," I say. "It wants to be a bridge."

She grins. "Next time one of us sees one, let's jump on the old Harley and ride right out to the end and grab on!"

If I were Emma, would I go find Ronny and force him into treatment and clean him up for Whitney? Emma's not real though. None of them are. They're puppets, with Austen pulling the strings. You can save a puppet from danger if you jerk the strings at the right time.

Whitney hitches herself up from the depths of the chair. "Katherine, what you said about everything being connected? That's the circle! That s what it is, isn't it? Our talking circles and the drum circle." Her eyes shine with discovery, inviting me to join in.

"Our most sacred symbol," I say, wondering at the way the mind travels its slow, circular path to see things that have been there forever.

chapter 28

The first thing I notice is the perfect red rose in a white bud vase on the back of the toilet. Then I see that Arethea has cleaned the bathroom. It must have been her because all of her personal items that were lined up on the back of the toilet are gone: her Jergens lotion and Colgate toothpaste and bag of cotton balls, nestled in a row along with a bottle of witch hazel and a jar of Pond's cold cream. The basin is sparkling and the floor has been cleaned so carefully there isn't a stray hair or speck of anything in sight.

Apprehensive and not letting myself ask why, I use the toilet and flush it, then wash my hands and dry them by brushing my fingers against one of the fresh guest towels. Everything looks newly laundered. I go into the room that used to be my own and Arethea is sitting there on the edge of the bed, the old black suitcase resting on the floor next to her white-sandaled feet. Both Arethea and the suitcase look ready to go. Her dress, a red-and-white polka dot that I especially love, is beautifully ironed with sharp creases down the sides of the elbow-length sleeves. She raises her eyes expectantly. How long has she been waiting, ready like this?

"Arethea! What—"

"It's time, Katherine, for me to go home now."

"But I thought—you're just starting to really get along, you and Mom. She likes it, having you here."

"Honey, I've done what we brought me here to do, and now I have to get home and water my flowers and make sure I can still git up that tree."

"What we brought you here to do?"

"Oh, don't let's pretend, Katherine. We know each other too well. You needed grandmothers for Victor that could love him with their whole hearts like the boy deserves. And he's got that now."

"But, Arethea, he loves having you here."

"Well, he knows where to find me. I reckon he'll be down to see me when he's a little older." She stands and goes to the dresser and picks up a black straw hat with a wide red ribbon around the brim. "He knows where I am and where I'll stay. He might like to take the train down there someday, like I'm goin' to do." She plants the hat firmly on her head. "And don't you say nothin' about that, Katherine, that's what I'm goin' to do. I've got my ticket and I won't be no trouble to nobody. Just a ride to the station, no more than an hour or two drive, and that's all I'll trouble you for."

"Arethea, you know I could take time off and—"

"And have us another one o' them car chases? You think we need another one to keep us runnin' good as some old fox? No, I'm gettin' too old for that." Arethea adjusts the hat to a more flattering angle and studies the effect in the mirror. Her voice takes on a softer tone. "Like I told you when we were down home, I've got me a man there. I don't want to leave him missin' me too long. Don't want him to go lookin' for another lady to take my place. A man who'll wait patient-like is not so easy to find." She searches my face. "Am I right?"

"I wish I even knew what to look for, Arethea."

"Oh, don't get all downhearted an' discouraged. You know well enough." I feel her eyes pierce into me and finally I meet her steady gaze. "You knew to come get me when Victor needed grammas who'd love him and like him. And you know you're part of a family, Katherine, not just a lone woman, and you'll do what you ought to do."

The old witch'll have me doing what's right for me and the boys even if I want to do the exact damned opposite. I think it even as some untamed need tempts me to rebel. "I'd hoped you could meet Mark ... in a better way."

Arethea's eyes widen.

"He's been kind of busy lately ..." I falter.

"Busy at what?"

"I'm really not all that sure."

"Maybe you'd best be finding out. There's more to that man than meets the eye, Katherine. No, that's just it, he *don't* meet your eye. He be hidin' something, and I'm not sayin' it just 'cause he acts like I'm some ghost you can look right through. No, he be up to something."

I feel a tremor pass through me, jolting my memory back to myself and Mark by the pond when he said the dam meant progress—yet didn't he know it killed the fish?—and then the flash of insight is gone. "When, Arethea?" I ask. "When does this train leave? By the looks of you, it's soon."

She turns and walks to the window. "I told the boys before they went off this mornin'. Told 'em I wouldn't leave till they come—"

Without knowing I am going to, in one quick impulse I move toward her and grasp her forearms. The flesh is firm and soft and I want to hang on forever. "Don't! Don't leave me. I need you."

"You need me, do you?" She puts a hand over my wrist and grips it. "Oh, you need somethin', girl. But it ain't me. No, it sure ain't me you be needin'."

"I want you near, Arethea. I need you to stop me from making the same damn mistakes over and over."

"You think that'd help, havin' me here?" She tilts her head back and laughs. "Hell, girl, you go right on finding everything out the usual way, by yourself, right when I'm here in your mama's house with her, waitin' for you to come home." She squeezes my hand. "We all just muddle along, Katherine, the best we can. Some of us have good hearts, fed with enough love or whatever makes a heart good, and we just have to hope that'll see us through."

Tony rushes into the room and throws his arms around Arethea's hips. He turns his head to speak to Victor, poised in the doorway. "See? She's still here, like she promised. So we can go to the train station with her."

Arethea lays a hand on Tony's head and smiles at Victor. "I'll need your strong arm to carry this heavy old suitcase o' mine, won't I?"

And then Ada is there standing beside Victor, holding forth a new Indian blanket. "This'll help keep you warm on the train," she says. She brings out a new pair of beaded moccasins from the folds of the blanket. "And you can put these on your feet when you're restin' in your seat." She thrusts the gifts into Arethea's arms.

"I'll be the envy of all the folks back home," Arethea says. "And how I'll love wearin' these beautiful moccasins when I sit an' read, all wrapped up in your soft blanket!"

Ada's face flushes. She says quickly to me, "Come help me carry the bag of food I got ready for Mrs. Washington's train trip."

chapter 29

I'm back in my room again. I stand in strong sunlight in front of the mirror, looking at my legs. I have walked a lot since coming to my mother's house. Sometimes I feel I am walking toward something and will get there if I can just make my legs keep on going; other times I am walking to escape something that lurked in the city waiting to destroy us and that now stalks me on these country roads. If I keep my legs moving, nothing bad will happen, nothing will catch me. Often I look over my shoulder and stop a moment to breathe in relief, seeing the road behind me empty of danger. I walk to stay young. I figured that out just yesterday. And I walk to keep from missing Arethea more than I can bear. A lot of things will become clear if I keep to myself, letting spirit move into parts of me it has not visited. Dangerous, though, to be walking away from Larry's memory and walking into the arms of a new man, even seeing the walking as a way to be ready for him. Clear mud. Does such a thing exist? My legs are the legs of a woman thirty-two years old and wanting to forget how old she is or that people expect her to make a decision. I let the skirt of my cotton dress fall back into place. I slept through the long morning, luxuriating in a whole bed and room to myself. The luxury has an empty quality to it, the emptiness of a house without Arethea in it. I yearn to plug up the hole. The image brings rueful amusement that I would think so concretely of the emptiness of a hole needing to be plugged. By a man?

I am alone in the house. They've all gone off, not telling me where. I pluck Arethea's week-old rose from the bud vase in the bathroom and start off toward the tribal center. Today I work only the afternoon. It is hot and still, the kind of day when everyone is inside to escape the heat.

At the office, I pull out the reforestation booklet I sent away for. It arrived in the mail last week and I haven't had time so far even to look at it. Too busy getting ready to sell off all the trees. Everything fraught with irony. I smile. I'll plug the hole with reforestation and learn how to bring the forest back after they've destroyed it.

The afternoon passes quickly, divided among phone calls and a report to type and the secret, intermittent reading of the booklet, which feels like a talisman in my hands and inspires extravagant daydreams.

The day is insistently summer. Robert is insistently Robert. Or Sky, rather. Something about this day, the heavy summer weight of it, has moved me back in time. How has he come into my life anyway? A moment ago, he passed by the window, waving to me, vivid and smiling against a backdrop of hazy greenness. I hear him on the porch, greeting the old men who have gathered now that the sun is lower and the heat is bearable. I'm certainly not going to fall in love with him, and it isn't clear he is going to fall in love with me either. That surprises me. Men usually do, given half a chance. He has become a part of both my boys' lives—they quote him, they wander around after him, waiting to be given jobs to do; Tony has begun to walk with Sky's lilting step and to wear a hat like Sky's, an old thing he found in Ada's closet that he pulls down over his eyes and tilts off to an angle when he wants to make an impression. I wonder if he even knows he is doing these things. He's still at the unconscious age. I myself am far from that state of mind. I am aware I wore a revealing yellow halter dress to work because I thought Mark would come by to pick me up. You never know with Mark, I am realizing. Now here is Robert. And again I remember, startled, that he is Sky, disembodied, no longer a man with a solid name.

"Nice dress," he says. "How'd you know we'd have another scorcher?"

"I was just hoping mostly."

He smiles. "That's a good way to make things happen. So." He walks over to the file cabinet and smells the rose I put there in a white pitcher. He notices everything. Men surprise you sometimes. It would be nice to get close to one who had some good surprises in store.

"So." He says it again. "Where's the boyfriend?"

"Who do you have in mind?" I ask.

"Why, Mr. Cool. Who else? I thought he'd be in here mappin' out his territory. But when I saw the coast was clear, I decided to come in and distract you from your work for a while." He sifts through a pile of papers on my desk, letting them fall through his fingers.

I adjust the straps of my dress and feel the lift of my breasts inside the soft cotton, and sense Sky's eyes watching me. "Want to walk over to the house with me?" I say. "It's too hot to work any longer. Wally went home an hour ago."

He looks at me thoughtfully and I am embarrassed. Maybe he reads minds. Maybe he knows I don't want to walk alone when I was counting on male company.

"I just came over to check on you, Katherine, make sure you're stayin' out of trouble." He grins. "I'm helping the kids. They'll be here all evening, workin' on their outfits."

"Oh, I forgot. Tony told me. I'm supposed to help with food. I'll go home and take a shower first."

He keeps grinning, keeps his distance. "Don't let the bogeyman get you!"

I don't want him to dismiss me like this. I want him to see there's a serious side to me.

"I've been getting to know Richard Dillon," I say. "We worked really late last night, putting materials together for a presentation he's making."

"Oh, what's that about?"

I see the double meaning in his eyes.

"Not what you think, Sky! He's not like that."

"I know." His glance at me is sober. "He isn't, is he? He's a real loner, that Dillon. He's a funny guy."

"What do you mean, funny?"

"Dillon's a breed. Breeds work harder. Haven't you heard that?"

"Work harder how?"

"At being an Indian!" Sky chuckles. "Dillon's the only guy in town who's got his own sweat lodge in his backyard! If he's not out choppin' wood for a sweat, he's burning the midnight oil on some scheme to get back our rights."

"Well, that's exactly what he's doing now. And I'm proud to be helping him."

"What's old Dillon got up his sleeve?"

"It's about the river. You know how when we were young it was so much bigger?"

"And had ten times as many fish. Yeah, I remember. I know what you're gonna say, Katherine. Those logging companies diverted it, way upstream. I've talked to Dillon about that. He's doing something, is he?"

"He's trying to. He's gathering data. To show the feds and local authorities didn't follow due process when they allowed the dam."

"How's that gonna get us anyplace?"

"We can't get the fish back. But we might get compensated for the loss. Because the feds were supposed by law to consult the tribe. And they didn't."

"Why do you look that way, Katherine?" Sky startles me out of my thoughts.

"Look what way?"

"Oh, kinda wistful."

"Dillon wants Victor to help. He told him he's a real smart kid." I feel tears coming and don't want to think why.

Sky takes my hand and squeezes it. "That'd be good for Victor, wouldn't it? Dillon's not a bad role model. Be good for Dillon, too. He's a lonely man." He drops my hand and goes out the door. "I'm headed for the longhouse. See ya later."

chapter 30

"Sky!" I motion to him above the heads of the children, and without hesitation he makes his way toward me, winding around hunched-over figures that sit cross-legged on mats on the floor. The smooth young faces are absorbed in the task of threading oversized needles through buckskin, securing thongs of fringe.

"What's up?" He looks eager and young, childlike himself.

"There's an old, drunken woman raving out there. The heat must have got to her. Somebody needs to do something. She won't leave. We were working in the kitchen and she showed up at the back door. She grabbed a trash can lid and she's out there charging around with it like a shield."

A change comes over Sky's features. I had thought he might find the story funny, but his eyes dull and his jaw drops, hardening the lines around his mouth. He passes a hand over his forehead.

"Did she say anything?"

"She's asking for Robert, so I thought I'd let you know, but she's raving, Sky, she's drunk out of her gourd."

He hurries past me, then does a half-turn. "Is she still out there, in the kitchen?"

"No. They made her wait outside. She was carrying on so bad nobody could work."

Sky heads off in the direction of the yard outside the kitchen and I follow. He outdistances me because he moves so fast, but I am close enough to see him approach the woman, who is collapsed in a heap on the step. The woman looks up as he approaches. I am surprised to see her run her hand through her matted black hair, as if to make herself presentable.

Sky takes hold of her by one arm and pulls her to her feet. He brushes off her clothing, which is torn and covered with leaves and debris. She looks like she's been rolling in the underbrush. But what strikes me most is that Sky is acting like a parent. Systematically, he turns the woman around and brushes off all sides of her. Stooped over, she submits like an obedient child.

Closer now, I see the concern on his face. He has been transformed from a carefree child to a worried parent. The woman lifts both dirty hands and smooths her unruly hair back from her face. She and Sky have the same finely drawn nose and chin and brow, and her eyes are like his, large, dark pools of somber light. But her face is puffy, and a scar disfigures one cheek.

"I'm sorry," I hear her say. "I need t'go someplace ... need you t'help."

"Where do you want to go, Janie?" His voice is empty, impassive.

"To treatment, Robert. Can you get me in?" It is a plaintive whine.

"How long will you stay in treatment? Till you feel good enough to walk out and go get a drink?"

He looks up then, some movement of mine catches his eye, and he sees me standing there, watching.

"Come here and meet her, Katherine." His voice is bitter. "I told you once you reminded me of someone? Well, here she is. Mom, this is Katherine. Katherine, this is Janie. Janie used to be quite a beauty, too, on her good days."

I move toward them, wanting to retreat, forcing myself forward, my mind a blur of anger at Sky for the way he is treating both of us.

In defiance of him, I hold out my hand to Janie. Janie looks toward me, eyes unfocused, and lifts her limp right hand a few inches, then drops it as though overcome by the effort.

"I'm drunk, Robert. Whatcha doin', introducin' me to your friend like this?" Her words slur. She is close to passing out.

"Sky," I say, "you're an alcohol counselor. Even if you don't want to help as a son, you've got to do something."

"Oh, do I?"

"I'll do it myself!"

"We'll do it together. It's no big deal. I could do this with my eyes shut, couldn't I, Janie?" Janie's head droops down to her chest, hanging there, swaying.

"Help me then, Katherine." He lets out a weary sigh. "Help me get her to detox."

Neither of us speaks again until we have gotten Janie propped up between us and are speeding down the road. Behind the wheel, Sky sits tense and erect.

"I know where to go," he says. "You're right. As an alcohol counselor, I know where to take her." His jaw is tight, as if from the effort of trying to keep from blurting out more anger. And I understand it, the frustration of dealing with an addict. But to think of me as like this woman! I close my eyes and hold my breath, to escape the boozy smell coming from Janie's clothes and skin. Holding my breath doesn't hold up thought. I don't drink often but I binge. Dad was a binge drinker. It didn't happen often, but when it did, it was bad. And it killed him.

I can't bear the sickening smell, the angry silence. I want to cut through and reach him. "You've done this before, I take it."

"Yeah, I've done this before. Maybe ..." he screws up his mouth into an expression I've never seen on him. "Maybe ninety-five times in the past thirty years. No, let's see. I'm thirty-seven." He turns his face to look at Janie, whose head bobs with the bumpy motion of the car on the rutted road. Her eyes are closed and her mouth is slack. "I've been doing this since I was about ten, let's say an average of five times a year? To be conservative. So what's that? I'm driving. You do the math."

"Ten years old. Twenty-seven years, five times a year. Five times twenty-five is a hundred twenty-five. I guess you underestimated."

"No. There were a few years she disappeared on me. Called me from Texas once? Said she'd run out of Tampax, could I bring her some. She was blubbering so much it took me awhile to figure that one out." His mouth is still set in the grim line I have not seen before, but he is trying to smile.

"How long since you last saw her?" I ask it quietly.

"Let's see. She always gets hold of me around the holidays. So I know we made this little trip back at Christmastime. She lives in the city, and she's got so-called friends there, so it's not always me who gets to her when she needs help."

"Where did you grow up, Robert?" I have slipped back into the other name, but I don't correct myself. It's what his mother calls him.

"In the city—makin' trips for her back and forth to the liquor store, tryin' to save my homework from various natural disasters. They happened around our house on a daily basis."

"So, were you a good student?" I try to keep it light. I yearn for him to be again who I thought he was.

"I was till I got hooked myself."

I feel a quivering all down my throat into my chest. "On what?"

"Heroin."

"I'm going to open the window," I say.

"Sure. Go ahead." He glances at me, his expression a mix of so many feelings that my brain feels stunned. I roll down the window and close my eyes, trying to draw comfort from the cool night air.

He goes on talking in the new, hard voice. "No, there's some things you didn't know about me. I'm a well-qualified counselor, though. There's not much they can pull on me."

I open my eyes. "How long have you been clean?"

"How long have I been clean. You know the lingo, don't you?"

"How long, Sky?"

He grins at me finally, and it feels like a sunburst. "I'll be eight years old next week."

chapter 31

On the ride home, a feeling comes over me. It is as familiar as hunger pangs. I can't believe I want a drink. I lay my palms flat at my sides and close my eyes and wait until the feeling passes and leaves just a memory of the intensity, the need, the wanting. Slowly I let my eyes flutter open. Now that Janie's smell is gone I become aware of the smell of the car, a sweetness that seems to reach my nose through my fingertips, cushioned against the soft, yielding nap of deerskin. I am sitting on an old worn skin. Sky has layers of skins piled up on the backseat and the clean warmth of them permeates the car and makes me aware of his body, firm and strong, only inches away. I edge toward him, wanting the comfort of his warmth. He was gentle with Janie when he led her into detox, protective even. We were entering alien territory and both of us felt it. Drunk though she was, it seemed Janie felt it, too. Her eyes were watchful and wary. She let us support her, one on each side with an arm around her, so we presented a united front as we went through the wide hospital doors that parted electronically. There was something dramatic about our entrance because of the opening of those doors and walking three abreast. It dawned on me, as a few heads turned in our direction, how alike the three of us must look, brown-skinned, slim, all about the same height, Sky just a few inches taller, both women with a mass of black hair falling forward onto their shoulders, Sky's braid trailing down his back, the three of us hunched over, myself and Sky as though in sympathy with Janie's fallen state. And there was something sad and shameful about it, to be Indian and to be bringing your mother in to be cared for by whites who would see her in the worst possible way, who would see an old, drunken Indian woman and chalk it up in some secret register of their minds so that the next time they saw you, or any other Indian, the layer of scorn and distaste that lay between you and them would be a little thicker.

"I want a drink." I say it aloud, not knowing I will.

"Damn you, Katherine." He looks at me and I smile, glad to have his eyes on me finally.

"I was kidding."

"Kind of a bad joke, don't you think?" He glances at me again and his mouth softens and widens a little, ready to smile with me.

I move closer, until my arm and thigh touch his. His body stiffens. I feel it in the arm that is up against mine and in the tightening thigh muscle.

"Relax," I say. "It won't hurt to make each other feel good. You can't think about that kind of thing too long. It drives you nuts."

"So you're going to drive me nuts instead?" I feel my chest swelling and a need coming over me that wants to sweep him off the road and into my arms. He'll start responding in a moment, I know the signs. But just as I think it, he pushes me away.

"What're you doing?" Surprise forces out the question.

"I'm trying to get you to stay on your side of the car. Look, I don't know what turns you on, Katherine, but for me, sex is pretty special. It's not what I do for relaxation when I can't have a drink."

I scoot over as far from him as I can and lean against the door, wishing it would fly open and I'd fall out. A pulse pounds in the side of my throat and I stare straight ahead and fling the words at him: "Just drop me off here."

"Here?" He looks at me with exasperation. "You know who you're acting like, Katherine? That's how she acts. When she's not too drunk to flirt, that's how she acts."

"Goddamnit, Sky, slow down!"

"I'll let you out when we're at your mom's." He speeds up and I have to endure and wait, seething, until finally he brings the car to a controlled stop and I am out and running for my mom's front door on a burst of adrenaline.

"Thanks for the help!" He calls it out his open window as he U-turns and heads the other way.

chapter 32

"Mom, what's that smell?"

I look up from the book I have been staring at, my thoughts making a blur of the words. I shift my weight forward to the edge of the couch and sniff. "What smell?"

"Like burning coffee."

"Oh, hell. That's what it is!" I leap up and into the kitchen and grab the pot off the stove. Victor follows me.

"Wait a second before you pour water in." He takes the pot from me and goes to the sink. I sigh and rub my hand up over my forehead and through my hair. Even my scalp feels lonely. I rub it over and over. Victor runs water into the pot and sets it in the sink.

"One more thing for your Grandma Ada to hold against me," I say.

He leads the way back to the living room. "Lie on the couch, Mom." He places a big cushion at one end. "Lean on this an' put your feet up, you'll feel better."

I settle in, grateful and a little surprised, but not comfortable or even wanting to be because of what I'm about to say. Are we always going to be at cross-purposes, cross-moods? With the gesture that has become habitual, Victor pulls his knife and a small block of wood from the pocket of his jacket. With deft strokes, he transforms the block into the rough beginnings of a bear.

"Victor?"

"What?"

"We're going back to the city, okay?"

"Mom! Why?" His face falls apart, and I turn away, unable to look at the thwarted little boy my words turn him into.

166

"I just mess everything up, Victor. And Mom said I have to make a decision what to do. I only got a leave for the summer. There's no way I can make the kind of money here I do in the city."

"Mom, we don't need that much money when we live here. Everything's different, it's easier here."

"What are you saying, Victor?" I roll onto my side to stare at him.

"I don't want to go back, Mom. I want to stay here."

"But there's nowhere for us to live. And you get tormented, Victor, just for who you are. More than in the city."

"Mom, they're starting to accept me. It just takes time. They had to get used to me."

"Used to you? What's there to get used to? Oh I know, I know. I just get sick of it."

"Mom, I'm writing a play for the kids to put on."

"*You* are writing a *play?*"

"Well, you don't hafta say it like that. You're not the only one who can write, y'know." He juts his chin forward, and his eyes shoot out defensive rays. "I told you we scrapped the old play. You probably don't even remember."

"I'm sorry, Victor. You took me by surprise. You never mentioned anything about you being the one writing it!"

Rain splatters hard now against the windowpanes, releasing tension the clouds have held all day. I feel freed by it, as if I, too, have been released from a nagging gloom. Victor frowns at the bear-shaped block of wood in his hand. "Now we're doing a play about the rainbow. That was the subject Sky gave me. He said I could write what I want."

"The rainbow. You're doing a play about a rainbow. Are there girls in it?" I try not to smile, teasing him. Suddenly I am lighthearted.

It is Victor who grins. "Sure! They're part o' the rainbow, aren't they? Remember I told you Paula gets to be a medicine woman? That's because I'm writin' in the part for her."

His eyes glow with hope that I will change my mind. What an awful power to wield. And it's not that Ada is pushing me that hard. It's that I am frustrated and mad at Mark, and ashamed to have Sky see how stupid I can be. I had been about to run away, start again. But the image of the rainbow works a gentle magic, forming an arc over my worries, making them seem transient. Only a fool would run away from a rainbow.

"The trouble is, Victor," I explain slowly, "we can't stay here at Mom's indefinitely, and school's about to start. The only houses available are one-bedrooms."

"Gramma said one of us could stay here with her." He shoots me a quick glance, then looks away.

"Why didn't you tell me?"

He stares at the floor, infuriating me. He looks as if he could go on staring at it forever. The smell of burnt coffee permeates the air. My eyes graze the wood carvings my father left behind, the bookshelves with his Steinbeck and Saroyan thrown in among the Victorians and philosophers, the small oak table laid out with beadwork, everything familiar and solid.

"Why didn't you tell me this sooner, Victor?" My mind races with questions. Is Ada offering that either boy could stay with her? But would I let either of them stay with Ada, and not be together, the three of us? Isn't it good, though, that Ada would talk to Victor about this?

"All you ever think about is your boyfriends." His voice is bitter. Well, he's right, I can't deny it. The realization hits as a kind of sad surprise.

"Victor, I'm not that mean. We'll stay till you do the play. But I can't think beyond that right now, okay?" It's the best I can do, the farthest I can plan.

There is a sudden flurry at the door, a scuffling noise and the sound of feet scraping. Then the door bursts open at the same moment we hear a knock, and Whitney falls in, looking surprised.

"Huh," she says. "Funny door you've got. Well, hello!"

My spirits lift. Whitney's wackiness makes me smile.

"You two sure looked somber when I came in." She darts bird-bright eyes from Victor to me. "You been plottin' somethin'?"

"We're plotting our future," I laugh.

"Well, good then!" Her tone is deep and resonant. "So let's have some hot chocolate and toast, a toast to the future, does that sound good? Homey-like?" She grins at Victor, whose eyes are fastened on her with delight. No wonder. For one thing, you never know what getup Whitney will be sporting. She has flung off her black leather motorcycle jacket to reveal black leather pants with long pink fringe at the waistband, into which she has tucked a purple-and-white-striped tee shirt. "I'm a transient in this world" is printed in silver glitter across her bosom.

She sprawls in a big easy chair with her legs spread wide apart and the shiny soles of her boots tipped up.

"Are those new, Whitney, those boots?"

"These? Naw. Where would I get the money?"

"Well, they look good. They're shiny on the bottom, you know? So I figured they were new."

"I got 'em at the Salvation Army thrift shop. Shined 'em myself. Listen, Katherine, what were you guys talkin' about when I came in? Something serious?"

"Aren't we always serious?"

"Oh, c'mon honey. You two are a mother and a teenager. What d'you expect?" She settles in more comfortably. "Anyway, I'd say you're doin' pretty good. Nobody's in jail. He's at home, talkin' to his mother—of all things." She tosses her infectious grin at Victor.

"I was telling Mom about a play I'm writing."

I marvel at this woman who can draw out even Victor.

"Great! I love plays. When can I come and see it?"

Victor leans forward in his chair toward her, his elbows on his knees. "I hope in a couple months. The thing is, Sky wants at least two plays. Mine's gonna be a one-act. He wants to make an evening of it."

"Don't look at me." Whitney shades her eyes with one hand. "I'm no writer. I'm more the active type. Don't know if I'm an actor. Just plain active, that's me."

Victor sighs. "None of the other kids wants to write either."

I decide to add my two cents' worth. "I've been kicking around an idea for a story."

His expression takes on an edge of curiosity. "Really, Mom?"

"It's just a fanciful idea that came to me out of the blue. It would definitely be a one-acter. It's a one-idea kind of thing. But I could see it being dramatized."

169

"Fantasy would be good," he says seriously. "The kids eat it up. Mine is a kind of fantasy, too. Real life gets to be too much to take sometimes, y'know? So the theater can be a way to set yourself free, to dream a different world."

Whitney slides forward on her chair. "Gee whiz, Victor. You're deep as a well. I like that, what you just said about dreamin' ourselves into someplace different. That's how I feel on my Harley, like I might just ride myself off to a better world. Like maybe there's really one out there someplace, waitin' to be found."

"At the end of the rainbow," Victor says, smiling. "Where the pot of gold waits for us."

"Yeah!" She beams at him. "You've got it, Victor, right there. You've got it!"

"So, Mom, why don't you give it a try? Talk to Sky about it."

I don't want to kill the thing that is happening, right here in my mother's living room. "I just might," I say gently.

chapter 33

"I'm going to quit smoking."

"How come?" Victor hears me over the din he and Tony and Sky are making, all talking at once and tuning the radio to a different rock station every few minutes. How anybody can make so much noise sewing is something I can't figure. Or is Sky using noise to cover the tension in the air between us? Ada has heard, too, and is listening for my answer. I know by the way her needle stops for a quick beat before its dive into the buckskin.

"I can't keep up with you, Tony," I say. "When you were running yesterday? I was on the other side of the shrubs, and I ran along for a while."

"I know, Mom, I saw you." Tony grins. "For a while. Then you disappeared."

I laugh. "That's because I fell so far behind."

"We gotta be ready by September," Tony tells me. "That's when we go out on our own for three days."

"I saw you, too." Sky glances at me. "You looked like you wanted to be left alone. And I've learned to respect your moods." He gives me a long, deep look. "So, you're starting a pure life?"

"No. I'm just quitting smoking." I flash my eyes at him, up through my lashes, shading my face with my hand so my mom won't see me flirting. And then remember what he said about Janie.

Ada dives in, changing the subject. She must have noticed. "Overalls in the toilet," she says, shaking her head.

"Overalls in the toilet?"

"That's what Ernie found," Ada reports, "when he was helpin' clean up after dinner. The dinner you missed. Out with that fella."

I look at Sky. "Want to be friends?" He mouths the question, then raises Tony's buckskin vest in front of his face to cover his mouth. All I can see are his twinkling, questioning eyes.

I let my own eyes show relief. It hasn't felt good to be at odds with Sky. I turn my smile, my sudden goodwill, on Ada. "Do you mean that Ernie who works in tribal court? The clerk guy?"

"Well, who else would I mean? We've only got one Ernie."

Is Ada matchmaking? The last thing I need is another man in my life! Does she think serious, plodding Ernie would get me on track?

"Gee," Sky says suddenly. "About this time, you'd be going outside for a smoke, Katherine. I kinda miss that. Can't we just go out for a few minutes and breathe, blow some air around?" I see he wants to tell me something.

"Okay." I stand up and stretch. "I'll take a breathing break."

Outside he falls down on the grass laughing.

"What, Sky? What?"

He twists over onto his back and rests his shoulders on my bare feet and grins up at me. "You want to know how those overalls got in the toilet? One of the guys got a girl out in the bushes and while they were out there, Steve stole his pants. Thought he'd teach him somethin', I guess."

"And you think that's funny."

He sits up and rubs his eyes, suddenly glum. "No, Katherine. I don't. But it gets to me sometimes, being in charge of every damned thing those kids do." His voice rises to a mimicking falsetto. "We don't know what to do with her, doctor!"

"What's that supposed to mean?"

"AIDS. That's what it means. I have to teach these kids to go against every instinct they have and—"

"I don't want to talk about this kind of thing," I say. "Let's go back in."

"Wait a minute!" He grabs hold of my arm. "I'm bustin' up, trying to cope with these kids and the threats out there waitin' to do them in, and they're not even my kids, Katherine. Two of them are yours. None are mine. And *you* don't want to listen?"

"I don't know why, Sky, I just don't. Maybe I'm irritable 'cause I'm not smoking and I want to. This was a really dumb idea."

"What was?"

"Coming out here together."

"Well, I used to hang out with you when you smoked. What's the difference? Now I don't even have to waste energy looking disapproving."

"You never did look disapproving. Not about that!"

"You're right. There's other vices worry me more. I guess I figure you need something to do that's bad for you. That's how it is at AA meetings, you know?" He looks at me. "You ever been to an AA meeting?"

I kick my toe against the step, wanting it to hurt. "No."

"Well, you wouldn't know then. There's a lot of smoking at most AA meetings. And some heavy Coca-Cola drinkers."

"You don't do any of that, Sky. How come? Are you some sort of monk or something?" Where is the meanness, this urge to hurt him, coming from?

"Whoa." He backs off a few steps. "Maybe you ... I don't know what to say, Katherine. Anything right now would be wrong, right?" He looks comical as he wards off imaginary blows and staggers backward, away from me.

"Oh, come on," I say. "Let's do be friends. I was feeling good up until you—I don't know what it was bothered me. Something did." My mind clouds, putting a screen between me and the something.

"Isn't golden boy coming by to take you out?"

"Oh, gosh! I can't believe I forgot. What time is it? Let's go in. Neither of us has a watch."

I notice a tightening in the muscles of Sky's face. Then I see where his eyes are directed, out toward the road. A truck has pulled up.

"God, he's here! How long has he been sitting there?" I run down the front walk and motion to Mark to come in, but he stares straight ahead. I open the truck door and climb up onto the seat. As always, the presence of him causes a stir, a pulling together inside me.

Finally he turns his head, slowly, and looks at my jeans and tee shirt. "That's what you're gonna wear?"

"No, this isn't what I'm going to wear. Don't you want to come in while I change? You could see the boys. And my mom."

"I've seen the boys," he says. "I came to take you dancin', Katherine. Are you comin' or not?" I consider explaining that Sky is there to help Victor and Tony get their powwow regalia ready for tomorrow, but he wouldn't care about that. And if he wants to be jealous of Sky, let him.

"I'll be about five minutes."

I'm hungry, I think, as I slam the door behind me. And Mark is mad and won't want to get me anything to eat. I brush against Sky, going past him to my room. Why do men take up my body and my mind? I glance back at the scene of the three of them working away, at peace for once, my mom and my boys. Ada is helping Victor with a difficult seam that has to curve, something I never learned to do myself, but he seems to be catching on. His nappy head is close to his grandma's head, and Ada is showing him the way to ease the stitch around. Will that annoy Ada, having him so close? She leans in and guides his hand. But then she draws back and pulls herself up tight, retreating. I sigh, knowing she has sensed me watching. I don't want to go out with Mark and leave them. I realize it like a sharp pain. I want it all to go on, this closeness, this dancing back and forth and around that Sky and I do. What I'll do, though, is start drinking fast to have a good time. Lose myself in sex. And suddenly I know why it bothered me to hear Sky talk about the kids and their craziness and the risk of AIDS. When we both drink, Mark and I, we forget to be careful.

This month they're giving AIDS tests free at the clinic. I read it on the bulletin board.

"Don't forget I'm in the first dance tomorrow at the powwow." Victor's voice is the last thing I hear as I fly out the door.

chapter 34

I lift my head and lower it quickly, downed by the throbbing in my temples. I lie very still and try not to breathe or think. Smells invade my nostrils. The bed stinks of sweat and unwashed sheets and vomit, and my own breath is a mixture of alcohol and puke. I am sickened by the smell and know that in a moment I'll have to run again for the bathroom. We have taken turns all night. I've been passed out most of the time, or fitfully awake. It has been one of the worst nights I can remember. We are on a futon on the floor. It is double-bed size and Mark's weight has worn it down to a flat, rocklike hardness. Mark is wearing a tank undershirt and nothing else. His back is to me. He looks like a huge, round-shouldered bear, deep in hibernation. I turn my head away from him and stare at the gray patch of wall just above the floorboard. There are brown stains on it. The throbbing continues, but maybe I'm not going to throw up again, after all. The shades are drawn and no light filters in. I need fresh air. I imagine getting up and finding my clothes, the too-tight black leather skirt, the red blouse. I imagine creeping out into the air. Something else is beating in my head, insistent, not painful, but insistent and steady like a drumbeat. I listen and feel the beat course through my alcohol-dazed body.

Slowly, carefully, I roll over onto the bare floor and raise myself to my knees, then push up with my arms to a standing position. I waver unsteadily. My feet are cold. I find the door to the backyard and turn the knob and step out, not realizing I had expected sunshine until I see the blackening sheet of sky. It seems to be spreading, moving in on me, but the air feels life-giving. Sultry and oppressive, pre-storm weather, exciting.

I lift my head on my neck and breathe in deeply and promise myself, or God, or somebody, I will never drink that way again. My toes spread out and grasp the cool grass. The drumbeat presses on, doing its work; I feel it in my feet now and pulsing up through the veins and muscles in my legs. It is part of me and of the earth beneath me. The powwow!

I turn to run back into the house but am slowed down immediately by pain charging into my forehead. I make my way toward the kitchen, trying not to breathe the smells as I pass through the bedroom. On the kitchen sink, there is one clean glass in the dish-drying rack. I fill the glass with water and drink it down. Then I fill it again and drink the second glass more slowly. The clock says ten after one. The Grand Entry was scheduled for noon. I've probably missed it. Tony will be dancing soon. There is no time to go home and get other clothes. The thought of going into the stinking bathroom to shower is repulsive. One of us didn't make it to the toilet in time, I don't even know which one of us it was. But I need a shower badly. I walk back into the bedroom, still naked, and Mark opens his eyes.

"Whatcha doin'?"

"Getting ready to go to the powwow. I'm late. Tony's dancing." I pick up my underwear from the floor and my blouse and skirt from a chair. "You coming?"

"Are you kiddin'? If I sleep twenty-four hours, maybe I'll be human again." He tries a smile, not successfully. "If you made some coffee ..." His voice trails off and his eyes close.

"I've got no time to make coffee." In the bathroom, I step around the splash of vomit on the floor and turn on the shower. I stand under the stream of hot water and feel as if I have died and gone to heaven, the heaven they let people like me into, a kind of *demimonde*. I laugh into the spray of water, thinking that word, trying to remember where I read it and what it means, keeping my mouth open and letting water rush in and out, sharp and clean against my teeth. I stay under a long time and use the bar of soap to scrub every part of myself. There is a bottle of shampoo on the shower floor and I use it to wash my hair. I get out finally and find a clean towel in the cupboard to towel myself and my hair dry. The part that doesn't feel so good is putting on yesterday's underwear and party clothes and the high heels. Mark is dead to the world again. I shut the door quietly behind me and it feels as if I am shutting the door on a whole lot of things, trying to put them behind me.

I hope so, I think, striding forward in my high-heeled shoes. The drumbeat grows louder as I near the powwow grounds. I begin to pass through clusters of onlookers, some of them white people come from nearby towns, the city even, to see the Indians dance. Mostly they are families, with children. I smile at a young mother with a freckled face and wide, expectant blue eyes, a baby in her arms.

"Are you going to dance?" the woman asks.

"No," I say. "Not this year."

I scan the crowd for familiar faces. Various people nod to me. I know them from helping Ada at community dinners and from my work in the office. As I edge my way into the dense circle of spectators, a voice booms over the loudspeaker: "Look at these kids, ladies and gentlemen. Now they deserve your attention, these kids do; they've worked hard to learn these dances of their ancestors."

Could that be Tony dancing already? I feel woozy, brushing my way past people who are almost all taller than I am. The ache in my head has settled now at the base of my skull. It throbs there, reminding me I drank way beyond the point of being able to remember how many drinks I had. I won't take aspirin. I'll tough it out and let the pain be my punishment. What am I doing to my brain though, will I have any left? Is that what hurts, my poor, stupid brain?

I am just behind the inner ring of spectators now, and I see the young boys dancing, each of them wearing furs and skins that represent an animal, their bodies bent forward or to the side, slapping their feet on the ground, shifting their weight from side to side, back to front, and there is Tony, bent over from the waist, shaking and swooshing his head around, gyrating with and against the beat of the drums, his feet taking magical leaps, his whole body agile like the—my mind closes in on itself. I don't know, or can't remember, what animal he is supposed to be. He is so intent, so focused on every beat, every movement, so careful and yet wild and free. Tears fill my eyes.

I sense the familiar presence close to me before I hear Sky's voice at my ear. "He's wonderful, isn't he?"

"He's wonderful, yes," I say.

"He's a natural." Sky's face lights up with a smile that is mostly in his eyes. He looks at me then, studies me for a moment, and I know he is taking in the puffiness around my eyes, the grayness of my skin. "He'll be really glad you made it." Then he adds, "Your mother's as tense as a rock. See her over there? Wave to her, why don't you, before she freezes that way."

I look at my mother, sitting with the other older ladies on chairs in the inner circle. I lean forward and wave my arm back and forth. The young couple in front of me, with blond hair rubber-banded into identical ponytails, move apart for me and a moment later my mother spots me. She nods her head slightly and looks disapproving, then I see her shoulders relax and see her turn to the gray-braided lady next to her and say something. The lady looks in my direction and nods.

I step back and right up against Sky. I hadn't known he was standing so close, and I am surprised how good the warmth of him feels. He looks startled. "I'll get you some coffee," he says. "You look like you could use some." His eyes are watchful. And again I think of Janie.

chapter 35

"Mom, let me help."

"I'm all done."

"I'll start on something for tomorrow then."

My mother doesn't say the words but I hear them, loud and unspoken. What is the matter with you? She says, "Sit down, Katherine. I'll make tea."

"I can't stand this!"

"Yes, you can."

"What are we doing?"

"We're makin' the best of things. It's what we've always done."

"It's not enough! I want so much, Mom. I want to be rich and happy and safe and—"

"Hush, Katherine. You have everything you need. Don't let the boys hear you."

"I'm not ready to be their mother." I hiss the words across to where Ada stands by the teakettle, waiting for it to boil with a wary patience, as if every task she does signifies something. "How did you get this way, Mom? Weren't you ever crazy?"

"Katherine, you aren't on dope, are you?"

"What? *What?* You can ask that? After Larry, you think I'd do that?"

"That's what he died of, is it?"

I seethe with anger at my own carelessness, but Ada pursues a different line of attack.

"What about the boys?"

"What about them?"

"They know you didn't come home last night." The demon pounding in my head returns. It makes me wild. "I'm an old woman, Katherine. I can't take this much longer."

"You say that so I'll respect you and not go against you. What you want is for me to be old and dried-up too!"

"You're raving. Here, sit down, sit still, and drink your tea. It's that man. He's in your mind, screwin' it up, isn't he?"

"What do you know about that, Mom? What do you know from your own experience that I could trust?" I laugh aloud at the image conjured by Ada's words, the image of Mark screwing up my mind as he screws the rest of me. The laugh hits the air, sharp as a slap.

She opens the screen door and stands staring out, and I glare at her implacable back. A sudden wave of frustration, violent and unreasoning, rises until it carries me to the front door and down the steps on the run. I don't stop running until I reach the riverbank. And like a blessing, peace descends on me, or maybe exhaustion, when I plop down onto the dirt. My thoughts drift out like fishing lines floating in different directions, my spirit a cloud, hovering over the murky water. I can almost see it, a cloud that hasn't decided whether to release its burden of moisture. Where did that come from? Myself a rain cloud, raining on Victor's parade! The image brings me to my feet. I brush off the seat of my jeans and start at a run toward home. I have to get there and talk to him while I still feel this sense of how I must seem to him, a heavy rain cloud of a mother, pouring cold water on his hopes.

The front door stands open, as I left it. Ada has closed the screen door against flies. I bang it behind me and rush through the living room into the hallway.

"Is that you, Katherine, makin' all that noise while I'm tryin' to nap?" I hear her grumble, "Who else would come tearin' in like that? Worse'n the boys. Hasn't changed since she was a teenager." Ada has become a mutterer and I listen in the hope of finding out what is going on with her. Never having been a talker, in her old age my mother is a mutterer. Maybe that's progress. I come to a halt at her doorway and look at the rounded form stretched out on the bed, patient and wary. When has Ada ever not been wary? You'd think dangers lurked at every turn. Well, they do. Maybe if I had ever had even a trace of wariness I wouldn't be a single parent raising a teenager, with his brother coming along fast on his heels.

"Mom, has Victor gone out?"

"No. Tony has, he's over to Adrian's. Victor's settin' out under your tree in the backyard."

I pause, preparing to dash out, still aiming to preserve my momentum. "My tree?"

"You sit under a tree long enough and then it's your tree." Ada closes her eyes and I walk away, shaking my head. Why do I have a puzzle for a mother? I don't want to be a puzzle to Victor. I want to be right as rain for him, clear as a running stream. There it is again, the maudlin impulse to be good. I've caught myself saying it aloud in bed at night like a mantra. Let me be good, please. But to whom am I praying? If I believed in a god, would that make me good?

"Victor, mind if I sit here with you?" He looks almost ready to take flight. If only there were a way to pin children down and keep them safe. I wish I were a bird and could fly around with Victor under one wing and Tony under the other.

"I'm sorry, Victor," I say, still standing, wanting not to forget to say it.

"For what?" His eyes challenge me.

"If I seem to be getting in your way sometimes, and then when I wasn't there to watch you dance, I don't mean to—"

"Seem?"

It's not the right moment, not the right words. Instinct steered me wrong. A sigh comes out. "I just wanted to say I'm sorry. That's all."

As I turn to go back in the house, Victor's body makes a slight movement toward me. Does he want me to stay and tough it out, argue through to some understanding? I'm not in a fit state to do that. An apology ought to be worth something. I never got one from Ada.

An unexpected impulse to cry stifles me when I think of Ada lying on the bed, worn out by a daughter who directs a lifetime of anger at her in one morning. Maybe she, too, has moments of wishing she were flying around with me safe under her wing. Is that possible? I don't go into the house. I go around it and keep walking.

Earth. It feels good to have it under my feet. Like the only sure thing. I remember the tree in the city growing through cement, reaching to the sky, offering a memory of what strength is to people who've forgotten. No matter how much gunk we layer over the earth it is still there, breathing, waiting for us to notice what supports us. I lay myself on the grass, aware of that support, and am almost asleep when I feel someone standing above me, not intruding, just there. Slowly, not wanting to lose the calm that has sunk into me and around me, I roll over on my back and open my eyes. At first I am not sure it is Sky, the sun blinds me. But no one else would be that much a part of the earth.

"The river's skin." I say it aloud, the first image in my mind.

"I know." He sits down beside me easily, and keeps a small distance between us. He, too, needs distance. With my skin I sense his need, my thin skin, like the river's. And then he says it aloud, my thought.

"My skin is like that, smooth and unbroken. How deceptive."

"You roam around as much as I do, don't you? Is that how you found me?"

"I saw you, Katherine, head toward the river. Might as well admit I followed you. This place is full of eyes and ears. Everything gets around, so we might as well be honest."

"What's that, a new theory of reservation morality?"

"Actually, in this mode of honesty I have to tell you it was Whit who said it. Not that the thought's original."

Again this skirting, fencing, staying away from anything that might bring our thin skins together.

"Why do we always end up talking about her?"

Sky fixes watchful eyes on me, listening. I feel his eyes touch me deep inside.

"She didn't see me. I liked that. I mean it's like she saw past makeup and earrings and—"

"Do you wear makeup?"

"Not much."

"Then is that what Whitney saw past?"

"She saw me, what I am inside. She just skipped all that part so many people find important."

182

"Yeah. I like that about her, too."

"You're that way, you know."

"I am?"

"It's one reason I like talking to you."

"Do you like talking to me?"

"It's restful and exciting. Both. At the same time."

"What else are you saying, Katherine? There's more that you aren't saying. You're throwing up roadblocks."

"Just that I wish sex could stay out of things sometimes." My face turns hot. "It complicates everything and makes it hard to get to what matters." I grin. "I mean to what *else* matters."

"It's usually there somewhere, isn't it? You're right. We hang on to sex because we know, so long as we're fuckin', pardon my language, or thinking about doing it, we're alive."

"Don't ask pardon. It's a word." I say it harshly. He has thrown me back in time to a scene of rumpled sheets, my own nakedness. I shy away from the insight Sky tossed out in front of us like a flashlight beam and retreat into abstraction. "I think sometimes about how quickly life can be snuffed out. And yet we act like we have forever. We even have the nerve to get bored!"

"Yeah, that's probably the one sin." His eyes are watching my face, and I feel him responding to something he sees there more than to my words. "How did he die, Katherine? Your kids' father?"

A shudder convulses me. "Suddenly. Gone before ..."

With one hand he rubs up and down my shoulder and gives it a squeeze, leaving his hand there. "It's all right."

"No. It isn't. It was as wrong as could be."

"Were you there, when he died?" He asks it as if testing the waters. I feel the sensitivity in his fingers, in the timbre of his voice.

"I was next door. They had to come and find me there." I am not able to say more.

"It's all right, Katherine. It's all right if you weren't there."

"It's not all right! Quit saying that! I can't stand it!" Sky draws back, and I stare into my shame, frightened by it.

After a moment, he leans across the space between us and plants his hands on my thighs. I feel the warmth tingle through my jeans. "Come back, Katherine. Don't go so far away." He crinkles his face into a grimace. "I miss you. Come back!" Would he look at me with eyes like that if I told him when my husband died I was in bed with my husband's best friend? Maybe it is only Arethea who can forgive such a thing. Or who has any right to sit in judgment of me. The last thought flits in as a surprise.

chapter 36

My mother appears in the doorway of my bedroom, like a little gnome standing there, watching me with wise gnome eyes.

"I need your help, Katherine. Over at the center. We're short-handed."

She'll never admit she might really just want me to be there, working alongside her. In the past several days there has been a subtle shift, a softening in my own view of myself that has carried some of its softening over to my view of Ada, too. It's also had the effect of making me see things I hadn't noticed before, such as that it isn't only Tony my mother keeps beside her whenever she can, despite the hostile, barbed edge of most remarks she throws in my direction. I lay down *Emma* and roll off the bed and onto my feet. I'll have to wait a little longer to find out whether Harriet and the farmer will be reunited, and that suits me fine. I like to savor the suspense, the delicious, long-drawn-out drama. Will the girl ever come to her senses, or will it be too late?

"You can go like that."

I look down at my jeans and faded flannel shirt. "You don't want me to put on something better?"

"We'll be in the kitchen covered up with aprons."

As we set off down the road, I ask, "What's this one for, this dinner tonight?" I slow my step so she can keep up.

"It's for Tillie Turnipseed's father. He's turning ninety-three. He's our oldest person here on the rez."

"Gee. I remember him from before I started high school, and he came to live with Tillie and her family in that little house. His face was so full of lines, I thought he might be a hundred years old even then!" I laugh, wanting closeness with my mother, a little joy.

"He hasn't changed much," is all she says. We walk in silence, except for the crunch of gravel as we tread along the side of the road.

"Mom."

Ada doesn't respond like most people would, with a "What?" or a "Yes?" or some bit of encouragement, but I plunge ahead anyway.

"I wish we could talk more. You and I."

"What about?" It sounds like a negation of the possibility.

"Oh, I don't know. The kids. How they're doing. All the things they've had to adjust to here."

"*They're* doin' just fine." She says it shortly.

I decide to ignore the implication. "Do you think so?" I glance at her in time to see her mouth set into a stubborn line.

"Don't know what good all this adjusting does 'em if you're just goin' to pack up and leave, right when they get all adjusted."

So that's it. I shoot off a spray of gravel with the toe of my sandal. She is right. I don't feel ready to make any kind of commitment one way or another. I am aware of my mouth settling into the same stubborn line as hers. We round the corner and the tribal center comes into view, with its long, rectangular lines of rough-hewn planks. I love the stark, simple planes of the building, the broad surfaces of unpainted wood. Only the totem in front is painted, in reds and blacks, and the bear grins at us as we approach. So does earnest Ernie, the tribal court clerk my mother wants me to find interesting. He always volunteers to set up tables for the dinners the women have. Ada commented at breakfast that he didn't use to volunteer as much as he has since I came on the scene.

"Hi, Ernie." I flash him a smile.

His brown face reddens. "Oh, hi, Katherine, I didn't see you." He averts his eyes, embarrassed. I edge past him since he doesn't move from the doorway, where he stands stiffly with a broom upended beside him.

"Sweeping up, were you?"

"What's that, Katherine? What did you ask me?" His eagerness is pathetic. Even my mother looks a little put off by his awkwardness.

"Just asked if you're sweeping up," I say. "Silly of me. Of course you are. I don't suppose you and that broom were planning to dance!"

Sky appears from outside, his arms filled with firewood. Loaded down though he is, he takes a moment to observe the would-be courtship in progress, and shakes his head slightly, chiding me, when my eyes catch his.

"Where do you want this, Mrs. Jack? In or out?" He staggers around comically with his load, knees bent, pretending he's about to drop the whole mess on the floor.

Ada lifts her chin and stares meditatively out the twelve-foot windows. "I suppose with all those clouds we can expect it might rain. And Mr. Turnipseed probably shouldn't be out in the air too long. Let's just plan on buildin' a nice fire in this big room. I'll ask the women if they want the tables set up here."

"Sure thing!" Sky staggers off toward the fireplace at the far end of the room. When he comes back, brushing the wood dust off his hands, he pauses near me. Ernie stands there with his broom. He seems to have forgotten about sweeping and is using it almost like a prop in a play, to give him something to do with his hands.

"Coming to the dinner tonight?" Sky asks.

"No," I say, "I have a date."

"I should've known a hot ticket like you would have better things to do." He walks off, leaving me feeling abandoned and a little silly. Ernie's expression is noticeably disappointed. So is Ada's.

"Okay, Mom," I say. "Tell me what to start on."

"Well now, don't rush things, Katherine. We'll just go on in and see what's needin' to be done." Ada pushes me into the kitchen ahead of her, and I find myself greeted by eight or nine women who raise their heads from their stirring, chopping, and kneading.

Tillie Turnipseed, a vigorous woman of at least seventy, lifts her eyes from the deep vat of dough she is immersed in to her elbows. "Oh, good, you brought your daughter again! The more the merrier, eh?"

I feel myself smiling, glad to be welcomed into this group of older women, most of whom I remember from childhood, like Alma Wilbur, who always had pies cooling on the windowsill to tempt us inside for a slice when we ran whooping from one house to another. Alma hands me an apron and sets a pile of apples in front of me to peel and slice. Alma's sister is sorting through huckleberries and has her hands stained blood-red. The women take up their conversation where they had apparently left it, drawing Ada in to ask her opinion.

"Should we have the drummers come in after supper, like we usually do, or before? Tillie's afraid her dad might fall off to sleep and all the noise would scare him to death if they don't start up till after."

"Then have the drummin' first," Ada says. Never one to hesitate long over a decision. Too bad it doesn't run in the family.

"Will your father say a blessing?" Alma Wilbur asks Tillie.

"Oh, yes, he'll be glad to. He's the only one left in our family still can speak Indian," Tillie says. "It's a darn shame. I never could learn more than a few words somehow."

"Well, the kids are learnin' it! Did you know that? My grandsons are learnin' Indian from that there Sky fellow. 'Lushootseed,' he calls it. He brings in elders who teach it to 'em." I can't help but thrill to the note of pride in my mother's voice. "He'll probably be havin' your father in on it one ɔ' these days, Tillie."

"Oh, I 'spect he will then. If he can tear 'im away from the grandbabies. I've got a granddaughter livin' with me, you know, and her three kids, and then my grandson has the house next to mine, and he's got five. They get Pop out there playin' softball every chance they get. They tell 'im they need nine to play!"

"I used to speak it myself," Ada says. "It's what I heard at home. I never knew the name though."

"Your dad still plays baseball, Tillie?" A stout woman with kind black eyes looks up from a pile of chopped tomatoes.

"He catches almost as good as he ever did. It's just his hearing that's gone."

The woman who asked the question purses her mouth and looks thoughtful. "I guess you wouldn't need to hear all that well to play baseball." Then she winks across the table at me, and I realize she is joking.

"That youngest grandson of yours stayin' with you plays some baseball, don't he, Ada?" It is a sharp-faced woman who speaks. I don't recognize her. She is younger than the others, maybe only forty.

"Yes, he does, Jolene." Ada answers quietly, busy with her knife, peeling a potato in a long, continuous strip. Her cautious tone is the one she uses when she expects trouble.

"He's quite a handsome boy, that youngest one," Jolene goes on. "Looks a lot like his grandfather, as I recall." Her mouth twists downward and a sly expression sneaks into her eyes. "Not like the other boy. Don't know who he looks like. Nobody around here, that's for sure!"

Ada's knuckles clench the knife handle as she raises it erect. For a wild moment, I think she is going to rush around the table and stab Jolene. My mother looks as furious as I am, and as frustrated. My fury is mixed with joy that Ada would care this much. The trouble is, anything either of us might say or do will only make things worse.

"Jolene, why don't you take this smelly sack o' garbage out to the dumpster, so we don't have to look at it." Alma Wilbur plumps a sack on the table in front of her. "Take hold from the bottom, it's wet and might burst all over you." Jolene's face is a study in surprise and indignation. But she hasn't been given a choice. She picks up the bulging bag as instructed and huffs her way out of the kitchen, letting the door slam behind her.

"She's always been a case, that one," a gray-haired woman says. "And her son Kirk's the same. Like a chip they carry on their shoulder. Ever noticed she leans off in one direction, kinda pulled down on one side?" The women are still laughing when Jolene comes back in. She peers at them suspiciously.

"That fresh air do y'good, Jolene?" Ada asks.

Jolene acts as if she doesn't hear and goes to the sink and starts washing her hands with dishwashing detergent. Alma Wilbur steps closer to me. "It's you and nobody else they look like, if y'ask me. Not like the father at all." I try to smile. Alma means well.

chapter 37

I reach out my arm for him and nothing is there. I turn my head and open my eyes. The bed is empty on Mark's side and I now hear the murmurs in the next room that must have awakened me. Why is he on the phone so early? Odd. I stretch my arms and legs toward the four corners of the futon. My muscles relax when I let go. I feel thin and my stomach is flat when I lay my hands on it, and most of all I feel satisfied deep down throughout my body. "He's quite a guy." I say it aloud and laugh to myself, reliving the feel of Mark's firm flesh against mine, his whisper that I have the softest skin in the world.

His voice grows louder. He sounds different from the man who whispered to me. He sounds angry, or worried. How little I know him, really. He gambles, plays pool, does odd jobs; I haven't wanted to think about the aimlessness of that, because Mark himself doesn't seem aimless, he seems driven rather than aimless, driven by some need from deep inside. I let go of the thought and roll off the futon, then pick up his tee shirt from the floor and pull it on. When I stand up, it hangs to my knees. I stretch again, feeling my bare feet flat on the floorboards and my arms thin and strong above my head.

I'll make him coffee, and fry up some eggs and sausage. He gets tired of my low-fat routine. I pad noiselessly to the door and am about to push it open, but his voice stops me, the hard, threatening tone of it, like voices from the days before Larry died, when deals and threats were made, and lives hung in the balance.

"Just give me half, that's what I'm askin'—and you know what happens if you don't deliver."

I stand with my palm against the door, listening.

"Tribal council would find it pretty interesting to know they could get five times the price. Think it over, Tim. That lady of yours is gonna go on costin' you."

The phone clicks and I jerk my hand away from the door, startled, unwilling to be caught spying. In one swift move I am back under the down comforter with my eyes closed and my hands tucked under my chin.

Mark opens the door and enters. I feel the silence that follows. Is he looking at me?

"Katherine?" A pause. "You asleep?" He waits and then must be satisfied. I hear him go into the bathroom and turn on the shower.

My eyes fly open. Half of what? Who was he talking to? Uneasiness runs through me like the steady sand through an hourglass. I pull the tee shirt off and lie down again, not wanting him to know that I had been awake.

Tim ... that's the man from the BIA we are going to have dinner with tonight. Will Mark tell me what it's about?

I am still lying quietly, feeling small and fragile now instead of strong, when he comes back in, toweling himself dry.

"Hey, little turtle, you're awake!"

He eyes me closely and I smile to cover the doubts running through my mind, and then he is on top of me, taking me again, with no words at all this time, thrusting himself deep into me, almost smothering doubt, pushing it deep down. I feel empty and used when he is finished, though. He's done this before, seized and used me, like a receptacle. It makes me aware of a deep well of pain inside my body. It makes me want to be alone.

"I have to go home."

"To Mama?" He has rolled off me, onto his back, and he turns his head toward me, his eyes mocking.

"Don't make fun, Mark."

"I thought you like makin' fun with me. Makin' whoopee!"

I get up from the futon, no longer wanting to be near him. "The boys will wonder why I'm not there. I hate this part of it. Sneaking in."

"Whoa. What's this all about? Why the big mood change?" His eyes are fixed on me as he lies sprawled on his back, watching me slip into my jeans and shirt. "What's up?"

I see caution in his eyes, suspicion. I hadn't known I could read him this well. Reaching for space to think, I take the hairbrush out of my bag. I fling my hair forward and brush vigorously, feeling blood come into my face. When I flip my hair back, he is still watchful.

"Sorry," I say. "I meant to make you breakfast, but you look ready to go back to sleep and I really need to get home. Didn't mean to lay a trip on you." I lean close to the cracked mirror on the wall and run lipstick over the curve of my lips. I can see him in the mirror. He turns over on his side. "Just be ready for tonight," he mumbles. "I want you to look your best."

"Why is that, Mark?" I try to say it lightly.

He rolls onto his back and grins. "I want you to look as good as his lady. I want him t'know he's dealin' with a somebody. So dress up, baby."

Why does it feel so good sometimes to walk away from his house? Just to close the door behind me and walk away.

chapter 38

Tim Wilson looks beaten down by life. Is he fifty, fifty-five? Hard to tell. The lines in his face are deep creases, as if he's been burned by sun and wind and pain. Mark told me that after Tim's wife left him, in a matter of weeks he took up with Babs, the redhead who now sits across from us, jabbering about horses. We order lobster and steak around and over Babs's high-pitched monologue on the virtues of roans and palominos. She loves cowboy movies. That's where she got her start on horses. She hadn't known Indians still existed until Tim explained to her about the Bureau of Indian Affairs. "You don't look like Indians," she comments, as if conveying a compliment. No, we're wearing your kind of clothes, I want to say. That's probably what threw you off. The two of them, Tim and Babs, plan to buy a resort ranch.

I drain my bourbon glass and set it on the snow-white tablecloth. The cloth is thick like a soft bed, and I wonder for a moment if the glass will tip over. I drank it fast because I want to be sure to feel it. I plan to have one more and then quit. There's no way I can face the evening sober, but neither can I risk getting drunk. Mark made it clear that I'm to make an impression. He hasn't made anything else clear.

Babs interrupts herself to ask me, "Have you ever ridden?"

"No," I lie. I'm not about to tell of jumping from a fence onto the Turnipseeds' old pony and gripping the coarse mane with five-year-old fingers and flying into a puddle of manure. The story wouldn't go with the black lace dress I squeezed into with such care. I adjust the low neckline and then drop my hands to my lap when I see Tim Wilson's eyes on me. Making Babs jealous probably isn't part of Mark's plan, whatever Mark's plan is.

Babs widens her blue eyes. "I've only ridden for three years," she says. "I started when I turned twenty-one and Daddy gave me my own horse."

I register the age, even younger than I'd thought. What has this man gotten himself into? And whatever happened to Indian preference? The only thing Indian about Tim Wilson is his bolo tie.

"You work for Wally, don't you?" Tim asks unexpectedly. My brain makes a sudden connection, jolting me out of contemplation of skinny, self-obsessed redheads. Tim Wilson's is the signature on the letters Wally gets from the BIA forestry division. And then I remember Sky's comment about Mark being in the office talking to Wally while I was away. Or was it Whit who told me?

I smile, tempting him to say more. "He's a pretty good boss."

Tim downs his scotch and signals the waiter. "I'm more used to working with Stan Moss," he says. He and Mark exchange a long look, calculating on both sides. Mark is handsome in a tan sports jacket with a black shirt and black jeans. Babs has been directing more and more of her wide-eyed glances in his direction. Am I supposed to be distracting Tim Wilson so he won't notice? The thought hits me with a pang of bitterness and I think again of Whitney. Whit wouldn't put up with this bullshit.

The second round of drinks arrives and I take a quick, burning swallow.

"Did Stan Moss use to handle forestry?" I ask.

Mark enters the conversation for the first time. "Come on," he says. "We're here to have a good time. Let's drink to that ranch!"

It isn't until I feel a wave of dizziness that I realize I am on my third bourbon. By then it doesn't matter. Mark and Tim vie with Babs in telling horse stories and all I have to do is laugh at the punchlines.

On the way home Mark is pleased with me and both of us feel sexy. If we don't have more to drink, it'll be okay. Not like with Red, I don't want it to be like with Red.

"You know what I'd like, Katherine?"

"Hmm, let me guess. To take a trip? I see it in your eyes."

"You're right, almost. And with who?"

"With me, of course."

"But where, *where*, Katherine?"

"That's what I can't tell. I know what I'd like, though."

"Camping. That's what would do it for us."

"I can't believe we're thinking the same way." I close my eyes and relief settles into my shoulders. Or is it alcohol, numbing me?

"When can you get away? I have a few days next week. Would they let you off?"

"I'll ask Whitney to help out."

"Whitney!" He shakes his head. "I can't believe you two are friends. You're so ... feminine. And she roars around like somebody's uncle, like she don't know she's a woman."

"Mark, you ..." I stop short of saying "you have a problem." Instinct checks me. Or is it experience?

"Look, do whatever you want," he says. "Just be free to go. I'll take care of everything. Pack enough food for three days, okay?"

I bite my lip. I feel belittled. The food is a big part of it.

"Whatsa matter?" He lays a hand on the back of my neck and pushes his palm up under my hair, caressing my scalp with his fingers. "Your mom won't let ya get away?"

"I'll have to ask her."

"Do that." He pulls to a stop in front of his house, his hand warm on my neck, making my skin tingle and come alive under his touch. Controlling me with the pressure of his fingers, he moves an exploring hand down across my shoulder and probes it gently. "Get out," he whispers. "Come inside." I had meant to ask him to take me straight home. It is a vague memory, unimportant. What is important is the giddy, dizzy feeling of swaying with him up the front walk and stopping to caress his chest, my hands inside the black shirt, and his warm hands cradling my face, massaging my neck.

"One sleeping bag," he says. "I've got a double one I can zip together." He grins. "You don't need a tent, do you?"

"Who needs a tent?" I feel my eyes drowning in his. "All I need is you." My voice is thick, and he brings his face suddenly close and covers my mouth with his and sucks me into a kiss that carries me up to my tiptoes, reaching, pressing into him, wanting to be close, closer.

But when he drops me back down to the ground, his expression is smug. "Bring ham sandwiches an' chips," he says. "And plenty of beer."

Something in me stretches taut, ready to snap.

"My mom doesn't allow beer in the house."

"Well, fuck your mom."

Hostility gleams in my eyes and he sees it.

"I'll bring the beer then," he says. "Just forget about your family."

I follow him to the door, not liking always following him, taking his lead.

"I'll decide what to bring," I say. He hears the tension in my voice and turns.

"Sure, baby. Bring whatever you want. I'll pack it in."

"Mark?"

"What?"

"Sometimes ..." I draw in air, wondering why it is so hard to say. "Sometimes I like to be alone. I wondered if on the camping trip, if we could go off from each other, maybe for half a day."

"Half a day?" He frowns, uncomprehending. "You want to go off by yourself? Why?"

I shrink away. "It was just a thought."

chapter 39

"Wow, is it hot out there. Any more of that and I'd be a pancake. Whew!" Whitney mops sweat off her forehead with a big red kerchief she yanks out of the hip pocket of her jean skirt.

"I know. I've been moving around as little as possible."

She ambles closer to the desk. "What's wrong with you?" Her voice gentles when she asks the question.

"Nothing." I wonder whether to tell her. She has seen behind the mask again. "I wanted to ask if you could sit here and cover the phone for me a couple days next week, maybe catch up on some of your paperwork? I'll ask Wally if it's okay."

"Sure. I could do that. Except when I have clients scheduled. Where you goin'? I'm all ears!" She grins, plucking her ears up in the air with fire-engine-red fingernails.

"I like that pink tank top, the embroidery on it. Did you do that yourself?"

"Are you kiddin'? I couldn't sit still that long." Her hearty laugh rings out. "No, my sister-in-law made me this. Nice work, isn't it?"

I nod. My head feels heavy. It is an effort to move it.

"Somethin's wrong, isn't it?" Whitney's eyes linger on me, searching my face. "Tell me, you'll feel better."

"Oh, it's nothing. It's just that Mark is taking me on a camping trip and—well, that's the trouble. He's *taking* me. I'd wanted it to be this great adventure in independence, finding myself out there in the wilderness, a kind of emptying-out of all the junk in my head, and here he is telling me what food to make and bring lots of beer."

"Uh-oh." Her eyes flash an alarm. "That wouldn't work for me. I don't go anywhere at all with folks when they're drinkin'.'"

I sigh. "It'll be all right. It's just different somehow, already, before we've even started. Different from what I've been dreaming of."

"Come with me sometime on the bike. You can ride on the back. I could leave you up there a day or two, come and getcha. Hell, you wouldn't need food even. Get high on mountain air, that's all you'd need." She looks me in the eye with her direct gaze. Then her focus shifts. "Who was that leavin' when I came in? I only saw her from the back. Wasn't that my client I was talkin' to earlier, before I went to the clinic?"

I busy myself with a pile of papers, flipping through them. "Yeah. That was Lavina Green."

"Did you see her shiner?" Whitney grimaces in sympathy.

"I saw that and the bruises on her arm and the welt on her neck."

"Wow! She didn't show me those. I shoulda known. Wearin' a turtleneck on a day like this."

"We talked for a while. She's stopped by before, to talk."

"Well, good. The woman's got no friends. That maniac kept her locked in whenever he left the house! The day she changed her locks—you shoulda been there, Katherine, an' seen the look on the guy's face. I was inside, watchin' him from the window, with the phone in my hand, so he'd know not to try nothin'. I thought he was gonna shit green nickels!"

"You got her that far? To the point she could lock him out?"

"Took two years o' counselin'. And now she weakens and lets him in, and look what happens. Did she tell you her rent money got stolen? The asshole probably took it."

"No, it was her oldest boy. The one who's on crack."

"She told you that? Gosh, *you* oughta be the couselor." Whitney shakes her head. "I don't know what she'll do. I told her our petty cash just don't stretch to three hundred and forty dollars. We got her the deadbolts, but ... god, I feel bad about it."

"Don't worry, Whit. I think she found a way."

"Whadda y'mean? The woman's got no relatives here. No friends. How's she gonna come up with that kinda money?"

I feel my face flush. I lean down, pretending to search for something on the floor.

Whitney walks around the desk, bends over, and with her head hanging upside down, peers into my face.

I straighten up. "Look, Whit, I have a fund I try to keep up to five hundred. I've had enough emergencies to learn that one lesson."

"So you risk it on Lavina Green? Do you know she hasn't been in recovery all that long?"

"A hundred twenty-five days."

"She told you that too, huh?"

"She won't let him in again, Whit. I really don't think she will. Something's changed in her. I saw a new look in her eyes. A hard look, but I think what it was ..." I pause, biting my lower lip, "was courage. She's not gonna let her boy in, either. Not till he gets treatment. Sky's workin' on him, when he gets a chance."

Whitney pulls out the red kerchief and blows her nose. Then she wipes her eyes with the clean edge. "I guess I was wrong about Lavina havin' no friends."

"I couldn't stand seeing her lose her place and have nowhere to go but him." And I think of Emma, misguidedly trying to save Harriet. All Jane Austen's women had something in common: the struggle to find their place. And so often it meant relying on a man. Lavina picked the wrong one.

chapter 40

"Mom, I just heard a car drive up. You expecting anybody?"

"It seems early, doesn't it, for visitors. I wonder who it is."

I lean close to the window, then cup my hands around my eyes, not sure I'm seeing right. "It's Harry!"

"Well, don't stare out the window at him, Katherine. Go and say hi."

"Gosh, I will, Mom. I'm just surprised. It's been a long time."

"That's 'cause you never came home."

"Mom, don't." I ease forward, unsticking the backs of my thighs from the leather chair. The whole house has gradually heated up from days of temperatures above ninety. I adjust my shorts, go to the screen door, and open it on Harry's wife, it must be, a short, stocky woman with a friendly face, her brown eyes uncertain at the sight of me.

"Hi, I'm Harry's sister, Katherine." Three kids trail along the walk behind the woman, and a fourth, the smallest, holds tightly to her hand, looking down at tiny, dirty bare feet. Harry has his head stuck in the back of an old wood-framed Ford station wagon.

"I'm Maisie," the woman says.

"Come on in. Mom's inside."

The two oldest children, girls the same size and with the same round, black eyes, yell "Gramma!" and rush past me to grab Ada around the middle. I guess them to be twins, no more than six years old. Ada pats them on the back and smiles at the small girl hanging behind Maisie, trying to hide there, but peeking out with wide, curious eyes.

"How are you, Tammy? Come in and have a cookie at the table." Immediately the three oldest children follow Ada toward the kitchen. The youngest raises questioning eyes to Maisie, who nods, and the child lets go her grip on her mother's hand and toddles after the others.

"Come in and sit down," I urge Maisie, who still stands on the porch, glancing back toward the car, where Harry is unloading the trunk. "It's a little cooler inside," I add.

Maisie wrinkles her face in apology. "Harry's just settin' stuff there so we can sort it out." The lawn is stacked high with boxes, beside which stand two battered suitcases and a highchair.

"Harry!" Maisie calls out. "Your sister's here."

Slowly, Harry's lanky form emerges from the back of the car and he squints toward the house. When he sees me, a shy smile transforms his face. The smile draws me, running, down the three steps and along the walk to meet him. He approaches slowly, ducking his head and somehow giving the impression he is moving away from me.

"How're you doin', Katie?" Is it sadness in his eyes? If so, it has a hard edge. But the gladness to see me shines so strongly I am surprised I even saw the other emotion hanging back of it. He doesn't hug me. Instead he makes a show of wiping his forehead with his arm.

"Y'got the boys with you?"

"Yes, I do. They're at day camp."

"How old is he, your oldest one?"

"He's thirteen." Something passes between us when our eyes meet. Then he looks at the ground.

"That long, is it?"

"And you've got four girls!"

"Why don't you bring all that stuff in the house," Ada calls from the doorway.

"We're not stayin' that long," Harry yells back. "How're you doin', Mom?"

"Why not?" Ada demands.

"I'm lookin' for work. We're just passin' through."

"Well, you can look for it from here, instead of draggin' Maisie and the girls all over the countryside."

Harry grins at me. "She don't change, does she?"

"Get that stuff in here, Harry. I don't want it all over my lawn, now, do I? Help him, Maisie." Obediently, Maisie hurries down the walk and picks up two cardboard cartons.

"I'll help," I say. "It's too hot to be out here for long."

"Put it all in the back bedroom," Ada says. "That one I been usin' for storage, Katherine."

In my mind, I sift through the room situation. Mom and Tony share a room, I have my own, and Victor has the living room, and it is true there is one other room, smaller than the rest and so packed full of stuff I had forgotten it was a bedroom.

When every last box has been carried in, Ada settles herself on the couch. "I've got some spare mattresses in that back bedroom," she says. "Pile things up in there so's we can lay two of 'em out for the kids."

"Harry and Maisie can have my room, Mom," I say quickly. I hand around glasses of iced tea.

"That's right," Ada says approvingly. "You can have a little mattress, Katherine, in my room, and Tony can sleep next to Victor. Now, Harry, tell us what happened with your job." I sit down on the couch, feeling included by the surprise of Ada's offer to share her room and by the "us" instead of "me."

"Timber, Mom, you know how it is. No jobs anymore. Damned owls more important I guess than people."

"Crazy, isn't it." Ada shakes her head back and forth. She takes a long swallow of tea. "We can't just cut 'em all down, though, like white folks been doin' all these years. That's not our way, you know. Not to just cut and cut till everything's dead."

I watch my brother's mouth tighten. "I've got these kids to feed, Mom."

"Don't you worry 'bout feedin' these kids." Ada turns toward me and lays a hand on my arm. "Katherine. You go and start peelin' up some potatoes."

"I'll help," Maisie says.

chapter 41

"Whit, would you think it strange if—"

"Katherine. Nothin' you suggest am I goin' to think strange."

"Why is that?" I file the last of what had been a stack of folders so high I couldn't see over it when I sat down at my desk that morning.

"Because you are one original woman. I've noticed that. I hope it don't embarrass you for me t' tell you."

"No. It pleases me." I sit down, comfortable in khaki shorts and a tee shirt, and address an envelope for a letter I printed out earlier. "I don't know if men see us as we are. Even Sky."

"Hmm." Whitney's sculpted eyebrows go up.

"What's that mean? That 'hmm'?"

"Sky's different, huh?"

"Don't you think so?"

"Oh, yeah. He's pretty different. Different from old tall, dark, and handsome, that's for sure."

"Why do you say it like that?"

"Let's go back to where you wondered if I'd think you're strange."

"Oh, it's nothing really. I just wondered if you might want to go up on the hill and take a book and, I don't know, be quiet and read and get some air. It's been so damn hot."

"Read, huh?" Whitney's eyes widen and she puts a question in them.

"Well, it's just an idea. I've been wanting to take advantage of the peace out here. In the city there's nothing like this. I mean like hills, and the river, and lakes—with no people on them! But snakes, we don't have those in the city either."

"So that's why you want me along!" Whitney's laugh booms out through the small room. "When can you go?" she asks.

"You mean you'd like to? Really?"

"Sure. I'll bring my motorcycle manual to read. I may fall asleep, though, before I get to the exciting part." Whitney aims a wink in my direction. What creative spirit possesses her to combine the clothes she does? Pastel-flowered shorts flare out over her solid hips, topped by a royal blue blouse, worn under a loosely crocheted pink vest. Blue beaded earrings match the blouse, and a green-and-yellow beaded pendant brings out the flowers in the shorts. Accenting her white net hose are a pair of black granny shoes. What does Mark mean by "not feminine"?

"How 'bout in forty minutes? It's quitting time," I say. "I'll go home and make us each a couple of sandwiches and a thermos of tea. Does that sound good?"

"You kiddin'? You know I'm always hungry. I've got cookies I can bring."

"Come by my house for me?"

"Are Maisie and Harry still there?"

"They took the kids—mine, too—and went with Ada to visit a lady who's got three kids and no working car. Harry's good with cars. Whitney ..." I hesitate. "This is instead of the camping trip Mark and I were going on. He got too busy."

"Busy?" Her look is skeptical. "Okay. I'll be on the bike. You can ride in back. Them snakes will run for cover when they hear us roar up that hill."

All I find to make sandwiches with is peanut butter. Maisie used up the lunch meat and cheese. I slice a dill pickle thin and layer it onto peanut butter, thinking how much easier things are with women. It will be different from what I'd feel if a man, any man, were with me. Why did I ever think Sky could be a friend and I wouldn't feel any of that with him? I pause, holding the knife in midair, with peanut butter sticking to it. I do think of him as a man. What does that mean exactly? How do I feel when I'm with him? Young, life-filled, with deep thoughts, most of which I can share. An undercurrent of attraction. What do I feel when I'm with Mark? Even the question I resist. And I don't let my mind go into the answer. It is my body that answers, a kind of stiffening, a lifting, a tightening in my stomach and below.

I leave a note for Ada and am sitting on the porch steps next to sacks of picnic food and supplies when Whitney zooms into the yard. She leaps off and helps me stuff everything into the carrier bag.

"What is all this?"

"You'll see! It'll be fun."

"You ever ridden a motorcycle before?"

"No." I push down the quick fear. I want to take on the challenge.

Whitney gives clear, simple instructions. "Sit directly behind me and hold on to my waist. Move with me when I move. If I lean to the side, you lean with me—don't lean the other way. Think of us as one rider. And don't worry. I may look crazy but I'm careful. Careful and fast!" She flashes a grin meant to be wicked and we start out. The ride along the road is remarkably smooth. And when we get to the path that leads to the hill and the bumpiness starts, I follow instructions and merge into oneness with the woman whose broad waist I am grasping. By the time we attack the hill, I feel confidence in myself and Whitney both. We ride the bumps with style, lifting slightly in our seats. When we reach the top and the terrain levels off, she glides to a stop. We dismount and she strokes the Harley as if it were a horse.

"This here's my best friend." Her cheekbones are flushed and her eyes shining. "You did great. I hardly felt you there at all."

A glow of pride warms my face. "I feel as if I could do anything after that, do you know what I mean?"

"I sure as heck do. That's why I ride the damn thing. That and because I love it." She still has a hand on the Harley, caressing it.

"It's a funny beginning, though, for a Victorian afternoon." I open the carrier bag and pull out a red-and-white-checked tablecloth. I spread it on the ground.

"A what?" Whitney looks puzzled.

"Oh, I know I'm silly, but that's how I've been thinking of it. Two ladies, you know, having tea on a leisurely summer evening?"

"So what's that word got to do with it?"

205

"Victorian? That's the name of the century before ours, at least in England. Queen Victoria reigned for most of the century and they named it after her."

She settles herself onto a foam cushion I have produced. "How on earth did you get all this stuff packed in there? And what's England got to do with us?"

"I don't know. Or why I feel so attracted to the way things were then. It's not like I'd want to live that way all the time. Those dresses made life complicated, but something about the slow pace and the time given over to conversation and having tea and—oh, I know you had to be one of the rich to live like that, but ... I can't explain really."

"So we're like two Victorian ladies havin' tea?"

I giggle. Whitney has matter-of-factly poured tea into the lid of the thermos and is slurping noisily.

"Wait! I've got teacups and saucers. It's okay, though. Drink that first. I can see you're thirsty."

"You've got to be kidding. *Saucers?*" She looks on in awe as I unwrap them from cloth napkins. "Well, this is real nice. I'm beginnin' to get in the spirit of it, you know? Wouldn't we have had servants, though, to pour for us?"

"I don't think so. They weren't all of them that rich, really. And a picnic's always been a picnic—informal, that's the fun. They probably had servants at home but didn't bring them on picnics. I'm not sure. I'll know maybe when I read more."

"What are you readin' exactly?"

"It's a book called *Emma*. I'll tell you about it when I know how it ends." I arrange sandwiches and cookies and pour tea into my mother's china cups, nestling in flowered saucers. We munch our way through the sandwiches in short order. Then I replenish the teacups and we begin nibbling on cookies.

"Boy, am I hot!" Whitney peels off her vest and blouse and reveals a tank undershirt with the words TRY ME stitched in neon pink. "I've seen pictures of those dresses you're talkin' about. Lots of lace and some good embroidery. Real pretty. I wouldn't mind wearin' one of those from time to time." She stares off into the valley, a dreamy look in her eyes. She is vulnerable. Under all that dash and verve, a little girl peeks out.

206

"Why don't we ever feel like girls, Katherine? Do you know why?"

"Well, it's not because we're Indian."

"I think it is."

"You think everything is, Whit." I ponder the way she picked up on my thought process. Sky does that, too.

She shakes her head at the tablecloth, spotted with cookie crumbs and smudged with peanut butter. "We were pretty hungry, weren't we? Did Victorian ladies have appetites like ours?"

"No!" I laugh. "They had to fit into tight, awful corsets. It must have felt great to take those torture chambers off at night."

"Their sex lives weren't so great, from what I've heard."

'You *have* heard of them then!"

"Yeah. It's kind of all comin' back to me. Like a bad dream. No, I'm only kidding. I think I'll take a walk while you read, Katherine. If you see a snake, just hit him real hard on the head with that book."

"Thanks a lot."

She marches off into the bushes. I find my place and immerse myself in the book I have begun to think of as my own story. When Whitney at last reappears, I finish the paragraph I am reading before lifting my head. "Back already?"

"Gosh, Katherine. I've been out there for over an hour." She is carrying a sack.

"Really?" I yawn. "I do feel a little groggy. What have you got in that bag?"

"Roots I found down on the hillside. I went way back off the path and came across some stuff I've been needin'."

"Roots?"

"For medicine. And leaves to make tea with."

"How do you know they aren't poison?"

"Whooo, you been in the city too long. I learned from my aunt, when I was a kid. That's why I'm healthy. I drink this special tea every day. Want some leaves?"

"What would I do with them?"

"Just put 'em in water and let 'em simmer half an hour."

"Thanks." I accept the handful of leaves and tuck them into the pocket of my shorts. "My mother used to go out and gather roots, too. I guess I never paid much attention."

"Ask her to take you with her sometime. She'd be happy you want to know. You're lucky to have a mother around, Katherine."

I feel a sudden pang of shame. I grow silent.

Whitney lowers herself to the ground and leans against a tree trunk. "Wow. It feels good to sit down." She doesn't speak for a few moments and then she asks, too casually, "That letter you put in the mail? Looked like it was to the Bureau of Indian Affairs. Am I right?"

"You're right." I feel myself tense up, knowing something is coming.

"Whadda you do, take shorthand and write all his letters for him?"

"No, he uses a dictaphone. I transcribe them."

"Oh." Whitney has her blouse and vest on again. She extracts a toothpick from a pocket and starts chewing on it.

"Why are you so interested in that letter?"

"That letter to the Bureau?"

"Yeah, Whitney. That one."

"Oh, I just wondered if it had to do with the trees Sky and I were talkin' about."

"What trees would those be?"

"Old-growth trees over to the north end of the rez? It's prime stuff. Probably would go for several million. That many acres, it's a lotta trees."

"No! They're not selling it for anywhere near a million even. Oh damn, Whitney! I'm not supposed to talk about council business."

She darts a quick glance at me and looks away. "That guy you work for. What's your honest impression? Does he have any balls?"

"Gee. I don't know how to answer that. He's honest. I'm pretty sure he's honest."

"And?" Her eyes are keen as a bird's.

"Well." I sigh. "I don't think he's very smart. And he doesn't have much backbone. He's real proud to be on tribal council, and I think ..."

"What? What do you think?"

"He's easy to push around. Manipulate. By someone smarter. You know?"

"Yeah. I know. This isn't good, Katherine. I'm wonderin' how much I should tell you."

"Well, damn! I've sure told you more than I should have! Wally specifically said the logging deal is confidential."

"Interesting," she muses. "They don't want to give us time to organize a protest."

"What is it you're wondering how much to tell me?"

"Sky isn't sure who's involved. He only suspects. I don't think I can say more right now than that we know someone is influencin' tribal council to sell for way less than the timber's worth."

"Why would anyone do that?"

"It's even more tangled. They shouldn't be cuttin' those trees on the north end at all. Most of it's old growth. But if they're goin' to sell 'em, they ought to bring in millions, like I said."

"I don't get it."

"I know. We haven't figured it out either. Completely. Just let us know if you learn anything that sounds fishy, will you do that?"

"You already knew, didn't you, that the selling price was below a million?"

"Yeah, I knew. I had a pretty good idea anyway."

"How, Whit?"

"I can't tell you that." I give her a look, half-mocking, half-exasperated, and she leans forward, her eyes serious. "Ask Sky. And don't wait too long to do it."

Back at home, late that evening, I lie on the couch thinking. It feels as if my head will burst from the effort of spinning thoughts around and letting them fall into patterns.

My brother looks over at me during a commercial. "I can hear you thinkin', Katie, even over the yells in the stadium."

"It's a wonder I can think at all with that racket." Harry has brought his television in from the station wagon. I realize now how much I liked not having one. Victor is dozing against Harry's shoulder and Tony sleeps with his head in Victor's lap. They stay as close to their uncle as they can, and I know they love it that he will be here all night, he won't go away.

"You're doin' a pretty good job," Harry says. "Need any help?"

"No. Maybe. Yes! Have you heard whether there's going to be any logging work on the rez?"

A curtain goes down over his eyes. "Could be."

"What's that mean, could be?"

"Could be, come spring."

"Where did you hear that?"

"I been askin' around everywhere about work. You know that."

"Yeah, but exactly who told you there might be logging work comin' up?"

"Can't remember." His mouth closes in the way I remember from when he was a child. There is no use asking him any more questions. I go back to my tangle of thoughts, complicated further now by Harry's reluctance to reveal what he knows.

How could anyone benefit from a sale way below the going price, and who might it be? Aren't those the two questions that matter? The money has to be going somewhere or no one stands to benefit. A kickback. What is that exactly? During the Reagan years, a lot of government people ended up indicted and even convicted, and weren't kickbacks often involved? But how does one work? You do me a favor and I do one for you? That must be it. I sigh, and my brother glances at me. Am I imagining a glint of suspicion in his eyes? I go back to my unraveling. Someone is getting money because council is selling at such a low price. Do the council members even know how much the trees are worth? *I* hadn't, until Whitney told me. Maybe they don't. The tribe has never been that much into logging. We're a river-fishing tribe. We worry about dams upriver harming fish runs. Logging is not well thought of because it harms the fish. And lately council has been preoccupied with gambling and opposition to it from people like my mother. All the meetings have revolved around gaming. Some people are excited about the job opportunities a casino will bring, and others fear it will encourage drinking. Somehow that reminds me of Tim Wilson saying he was used to working with Stan Moss. I massage my forehead with my hand and decide to sleep on the subject. Maybe I'll wake up with a clearer head.

"Hey, brother! I hope your team wins." I pause to touch him lightly on the shoulder as I pass by on my way out of the room.

Maisie is already in bed. She goes to bed when her kids do. Harry's eyes rest on me for a second, alert, with a question in them. I can't resist a further probe.

"Think you might wait around here till spring then?"

"Hmm." He turns his eyes back to the television.

chapter 42

Mark is wooing me back, making up for the camping trip he put on hold because of "business" that came up. He throws out vague hints about something big that may break and make a camping trip look "like small potatoes." He has brought me to the scene of my seduction. The pond shimmers in late afternoon sunglow. He sits close beside me, giving me all his attention.

"In the dream it wasn't like this," I say. He pulls a reed up by the roots, clean, and puts the hole to his mouth and blows, raising his eyes to look at me, all one sensuous movement.

"Yeah?"

"It felt safe, like this, and with a hint of danger, like this, sitting here with you, but there was something pulsating underneath, a kind of beat." I stare into the water below us and pick up a stone and toss it in. We watch it sink.

"Pulsating, huh?" He shifts his weight to lie on his side, propped up by an elbow. He looks at me through narrowed, teasing eyes. The reed dangles from the corner of his mouth. "You're always like this, aren't you?"

"What do you mean?" I smile, more at the undulating water than at him.

"Fulla this kinda talk. I mean, I never knew a girl talks the way you do. Pulsating!"

"What do the girls you know talk about?" I take hold of the other end of the reed he has let fall from his mouth, and put it in my mouth and chew on it, watching him. I am at that point in drinking when a kind of clarity sets in, however briefly.

"Oh, the bills they gotta pay and how they're gonna pay 'em and what kinda haircut I think they ought to get. Nail polish.

That kind of shit." He drinks from the bottle of wine that has been sitting on the ground beside him and then hands it to me.

"What kind of haircut should I get, Mark?" I feel my eyes glittering and lower them, not wanting him to see the rebellion. He is answering me, but my focus has left him and soon I'll think of a way to be by myself. This isn't going to work. I've known it since the night before the powwow, waking up in that stinking bed, and somehow he charmed me back again. I wonder sometimes if I have good sense. Of course I don't. Nothing to wonder about. No more than Harriet, or Emma Woodhouse herself, so far, the way the story's going. It's easier somehow to see what Harriet or Emma should do. It would be difficult to stay with Mark cold sober. I drink from the bottle, not wanting this much clarity.

"Katherine." He leans into my space, eyes pleading. I try to lean back, away from him, and not get caught in those eyes again. He can turn it on at will, the charm, and reel me in like a fish, unless I struggle.

"I was thinking," I say. "I was thinking we could bring my mother next time we go out like this. She likes to hunt for roots."

He intensifies his gaze and a glint of humor flickers in the dark pupils. "You puttin' me on?" He draws me into a long, slow kiss, and we stand up, still kissing, then head for the truck. He gives me the bottle to finish off what is left and afterward hurls it into a blackberry patch, grinning at me. "Let's go home and do some pulsating!"

The interior of the pickup is warm from the sun. On the ride to Mark's place, our hands intertwine, turning and caressing in a long, unbroken twisting around and over and under to get closer, a warmth like sex, or anticipation of it, burning through wrists and fingers and palms and sparking out messages.

"I've never held hands like this before." He murmurs the words.

The instant we get inside the house, I slip out of my jean cut-offs and camisole top. Mark drops his jeans and we are naked, clutching for each other like lovers in a French movie I saw years ago, with Larry. The thought flickers and disappears into

213

the intensity of twisting and turning in the sweat of each other's bodies. It's the best lovemaking we've had.

Afterward, I rest my chin on his shoulder. "Mortality. There has to be a reason for this. Some end to it. And that has two meanings, doesn't it? An end to the suffering, the fun? An end to all of this, I mean it has to stop, right? And yet ... what was the other meaning?" I scoot up to sit with my back against the wall.

"You do always talk this way, don't you." He looks at me wonderingly, his face smiling, happy.

I see the wonder and the smile, see why I've come back for more, and why he has. He reaches over to the low shelf next to his side of the bed, where he keeps his wine supply, and uncaps the nearest bottle.

"Red wine is good for the heart, give me some," I say, and drink. "Hey! That fits in!"

"How? What?"

"Red wine and mortality. I keep forgetting! Darn! I see the connection and then it snaps. I lose it. Did you know that's the most profound it gets, when we see that everything is connected? Everything! I mean, think what that *means!*"

He shakes his head back and forth, looking baffled.

"There's got to be an end to it," I say, fighting off grogginess, trying to keep hold of the glimmer of logic that taunts me. "See, that's it, the other meaning: there has to be a point! See? See, Mark? There has to be something at the end, somewhere we're going."

"Settle down, baby," he invites me. "Settle down here beside me. I'm a big, lonely, hardworkin' man and I need comfort." He reaches out and cradles my breasts in his hands, but I squiggle out of his grasp, out of the bed. I walk to the small space between the bottom edge of the futon and the wall and stand facing him.

"It's hard to talk about mortality, Mark, and interconnected-ness, when you treat me like some kind of slave girl."

"Oh, she's pouting!" He makes a pouty face, so out of place on his strong features that I laugh.

"Come on," he says. "I can't wait much longer."

"And what will happen if I don't?" I ask. Struck by a thought, I press on, desperate to make him see. "Mortality again! We can't escape it. You just brought it up! What did you say, that you can't wait much longer? But see, the thing is, we never know how much longer we have." I slide down to the floor, my back against the wall. "Amazing, isn't it?"

"No," he says, and sits up on the mattress. "You're what's amazing." He smiles in a bemused way that tells me he doesn't understand, he doesn't share any of these thoughts. "Who wound you up today, Katherine?"

I leap up with alcoholic energy and run to the window, open it and lean out as far as I can, and stand with my bare feet planted solidly on the floor, taking deep breaths of honeysuckle air. Pride and the desire to control are not my failings. Emma and I are different there. Could we learn from each other? But Emma's not real. Either I am drunker than I thought or this is clarity.

chapter 43

Sky looks startled to see me. I have never come to his office before.

"Come in. Sit down." He motions to a deep, comfortable armchair and I sink into it, conscious of the contrast my bright yellow halter dress makes against the faded green fabric. He sits in a more worn version of the same chair, across from me.

"Is this where you sit when you're counseling?" I ask.

"Yeah, I stay away from my desk. Too intimidating."

I study the posters. I recognize Leonard Peltier and Russell Means. My eyes shift to the wall behind Sky's desk, where a window looks out onto the scrub trees.

"The masks are beautiful. Where did you get them?"

Sky lifts his eyes to the wall hung with carved wooden masks. His face looks drawn and seems thinner.

"These are all from northwest tribes. Mostly Tlingit and Haida. Actually ..." He stops and clenches his mouth as if trying to get control of the muscles around it. "Actually they're my mother's. I keep 'em here because she loses everything."

"What's wrong, Sky?"

"Why? Do I look that bad?"

"You do. I came here all full of what I have to ask you, but there's something wrong, isn't there?"

"Yeah, there's something wrong. Janie's ready to go into inpatient treatment and I haven't got the money."

"Can I help?"

"You got two thousand?" He smiles, a wan smile.

"They want that much up front?"

"I'm negotiating. The trouble is, even aside from the money, they can't get her in till next month." He stares at the floor. "She'll never make it."

"Where is she?"

"She stayed with me last night. I had to go buy a quart of beer and give her sips every half-hour so she wouldn't go into DTs."

"Was there anybody to help you?"

"No." He looks at me. "I thought about last time, Katherine, when you went with me to the hospital. I didn't want to go that route again. It's never worked. I thought if I could keep her with me—"

"Who's with her now?"

"Alma. But that's no guarantee Janie'll be there when I get home."

"You don't want to count on anything, do you?" I rise out of the deep chair and go and kneel beside him. I lay my head in his lap. "You look so vulnerable and tormented. And handsome. Sorry to mention it right now, but you do." His hand moves to my head and strokes my hair. When I turn to look up at him, his eyes seem weary and amused.

"God, Katherine. You're too much."

"I know. And I've been stupid, haven't I?" I lift my head from his knees and rock back on my heels and balance there.

"Sit down, Katherine. Get back over there in that counselee chair." He is grinning now. "What the hell did you come in here to find out? You pick the damnedest times to come on to me."

"Is that what I'm doing?"

"Cut it out."

"Okay. Truce. For now." I love his energy. Even when he is tired, he exudes a clean, biting energy that makes me want to be closer to him.

"Your hair is soft," he says. "What did you come here for?"

"To find out what you know. Or suspect. About the trees."

He watches me for a moment, as if assessing something. "Don't take this wrong, Katherine. Don't get mad."

"Why would I get mad?" We are both fixated on each other, like cats waiting to make a move.

"I don't want you to think I'm trying to cut out your boy-friend. Anyway, I don't have proof. Proof's what we need. It's where you could help us. Maybe."

"What is it you suspect Mark of?" I keep my voice level.

"I suspect he's working with somebody from the BIA to screw the tribe."

He waits, his eyes on me, challenging me.

"What makes you suspect that?" Even as I ask, I marvel at how little surprise I feel. Have I known and just not faced it? I think of the dinner with Tim and Babs and hear again the phone conversation that ignited doubts, and now my mind jumps onto other doubts.

"I'm sorry," I say. "I missed what you just said. I was thinking of you and Whit telling me Mark had come in to talk to Wally while I was gone."

"There's that."

"But what else? What did you say that I missed?"

"Part of you really doesn't want to hear this, does it?" His eyes are gentle.

"No, part of me really doesn't. But lay it on me, Sky. Lay it on me."

"Last year, when Mark went over to the Bureau office to check out adoption records, trying to find out who he was, I gave him a ride there 'cause I was goin' anyway. I hardly knew him—still don't—and he asked me a bunch of real nosy questions. I didn't like that. It made me wonder about him."

"What was he asking you about?"

"At first I thought he wanted to know about environmental stuff. That's why I was over there at the damn place, to try and get them to come out to the rez and tell folks about the long-term implications of logging—and especially of cutting old growth."

"He wasn't interested in that." I swing my legs over the arm of the chair and ease my sandals off, letting them fall to the floor. I want to show I don't care, and at the same time I am aware of feeling fragile and afraid.

"No, he wasn't. Old Mark wanted to know who I planned to see. Who has the power in forestry, he wanted to know. Well, the BIA gave me the royal runaround, about what we've come to

218

expect, right? And while I'm being shuffled around, I happen to see Mark back in forestry records, flirting with the file clerk. So on the way home I ask him, hey, Mark, I thought it was adoption records you were after? Weren't you romancin' the wrong lady? And he evades me, starts pumping me for info. What do you know about Stan Moss, Jr., he asks me. Well, I'm not some damn well to be pumped. I didn't tell him zip." Sky glares back at one of the masks.

"What was it you didn't tell him?"

"I didn't tell him what I'm sure he had no trouble findin' out from his drinkin' buddies, that Stan did time for embezzlement."

"How could he get elected to council?"

"Bless you, Katherine! You look shocked."

I swing my legs back and touch my bare feet to the floor. "There are still things that shock me, Sky. Whatever you might think."

"Sorry. Honestly. I'm sorry."

"Go ahead. I'll get over it."

"You don't look like you're over it."

"Just tell me, Sky. I have to hear this."

"Stan Moss, Jr.'s old man used to beat the hell out of him. Then Junior grew up and beat the hell out of his wife. He went to jail for that, too. She put him there. When he got out, he almost killed her, with her sister at the door yellin' at him to stop."

"And did that put him back in?"

"No. He threatened to kill her and the sister both if they testified. Everybody knew he'd do it, too."

"That was twenty-five years ago," he says, in answer to my stare. "Some folks laid it to his bein' young and crazy. And those same folks hope they'll get casino jobs because Stan knows they voted for him."

"And maybe logging jobs?"

"Yeah, maybe logging jobs."

"I still don't see what you've got that ties Mark in."

"Only that he and Stan Moss, Jr., are like this." He holds up his index and middle fingers, closely touching. I feel my skin begin to crawl.

"How do you know that?" I ask.

Sky presses his lips together and looks away from me, then back. "Stan Moss, Jr., runs prostitutes," he says. "Mark's been seen out there a lot."

"By whom?" I ask. An improbable smile crosses my lips.

He sees it and blushes a deep brown-red. "By me."

"You go there?"

"Shit, Katherine. I went there for Janie. Stan Moss got her to do it for drugs. She hardly knew where she was when I picked her up." He looks away and lays his hand across his eyes. "She thanked me. She did know enough to thank me."

"I'm sorry, Sky. I thought you were there ..." I hesitate. "For yourself." How wonderful it would be to have a man who cared enough to keep rescuing. And why do my thoughts suddenly go to Victor and Tony?

"You've probably wondered about me," he says. "Dammit, Katherine. I don't want to mess around with clients. Hell, half the women on this reservation have been in a class of mine or in this office—as clients," he adds. He raises his eyes and his look turns faintly mischievous, the Sky I know. "You're a visitor. And you decided not to join my class, remember?"

chapter 44

"You know they can't keep it."

I look up quickly to catch my mother's expression, trying to see behind it. How did I get this way, suspecting motives, strategies? Did she do this to Dad? But something *is* there, behind her eyes, I'm not imagining it. It is indignation, fury, and somehow it subdues my next words.

"Mom, it's a very little fawn. The kids'll care for it till it's big enough for Harry to ..." I'm about to say "take it back to the forest," but I am stopped by a vision of those huge, trusting eyes out in the wilds. It was a mistake, Harry never should have brought the fawn home.

"Your crazy brother! What'll he do next?" Ada sputters.

I press a fist against my mouth to cover a smile. "What *could* he do next, Mom? There aren't that many motherless babies out there."

"Spotted owls," Ada mutters.

"What?"

"You heard me. He says he doesn't care about them. But it looks like if something falls right in his path, he has a heart."

Is she raving? Sometimes it seems so clear she is talking about something else, strewing clues along a path, daring someone to follow, read the clues, and see inside her.

"Shouldn't ever have let that animal in my house," she goes on.

"Mom, it was only in the house one night."

"Yeah, now they all sleep out there in the yard with it!"

"We've only been letting two of them at a time sleep out there."

221

"I saw Tony sneak out with his blanket last night when he thought I wasn't watchin'."

"He loves it so much, Mom. They take turns, you know, feeding it from the bottle."

"Oh, I just don't want to *hear* about it, Katherine. Can't you ever leave me in peace?" She gets up from the porch step and stomps inside, banging the kitchen door shut behind her. I stare at the closed door. Another clue? What is this about? Babies left stranded, mothers killed, shot by white hunters. There's a story here somewhere. Or a poem.

Let me rest in peace before the grave swallows me, let me find a piece of heaven here.

The words float by and a startling vision comes of the forest gone, not there, no place for the deer to go home to.

chapter 45

I swing along, kicking up dust with my sandals. I lift my face to a floating mass of clouds and breathe in cool, fresh air, wanting to draw strength to get through the next hour. Grasping one hand with the other, I press soft skin and solid bone underneath. I yearn to reach Mark with that solid softness and break out together from the web spinning closer and closer around us. Some part of me—I know which part, as even now my thighs swish together and my pelvis responds—some part of me has entered into silent complicity with him. I heard him, on the phone, say "What if council knew they could get five times the price?" How could I suppress that?

A chugging noise breaks the morning stillness, and Sky's ancient Buick looms into view. Whitney sits straight and alert a couple of feet away from him on the wide front seat, looking ready for anything. Loaded for bear, I think, remembering Whit's proud demonstration, twirling the pistol. She gives me a side-to-side wave of her hand as they stutter to a stop, a couple of houses before they reach Mark's. What a getaway car! It's a joke. But Whitney insisted on being here, on the spot, to stand guard. "In case Mark gets ugly," were her exact words. I shiver, recalling the glint in her eyes.

I step up to the front door, knock, then push my way inside, not allowing myself to hesitate. The familiar thick scent of hunting gear and unwashed sheets hits me like a slap.

He appears in the bathroom door, a genie in a cloud of steam, with a towel wrapped around his lower torso. If only we could fall into bed and forget there's anybody else. But I have to find out how much of what I fear is real. I move into the room and stop a few paces away. If I come too close, I will be dwarfed by him. I hold my feet firm on the floorboards, my arms at my sides, and my fists begin a small clenching, flexing motion. The movement feels good, there is power in it. It helps me steel myself against the physical pull of him. I see the unease that has always been there deep in his eyes, that he usually covers with a grin.

"What's up, little turtle?" He is about to take hold of my arm, the arm with its fist silently clenching, and I will myself not to be drawn back into him, into the sex of him, not to be drawn too soon to that seeming safety. I step backward.

"Mark, I need to talk to you about the night we went to dinner with the BIA guy."

"What silly idea have you got in your head now?" He moves up on me and lays a hand on the back of my neck and squeezes it between his thumb and forefinger. It makes me feel like a female duck, it makes me want to skim across the water to get away.

"What was the point of that dinner, Mark?"

"You wowed him, baby, you did me proud. You were the classiest chick in the place."

"But why were you so anxious, Mark, to impress him?"

"You're readin' me wrong, Katherine. Not anxious. I just want him to know he's dealin' with class."

"What kind of dealing are we talking about, Mark?" I wince at my directness. It is not the right way to approach him.

"You don't need to know that, Katherine."

"I do need to know." My stomach tightens, the way it always does when I am close to him, but I can't tell if it is from wanting him or from fear.

"How about slippin' outa those jeans and warmin' me up on a cool morning?" He eases his fingers down under my shirt, reaching down my back, taking possession of me. I feel myself respond, feel a shudder go through my flesh, and I draw away.

"Get dressed, Mark. Please. I can't think when you touch me."

"Nice to know I have that effect!" He grabs a pair of jeans from the chair and I turn away and walk toward the window, not trusting myself to see him naked in the moment before he pulls them on.

"If you're doing business with him, Mark, and using me to help wrap the deal, I want to know what it's about."

"I can't tell you more, Katherine. It would put you in danger. People might try to make you talk."

I turn back to confront him. "Like who, Mark? Who might want to make me talk?"

For the first time, his face shows annoyance. "Like that little creep Robert, for instance. People like him, who don't know shit about anything that matters."

"What matters, Mark, to you?"

"You and me gettin' rich, baby! And livin' like we deserve."

"What if it means other people losing money?"

"Some people belong at the bottom, Katherine. They sink there, no matter what. There's a lotta losers on this reservation and I don't plan to be one of 'em. And I know you don't! You and me recognized each other from the start, didn't we?"

I yearn for distance from his words, his claims on me. A pounding starts in my chest and I raise my voice to speak over it. "You don't mind stepping on them, cheating them even, to come out a winner? Is that what you're saying?" My voice won't stop quivering.

"Hell, Katherine, you sound like somebody else!"

"Maybe I sound like *me*, Mark. Maybe this is the way I am. Maybe I want to understand what I'm involved in. It's about trees, isn't it? Cutting them down and selling them to that paper company?"

"Well, sure it's about that. I thought you knew that. I mean, what's the big deal you're makin' of it?"

"You're out to get that money, aren't you, and the tribal members won't get a fair share?"

He moves up close and takes hold of my arms and pulls me an unwilling step closer. His eyes gleam with the intensity that always reels me in, sucks me up.

"I don't want you to spoil it with questions. Don't worry about those little people, that's just what they are. They'll get their lousy five hundred up front! They think little, they dream little, they'll always be like that." He runs his hands down the sides of my arms. "They'll never be like us, Katherine, can't you see that?" His eyes plead with me.

I shake my head slowly, holding his gaze. "Mark, some of those folks have broken washing machines sitting in their yards and no money to get a new one."

"Katherine, we're different from them. This is the deal that's gonna show the world who we are. We'll know what to do with that money. Baby, you'll look great in a Jaguar!"

I feel it now, the distance between us. Odd that it would become real to me when he is so close I can see the fine pores of his skin. "Is it a cut you're getting because you found out something?"

"Listen, it's a cut I'm gettin' because I'm a smart guy! I'll be wearin' a three-piece suit and lookin' like a million-dollar man when this comes through."

I take a deep breath, but can't control the pounding. "How long have you lived here, Mark? Two years?"

"Two years. Not quite. I don't know."

"Doesn't it mean something to you that you're a part of things here, that people accept you and trust you?"

"Hell, they don't trust me. Nobody trusts anybody, if they have any sense. That's the only way, Katherine, don't you know that?"

I can't reach him. And now I can't even see him clearly, through the confusion I feel. "I guess I've been kidding myself or dazzled by you or I don't know what. We've gone along all summer just drifting, caught up in each other. I've neglected the boys. Mom's fed up with me."

"Your mom doesn't want you to have any fun, Katherine. She never had any, and she doesn't want you to."

My mother's face fills my mind, her eyes full of pain mixed with love. "It doesn't mean she's a bad person, or that she doesn't love me. You don't have a mom, Mark, that loves you like mine."

"Hey, why're you cryin'? I don't like to see a woman cry. Okay? Cut it out!"

"Dammit, Mark, I'll cry if I want to!"

He backs away. "What is all this?"

I wipe my eyes with my shirtsleeves. "Mark, I wanted to believe you care about the same things I do. Well, it couldn't be much clearer that you don't, and I feel like a piece of shit."

"What the hell does that make me? Huh? What the hell does that make me?"

"It's not you I'm talking about now. It's me."

"The hell it isn't! You go all moral on me and think you're too good for me. Just like the fuckin' white people I grew up with. I hate that!"

"What about your own Indian people, Mark?"

"Look, Katherine, I don't want you gettin' off on these side-tracks. Nobody needs to know what I'm doin'. Don'tcha see that? This is my big chance, and I'm gonna clean up."

I close my eyes and see the truth swirl past. He doesn't consider anyone's interests but his own. There is nothing there in his head but his own scarred ego. "Did you find out that BIA guy has been cheating the tribe on this, all along paying them less than the trees are worth?"

The expression of surprise on his face is instant. "Yeah. How do you know that?"

"And Stan Moss, Jr., is behind it."

"Yeah. He had his own sweet deal goin' and, unluckily for him, I figured it out. That dumb old Wally still hasn't caught on!"

"So you're going to split the kickback with Stan and the BIA guy."

"Katherine, you're pretty shrewd." He tries to project a grin to cover his uncertainty. "Were you ahead of me on this or what? Maybe I'll let you plan the next one."

I feel something go out of me, leaving my arms hanging loose at my sides. "There won't be a next one."

"There's where you're wrong! This is only starters. You won't believe the places we'll go. And you're the little lady I want beside me." He feels me slipping away and he turns on the charm, trying to pull me back into the dream. I see what he is doing and yet I am distanced from it finally, so that it feels natural to step away from him, to a chair, and sit down, moving out of his field of force and into my own.

"How did you find out he used to work a kickback with Stan Moss?"

"That Babs is a talker." He smirks, unable to keep from showing off. I don't even want to know how he got to know her well enough to find out.

"Is the contract signed yet?" I keep my voice cool, passion-less. He doesn't like that. I notice a cruel edge at the rims of his eyes. At this moment he looks ugly. Why had I thought him so handsome? I take a breath. "When is the signing set for?"

"Look," he says flatly, matching my new, flat tone. "The contract is nothin' to do with you."

I know, though, from some space between my first ques-tion and his body's answer; between that and my next question I got my answer. I still don't know when, but I know it hasn't been signed yet; I can sense it in his desire now to be gone from me. There are things he has to do.

A stab of pain shoots like a needle into my left eye. I place my right hand over my eyes and wait. It has happened before, a sign of tension striking back. With an effort, I speak over the dull roar in my head. "Mark. What makes you think I'd want to be part of cheating my own people? What have I done to make you think I'm that low?"

"You're shaking, Katherine. What's wrong with you?" He lifts his head, alerted to danger. He hurries toward the window.

"I'm going to report it, Mark."

I watch the panther-like turning of his body, ready to spring, and recognize the moment Whitney foresaw. Quickly I say, "Sky's waiting outside, with a friend."

He wavers, the sinuous threat of his movement suspended, and I see him thinking. It might be going to happen soon, I can read that in his eyes, the calculation: can the contract be signed before I report it? And then, could it be undone once signed? The smooth lines of his face contort with worry, and suddenly I see how small a man he is, how pitifully cramped his dreams are, dreams that have only to do with his own thwarted cravings. He turns to the window, raises it and leans out. He must see the car parked nearby, waiting. Deep down in my throat, dammed up there, a strong tide of laughter threatens to burst forth when I picture Whitney, the pearl-handled revolver in her lap.

"Dammit, Mark, I don't know why I'm even telling you. I guess it's to give you a chance."

He wheels toward me. "What the hell do you mean, bitch?"

238

There's a point at which a man like Mark calls you "bitch." It hits me like a fist in my face. Sky wouldn't look at me this way, all pretense gone, because Sky isn't pretense. He has told me all along what he has to say. He is searching and he hurts me sometimes by fidelity to his own needs, but he would never flash on me like this, a mask lifted to reveal hate. Or is it even hate? Am I simply in the way?

I move swiftly, pull the door open and step through, breathing in the clean, fresh air.

The car pulls up, engine revving, waiting for me to make my getaway. From what? What am I getting away from? My stinking self is still right here with me. Why that word, "stinking"? Walking out the door, I felt free, even brave, like someone doing a good thing, but reality reminds me now there is no being free from mistakes, from consequences and the stench of them.

Whitney reaches back and pushes open the back door for me and I get in. I slide to the far side where I hope I'll be invisible to Sky. I feel like a mass of beaten jelly.

"Did he admit it?" Whitney's face is eager, fox-like.

"Yes." I can't bring myself to say more. Just that admission ought to be enough.

"I knew it."

There is nothing to be overjoyed about. This is not that kind of coup. Yes it is, though. We can act to stop the dirty, stinking deal. That is what stinks—the deal. Not me. But yes—the guy I chose to be Prince Charming. Wrong again. I lift my legs up onto the seat and sink into the side of the car, leaning against a door that could fly open at any moment and leave me lying in the road. It would be a relief to turn into a medical emergency instead of this woman who looks good to everyone, yet feels like a raw wound.

"I wonder what his next move will be," Sky muses.

"He'll run." Whitney's strong chin juts out. "Rats run." She is so definitive and sure. How can anyone be that way?

"We can't count on it. What do we do now, Whit? Go right to council? Call a meeting? What?"

Interesting that he looks to Whitney for direction. He's not all that strong. Just determined. And honest. With shame comes clarity. I have never felt my mind so clear.

"What makes a guy act like that?" Whitney asks. "He really planned to do us all in. Is that the scope of it, Katherine?"

"Yes. And I don't know what makes an Indian do in his own people." I don't add, "or why I went along with him as long as I did."

"I think I know," Sky says. "He must have been wounded somehow, as a kid. And he never grew whole. Maybe he got put down for being who he was, a brown-skinned Indian, and never felt part of anything he could be proud of. It was way too late by the time he found us."

"Yeah, well, okay," Whitney says. "I'm sorry I started all this. What we need to do is act before he does. And Sky, you've driven us right to the tribal center, so I guess we know what we do next, right? We just need to tell our story." Her hand reaches for the door handle.

"I don't know why we can't sit down a moment and think this through rather than go off half-cocked."

"Okay, Katherine. We are sittin' down. What do you have in mind?"

"We have to talk to Wally before Mark gets to him." I pull myself upright, the clarity still with me. I push down the part of me that wants a drink, that wants to escape. "Let me talk to Wally. I can explain it so he'll understand. And I hope without making him feel like a nincompoop. The trick'll be to keep him from getting defensive."

"Yeah, the man must know he's no Einstein. Do you want me to come with you?"

"No, Whit. It's best if I talk to him alone."

Sky turns and smiles at me, as if I'm one of them now. Earned my place. I haven't. I've just proved to myself once more I don't know what I'm doing where men are involved. And I've never felt so alone.

I pause, my hand on the door. "This isn't going to work." I look out at the brightening sky. It feels as though there is all the time in the world to bring this to the light of day and look at it, as though it would be foolish to do otherwise. I reach inside the front of my flannel shirt and finger the small medicine bag Whitney made and hung on my neck yesterday. It is mine to keep. I wore it all night. Whit said it would protect me in Mark's house, the house of the ogre, it seems to me now.

"What do you mean?" Whitney turns and fixes bright eyes on me. "Why won't it work?"

She's really listening to me. I'm one of them now. In some way I have proven myself. Sky twists around in the driver's seat, watching me.

"Wally won't have the nerve," I say. "And even if he does, Stan Moss will find a way out of this or around it. He won't get caught, that's for sure. Think about it!" I consider it, then go on. "He never has been caught in however many years he's been getting away with this—well, you said he went to prison, Sky, a long time ago. But now he's got a lot of people scared of him."

Whitney looks at Sky and bursts into a laugh. "Maybe we ought to be scared of him, too!" Her laugh eases away tension, but I sense that all three of us realize the truth of her words. "Sky," Whitney turns to him. "What did you say about Richard Dillon? He suspected?"

"He's a smart guy, Dillon. Reads all those books, studies everything carefully. He figured out what's going on, but he hasn't done anything, couldn't prove it, you know?" A look of pain creases Sky's face. "He also guesses Stan uses his whores to sugar the deal."

Whitney straightens. She is wearing maroon cotton shorts, matching ankle socks, and a man's white shirt tied at the waist over a silver beaded top from the twenties. She reaches down into her black leather bag, like a doctor's, and pulls out a fringed deerskin pouch. "I forgot!" she says. "I brought tobacco and we haven't used it." I stop just short of saying "I gave up smoking" and wait. Whitney isn't about to propose we all have a smoke, or is she?

"Sky, drive down the road to that big cedar tree. You know the one. Right by the road, down near Turnipseeds'."

Sky starts the motor and off we go, thumping and bumping. His car needs work. He could sure use that up-front money. All the tribal members could. It's such a damned temptation, and then, in a week maybe, it's gone, and in some cases little to show for it and certainly nothing as lasting as a tree. Where the hell are we going? I feel relaxed, trusting.

231

"Here we are!" We pull up across from a giant cedar and Whitney turns to me. "We'll pray to that tree and ask its blessing on what we're goin' to do."

What *are* we going to do? I ask the question silently. We all pile out and Whitney leads us to the tree and indicates we are to stand around it, on different sides. She opens her pouch of tobacco and Sky takes a handful. I do, too. I wait to see what comes next. Whitney closes her eyes. God, help me through this, I pray. Help me to not mess up. Help me to stay with these people who are good, and to think straight. Whatever happens, I'll be okay. I'm not alone. We're in this together, Sky and Whit and I, and we can get Wally to see straight, too. And even Ada's on our side, and I know Victor will be! Tony, too, when we explain about the trees. I open my eyes to the heavily etched tree trunk, old and solid, and see Sky watching, waiting for me. Whitney throws her handful of tobacco onto the base of the trunk, sprinkling it against the bark. Sky waits, and I know I am next. I shake my handful of tobacco onto the exposed roots that lie nearest me. Sky does the same. We reach to join hands around the tree. Only our fingertips touch. We step closer to the tree so our hands can interlace. It feels as if we are embracing the tree and each other.

"Grandfather," Whitney says, "thank you for bringin' Katherine home. We love her. She's a beautiful soul and wouldn't hurt a tree or another person. She's only hurt herself. Help us all, Grandfather, to stop hurtin' ourselves. Help Janie get her mind and body free of alcohol. Help us all, Grandfather, keep the poison out of our minds and bodies. And Mother Earth, help each of us here t'do what we have t'do." She and Sky both give a squeeze to my hands and let go. We all troop back to the car and get in.

"I'm hungry," Whitney exclaims. "Anybody got anything to eat?" Sky pulls a bag of potato chips from under the seat and hands it to her. "This all you got?" Whitney's broad smile is back. He opens the glove compartment and an apple rolls out. She picks it up and hands it to me, then reaches in for two more and gives one to Sky.

"Symbolic," he says. "Eve in the Garden of Eden. Only there's three of us."

Whitney's laugh rings out. "Well, it's not one of us that's the snake!"

Halfway through his apple, Sky stops. "Katherine's right. Wally can't handle this alone. We'll have to call a meeting, get everybody involved." He leans forward over the steering wheel, like a runner ready to start. "That'll give us a chance to talk about reforestation!"

Three Turnipseed children draw near the car. Sky opens his door. "Want an apple?" Three heads nod in unison. He brings out the last of the apples and tosses them to the kids. "Hey, Burt," he says to the oldest. "Tell your gramma we're goin' to need to set up a tribal meeting. I'll be callin' her on the phone, but tell her Sky says it's urgent—we've got to do it today."

"You want her to make food?" Burt's eyes are comprehending.

"That would be great. Ask her to talk to the other ladies, too."

The kids take off running.

"Sky." I hesitate. "You know my brother Harry? I think he's been counting on logging jobs coming up."

Sky grins at me, the wicked grin I haven't seen in a while. "I was thinkin' about him, Katherine, just a minute ago. You know what? He could speak out on correct logging practices, what it does to a forest to cut down old growth."

"Harry?"

Sky bursts into a laugh. "You should see your face, Katherine. Yeah, Harry! He can speak from experience. I'll talk about how there'd be more jobs if we move from logging to reforestation. Give us months, years even, of work."

"We've got to get that up-front money out of everybody's minds, don't we?" I say it slowly. "But how can we get people to think beyond that?"

"Grandchildren. Children and grandchildren." Whitney's tone is serious. "Get folks thinkin' about them."

"I still don't see how we can make this come out right. I've been going over and over it in my mind."

Whitney reaches back and lays a hand on my knee. "We don't control the outcome," she says. "All we have to do is get up, each of us, and tell what we know. Let folks put it together themselves."

She's right. I sigh and sink back.

"Dillon can ask for more bids," Sky says. "Once we bring to light that the deal's fucked, Dillon can get up and demand that the tribe get bids from other companies. Or the BIA. Whoever does that part. It's ironic, isn't it? People will be more anxious than ever to sell the trees! They'll realize they can go to some other company and get a lot more money."

"We still don't have proof." I express the worry that won't leave my mind. "What proof have we got?"

Whitney looks back at me and then turns to Sky, her face comical in surprise. "God, she's right."

"Katherine, can you get statistics from other Bureau offices, find out what timber's goin' for? Would they tell you that?"

"Probably not," Whitney says.

"Wait!" I lean forward, my head up between the two of them. "Wally's got those stats. It's part of what somebody at the Bureau sent him. He had me ask for everything relating to timber and this one clerk got fired up and sent him stuff from all over. All kinds of stats! Wally was so confused he just piled it up in a corner. I spent an hour or two sifting through it. I can find what we need. I *know* I can! Just drop me off at the center, Sky, and give me some time alone with Wally."

Whitney beams at me. "I know you can do it. You've got the clearest mind when you use it."

"Thanks. Maybe someday I'll learn to use it on a regular basis. Maybe it'll carry over into my love life!" We both erupt in giggles and Sky looks at us wonderingly.

Then a light glimmers in his eyes. "And I'm up for making an activist out of Harry. He knows the facts. We've just got to give his viewpoint a hundred-eighty-degree twist."

chapter 46

The cedar's spirit glows warm inside me. I know now why we took time to fling our handfuls of tobacco. The tree's spirit strengthens me as I walk up toward the tribal center. It keeps me focused on what I need to do. I walk through the open door of Wally's office and find him sitting at his desk, staring into space. I catch that moment before he knows I am there. His expression is puzzled. I've seen him look that way before. As if he just doesn't get something. I feel a familiar flash of pity.

"Katherine!" he says. "This isn't your usual day." And then, kind man that he is, he adds, "Welcome, good to see you."

"I need to talk to you, Wally."

He motions for me to shut the door, no doubt picking up on the urgency in my voice. Now he looks worried as well as puzzled. "Sure, Katherine, sure." Wally repeats himself when he's nervous. I've noticed it before.

He concentrates on my chest, not looking me in the eye, but I've gotten used to that. I plunge right to the point. "Wally, has it been signed yet, the logging contract?"

He has on one green sock and one red. How is that possible? Is the man color-blind? And why am I noticing the color of his socks when I had thought I was totally focused? Probably because he isn't answering. He fidgets with the pens lined up in front of him on the desk.

"The logging contract, Wally. Has it been signed?"

"Yep, Katherine," he says, at last. "They've all signed it." My heart does a dip. I actually clutch at it, as if to catch it falling. Then something in the words he has chosen reaches me, filtering through slowly.

"*They've* signed it," I repeat, watching him. "The BIA. And the company. But you, Wally, have you signed it?"

He sighs and leans down to pick up a pile of papers from the floor. He plops them on the desk and pushes them toward me. "Not yet," he says. "Nope, not yet. And it's not me, you know, Katherine, who actually signs. It's Virginia. Our chairwoman. Soon as I put it in front of her, she'll give it the official signature. Make it official." Hope surges through me as he goes on talking. "Maybe it's good you took a notion to come in today, Katherine." There is confusion in Wally's eyes as he lets his glance touch the pile of papers. "They're pushing me to give Virginia the okay to sign, and I thought I'd do that today, but there's a coupla things I don't quite understand. Maybe it don't matter ..." His words trail off.

I lay my palms flat on his desk and lean toward him. "Wally, it matters a lot. Who is it? Who's pressuring you to sign?"

He scratches the top of his head, screwing up his face. "That's what I don't get," he says. "You know that guy Mark? The one comes to walk you home sometimes? Well, he's taken this interest in the trees and been workin' with Stan on the negotiations."

"But council put you in charge, Wally."

"Stan offered to help out. Told me he's used to all them fancy contract words—and dealin' with the Bureau man. Says he knows him from way back." Wally stares off into a corner.

I try to think how to approach him, how not to hurt him. I remind myself we've got some time now. If the tribe hasn't signed, we've got a little time. Unless Mark shows up. I feel my skin heat up at the thought of him, releasing the scent of perfume I dabbed on at the last minute before going to confront him. What had I been hoping?

"Maybe if we went over the key phrases together," I suggest.

Wally brightens. "Hey, good idea, Katherine. That's what I was wonderin', you know, just what the—whadda you call it— what the key phrases are. I have a little trouble findin' 'em."

He hands me the top batch of papers, stapled together, and I take them and quickly scan through the first pages. Mostly boilerplate. I learned to skim those sections fast, working for Allen. Soon I come to the meat of the contract. "Here it is, Wally," I say. "This, here. It's the price clause. Buried down in the middle of page five."

"Oh yeah. I was lookin' for that," he says. He takes off his glasses and wipes them on his shirtsleeve.

"We'll compare it to those stats the Bureau sent you," I say. "Remember?"

"They're stacked up in that corner, Katherine. You think you can find anything in that mess?"

I drop down on one knee and begin to page through the sheets, looking for a chart that shows the prices other tribes have gotten for timber stands. I hear Wally rustling cellophane, and the tantalizing aroma of smoked salmon reaches me just as he puts a piece in my hand. "Try this," he says with a grin. "Brain food." Munching on the dry salmon, I finally come to the chart I knew I had seen before. I stand up and lay it on the desk, next to page five of the contract. Pointing with a finger-nail, I show Wally the comparison figures.

"Wally, it's real low, the bid. Compared to what other tribes have gotten." I run my fingernail down the page. "And here's what I was afraid of. The old-growth trees? We'd be giving them away, Wally, if we sign this. I've talked to Sky, and he and Whitney are worried we're being taken. The Bureau guy is pulling something."

"Is that so?" Wally takes a moment to remove and adjust his glasses. "Sky thinks that?"

"He's sure of it, Wally. We're all sure of it." I watch him go behind his desk and sit down heavily in his chair, and then I ask, "Is Richard Dillon in today?"

"Yeah, yeah. Dillon's here." Wally frowns. "Dillon wouldn't be in on anything underhanded, Katherine." His troubled eyes flit across mine and I try to read in them whether he trusts me as much as I hope he does.

"I know," I say, nodding in agreement and seating myself in a straight-backed chair off to one side of his desk. "We need him, Wally, we need Richard Dillon to look at this and help us decide what to do."

Wally purses his lips and nods back at me. "Good idea, Katherine. Yep, that'd be good. See what Richard thinks. It's best not to rush these things."

The door bursts open, slams against the wall with a crash, and Mark strides in. "Hey, Wally!" He hesitates, seeing me and discarding me with one uneasy glance. "I been phonin' and couldn't get through. Switchboard's busy. So I thought I'd come on over."

"And why's that, Mark?" Wally tips slightly backward in his chair.

"Stan said soon as you've gotten Virginia Kelly to sign off, I can hand-carry the contract to the BIA, so you'll be sure to get it in by the deadline." Mark's eye twitches, and I notice beads of sweat on his forehead. It's the first time I've seen him sweat.

Wally brings his chair back to an upright position and takes off his glasses. He begins polishing them with a white cloth he draws from his pocket. The silence is profound; I can hear Mark's breathing and his effort to control it. I get the feeling Wally keeps silent just so we can hear that.

He puts his glasses back on, adjusts them, and for once I see him look somebody straight in the eye. "Now what deadline is that, Mark?"

"You know, Wally. Stan said we had to get the contract in real fast or we might lose the deal." There is pleading in Mark's tone.

"Oh, I wouldn't worry about that." Wally studies Mark's face. He seems to be enjoying himself.

"She's been talkin' to you, hasn't she?" Marks turns on me, a sudden vicious twist, and Wally half rises from his chair.

Mark struggles to get hold of himself, but he can't control the wildness in his eyes. He must see it starting to slip away, his chance to be somebody, to be rich. Rather than pity, I feel shame, that I would give myself to a man like this.

"She's lying, you know that, don't you, Wally? She's one o' those perpetual liars, whatever they call 'em. Can't help herself. She told you the price is too low, right? Well, she's crazy. She looks normal, but she's crazy."

"Wait a minute here." Wally rises to his full height and steps out from behind his desk. "What makes you think Katherine would tell me the price is too low? Why would you think that, Mark? Why do you come up with that particular lie for Katherine here, this crazy woman you're tellin' me to watch out for?"

Confusion takes over in Mark's eyes. "I was just guessin'," he says. "Look, Wally, I'll run an' get Stan. He'll explain the price and all. He's the one knows the details." Backing out the door, Mark collides with Sky, then Harry.

"You'll find Stan Moss at that house he runs," Harry says, his voice cool. "We saw him headin' out there."

Mark flinches. "What house?"

"Sky's been tellin' me about the different ways old Stan's found to make himself some extra bucks."

"You'd listen to a guy like this? Look, Harry, he don't know nothin', he makes up stuff."

"Like Katherine here?" Wally makes the question sound almost innocent. "Mark, you go get Stan, if you want. But I've already heard what Stan has to say. I'm gonna get Dillon in here, get Dillon's opinion on this here contract."

Mark's face contorts. He moves closer to Wally and hisses, "This deal is supposed to be confidential, damn it all, Wally!"

"Is that so?" Sky asks. "Seems like a deal to sell our tribe's trees is hardly a secret from a council member. And tribal members have a right to know what's goin' on, too, don'tcha think? That kinda makes you the odd man out, Mark."

"Yeah," Harry puts in. "Just why is it you're involved in this deal?"

I see in Mark's eyes his realization that he has lost, and in the same instant I see the little boy, hearing once again that he doesn't belong. In his twisted way, had he thought this scheme would make him an insider? Now I can't help feeling sorry for him. He is Stan Moss's victim as much as Janie was, as much as all of us will be if we don't act.

"Shall I go get Richard Dillon?" I ask. Wally nods, and Mark shoots me a look full of hate. He knows as well as I do what will happen when Dillon throws the light of his honesty and intelligence onto the papers sitting on Wally's desk.

"I'm gettin' outa here," he says. The rambler. The gambler. Moving on. As he passes me, he leans down and mutters in a choked voice, "It coulda been different, Katherine. If you weren't so stupid."

That's what he'll leave believing.

❀ ❀ ❀

Late that night, I lie alone in bed, the meeting a vivid film running and rerunning through my mind. Two circles of drummers, thundering the power of tribal memory through the rooftop into the night sky. People toted in folding chairs, and Tillie Turnipseed's father brought his metal armchair from his front yard. A great-granddaughter carried it for him. Most people ended up standing, and everybody rose when Mr. Turnipseed offered an opening prayer. There were maybe three hundred people; almost the whole damned tribe showed up. I remember Ada and Victor and Tony, and Maisie with the four girls, sitting up near the front, looking proud. And I sat in the long line of chairs facing everybody, right next to Wally, so I could hand him slips of paper with numbers he needed, and Richard Dillon on my other side, and Tom Matthews, Diane John, Virginia Kelly, and Frank and Rudy Vitello next to Wally, and then Harry and Whitney and Sky. I remember Harry's face growing almost happy when Sky introduced him as the forestry consultant who would present an experiential point of view. People listened to him with more interest than they did the tribal biologist, who went all scientific on us and lost most folks. It was seven o'clock when the meeting started and nine-thirty when everyone finally lined up at the food tables. By the time the petition to recall Stan Moss, Jr., reached me, halfway down the line, it had four full pages of signatures.

chapter 47

I stand naked in front of the mirror, brushing my hair. Ada and Harry and Maisie left an hour ago to take the kids to an air-conditioned movie in town, and temporarily I can reclaim my room and my mirror. My hair has a healthy sheen, like hair in magazine ads. It never used to have this shine in the city. My eyes are alive, too, with a sparkle in them, my skin tight and brown and smooth all over my neck and face and body. How deceptive, to feel so muddled up inside and screwed around and empty and yearning and pulled toward something I can't even name—and look like this. The picture of health!

My image reminds me of Dorian Gray. It was my last year in high school when I read that book. For the second year, Mrs. Dickson was my English and drama teacher, filling me with the fire of her own love for words, for ideas expressed cleanly, daringly. Mrs. Dickson had met and married Mr. Dickson when her hair was already gray and dry and sparse and her white face had long, gaunt lines. She was built like a board. If you looked at her sideways, there was almost nothing there. But not like a board, really, more like a willow that swayed over us. Her faded eyes turned bright and intense when she moved around the room giving back essays, the margins filled with comments in her tight, small script. As unlike me in looks as could be, but something in us the same. I sweep the brush back to get the hair away from my face, and then lift it from the back of my neck, relishing the memory of my teacher reading the poems I brought her. Mrs. Dickson was at her desk in the empty classroom by seven each morning. It was restful and comforting to know she would be there, to skip breakfast and be the first one in that room and breathe in the serenity of her. Serene, yes, but anger could break through and little spots of red appear high on her cheek-bones, if she believed a student was not trying hard enough, not working to the edge of where she could go and trusting that to be the jumping-off place. "You are hiding from the pain," she said. "You try to cover it up, Katherine, with birds flying and eagles soaring. You have to let yourself feel the pain and sink into it. It won't swallow you. Those wings you dream of won't let it. Think how the bird escapes, taking wing at the last possible moment."

How can every one of those words still be here in my mind? I fling myself on the bed and roll over onto my back, then wait for a breeze to filter through the open window. I close my eyes and smile, remembering gossip about Mrs. Dickson, imaginings about what kind of man could possibly have broken through her armor of gentility and married her after all the years the students knew her as Miss Price, the strictest of teachers, devoted entirely to literature, drama, and themselves. I was in her hands at least two hours every school day, more when the term play was in rehearsal. Mrs. Dickson had been waiting one morning, her papery, slen-der hands clasped in front of her on the desk. "Katherine," she said, "I want you to try out for the part of Laura in *The Glass Menagerie*. We're doing two plays this year and everyone will think of you for *Cat on a Hot Tin Roof,* but you can't have both parts." I answered, "Yes, Mrs. Dickson," not knowing either play. "Is it a big part?" I ventured. I remember every word of the an-swer. "It is a very important part. It is a girl who is afraid of the harshness of the world. She senses how fragile and precious beauty and kindness are. She is crippled, she walks with a slight limp, and she is very plain on the outside." Is she Indian? I won-dered, and kept that question to myself.

Mrs. Dickson had looked at me thoughtfully, lovingly, I wanted to believe. "When you try out for the part," she said, "wrap your hair tight into a little chignon at the back of your neck. Can you do that?" I nodded. "And no makeup, of course." Her eyes were sharp, critical. "Not that you need a speck of that makeup in the least! At any time!" The words felt like a slap. I tried to make the change subtle, but gradually I wore less and less eye makeup and foundation and hardly any blusher until finally my face was always just my face, with little or nothing hiding it. I felt better, freer, and even at this moment a rush of gratitude flows out toward the woman who set me on the way to freedom.

I was chosen by the casting committee for the part of Laura. The long weeks of rehearsing before and after school were the happiest of my life. But the night of the performance came and the play ended and there was no applause. I hadn't known I was waiting for the applause until it didn't come. And then I heard the scuffling of many feet and a rustling murmur ran through the auditorium and I thought they were beginning to leave. My heart sank. At first I wasn't conscious of the slow, gradual rumbling. It built and mounted until it grew thunderous, and then I heard cries of, "Bravo, Laura!" And my eyes filled with tears and I felt the connection between myself and the audience like a living, breathing cord stretched taut between us, I swaying on one end and all the people who had witnessed the sweet, raw insides of Laura on the other.

"Do the same with your poems," Mrs. Dickson said afterward, her hands resting on my shoulders, where now I put my own fingertips. What did she mean? "It is not just your pain you feel," she said. "You know that, don't you, Katherine? It is the whole world's. It's the man wearing too many clothes, all he owns, sitting in the library reading room, resting his head on the table because it is too hard to hold it up anymore."

"I wish I were spirit," I sigh, and I get up and pull on black shorts and a beige tank top with sandals for walking. I move at a fast pace, nodding to people I pass or calling out greetings, but hardly aware of doing it. And then, when I reach the point where there are no more houses, I turn into a tree-shaded lane, thrusting branches out of my way as I move along, inhaling the smell of dry, sun-warmed earth and feeling its goodness under my soles and the joy of walking on it. I stop when I approach the grove by the pond, charged full of memories. The shimmering water beckons me to come close and sit beside it and gaze into its shadow patterns. Behind me is the biggest and oldest of all the trees in the grove. I pull my knees up and clasp my hands together and wait. It's not coming from inside this time, is it? It is a person I am waiting for. I curl up on my side and fall into a shallow sleep that grows ever deeper. When I awake, the sun is low in the sky and I wonder if I am wrong, but I go on waiting, disappearing into memories, letting them go by and past me, remembering Larry, but for once not guiltily, suffering instead a kind of hopelessness. The boys seem far away. But they have grandmothers now, whom I brought together for them, and cousins and an aunt and uncle, and I can be in this far-off place and rest and feel hopeless and they will be safe.

I hear him coming. His steps are firm on the ground and he deliberately crushes down into dry leaves to make a sound I will hear. He stops a few feet behind me, but I don't turn my head to look. I am still caught firmly in the hopelessness and the safety.

"Katherine? Am I bothering you?"

I shake my head no. The other one never would have asked that. So I would have known him by his words, no need even to recognize the voice, the springy footstep. In a moment, a short little flash of time, he is there next to me, a little distance away, kneeling, rocking gently back and forth, balanced on his feet.

"You look so incredibly small," he says. "You've been here for hours, haven't you." It is a statement, something he is looking into me and seeing.

I can feel my face honest, free of makeup, of subterfuge. "I've been remembering something."

He sits near me, but not too near, and pulls his knees close to him the way mine are. "I'd like to hear. If you feel like telling."

"It's not what you think. It isn't really Larry I need to tell you about. I'm just realizing that."

He glances at me, a warm glance that encourages me.

"I remembered a teacher I had, who helped me see that the best part of me is inside, and I don't need to be ashamed ..."

"Go on," he says. "Ashamed ..."

"Of the pain," I whisper. "The pain of being me, and my father going with other women, or one anyway, and my mother closing down."

"And?" His voice is like a bird's wing dipping.

I look up into the sky and feel pain etched on my face. "This teacher knew the best part of me," I say. "She knew how much I

244

loved learning from her and being with her and she knew, too, I think, about the way my life was." My voice drops. "Boys."

"She trusted me, though." I say it urgently, looking straight at him. "She trusted I could put that aside and devote myself to the part of me that was like her. And I did!" I press my lips together against unexpected tears.

"Go on," he says. He watches with quiet eyes, not judging.

"I think," I say, and take a deep breath, trying to make some sort of joke out of it, "I think she thought I really could go on from there to become a poet or actress or playwright. I think she thought I could go on working hard and turn all the pain into something useful. Without her. I think she thought maybe I was strong enough to do that!" A bitter laugh comes out of the tears.

"You can," Sky says.

I want to hear it again. "What?"

"You heard me. That's why you're here, back home on your reservation. It's even why you're here in this spot today." His voice has a gentle, teasing huskiness that is familiar. I have heard it in my father's voice.

"Do you think so?"

"Yes. I do. But it's what you think that counts."

"Sky, I don't know what to do. I want to do more than write poems. And I'm too old to be an actress. Dammit all. I want my life to be worth something."

He lies back and closes his eyes.

"Do you hear me?" My voice is close to a scream. "I want you to tell me something, help me!"

"I can," he says. "Just listen and wait. There will be chances all the time. Some little and some even big." He sits up, full of vigor, and takes me by the shoulders and I imagine for an instant that he is going to shake me, or kiss me. "And write poems," he says. He smiles so heartbreakingly I want to laugh, or cry, or write a poem! "Anytime, anyplace. Just write. You can be the world's most unsuspected treasure."

"I did for a while when I first met Larry. I wrote about how the world looked to me and how light my body felt and I tried to write about his eyes, but I never could find words."

Sky sends his eyes away from me, out to the water. "Did you write about the pain that came after?"

"No. I've been hiding it, really deep, in a place nobody can find. Not even me. Isn't that funny?" I lower myself back to the ground, my knees in the air.

"Yeah, pretty funny. Pretty funny we didn't run into each other sooner. I go down into that place a lot."

"You know what's good, Sky?"

"What?"

"Now when you talk to me, I feel like it's me you're talking to. It used to be you didn't really see me. You were seeing Janie."

"I see you, all right. I see you even with my eyes shut." For a moment I imagine he is about to roll over on top of me. Mark would have. But Sky flattens his palms against the ground and jumps to his feet, and I sense he is protecting himself from the urgings of his body. "Walk home together? I don't know about you but I've got to stop thinking. Too much for one day."

"Can we walk home without talking? There's something inside me trying to bust out." Fusion. People think it's fission that busts out, but it's fusion. Something wants to fuse. And I have to be alone.

"A poem." His face is solemn. He holds out a hand to help me up but this isn't what I want. This isn't how to do it. I don't want to be drawn up and homeward by his vigor. A wrenching starts up inside me.

And then, shifting with a movement of the earth beneath me, a movement within and around me, I want him gone. Something jolts inside me, pushes me forward and onto my feet, and I almost topple Sky with the movement. But he is not part of it. I need him gone.

"Go, Sky. I was wrong. I need to be alone—" I fling myself back onto the ground, drawn to the earth as to the belly of my mother, a baby suckling at her breast, and I turn my face into the dirt and murmur, "Leave me. Please."

"You want to be alone? I can dig that." He sounds awkward, he wants to sound cool.

I hear him, but I don't want words. His retreating footsteps bring relief, and I swivel my head and watch him turn back once

246

to look at me, then he goes. A long, hungry, laughing sigh ebbs out of me and I rub my face into the earth and scrunch my hips forward, my squirming pelvis leading me. My body's overpowering urge is toward the earth, and I squiggle forward on my stomach, inching closer to the living roots of the giant maple, roots that thrust out powerfully. I wriggle myself onto the top of the biggest root, long like a bone jutting out, and I straddle it and rub myself into it and feel the bone of my pelvis in contact with its hardness. I am connected, rooted in the earth. It is where I want to be, on my belly, wedded to the earth, attached at the center of my being. I grasp a clump of weeds with one hand. My other hand claws into the dirt. A thrusting begins, a rhythmic pulsing against the root. My pelvis throbs against the hardness of the root and I thrust against its bony ridge. I keep the rhythm going, the pounding inside me rising and building until I explode and spill over into the earth, panting, feeling the juices of the ancient tree come alive and run out into me and my own juices run wild with the ecstasy of finally being free.

Spent and wet and satisfied, I lie inert on my mother, the earth. I feel oneness with all things.

chapter 48

"Katherine!"

I hear my mother calling to me and trace the voice finally to the backyard. Ada stands sniffing the air suspiciously.

"Do you smell that?" she asks.

I sniff, too. "What?"

"That tang in the air, the sharpness ..."

"Oh, you mean rain!" I laugh. "Doesn't it always rain on moving day?"

"Well, you're cheerful about it anyway." My mother sounds happy. We stand side by side, both taking deep, easy, satisfied breaths, I for once able to feel tall, next to her.

"I love it," I breathe.

"What do you love?"

"Being here with you, Mom. Having a home."

"Hmpff!" Ada snorts. "Who's goin' to help you move?" She looks at me sideways.

I smile. "It won't be Mark. He's left town."

"Hmm. This is not your home, you know." She rubs her arm, as if to rub off the scent of sentimentality. "You'll be all on your own over there."

I bite my lower lip to contain my smile. "I won't be far away."

"Do you plan to wear those shorts?" she asks.

"Yes. Why?"

"Just askin'."

Why does she do this to me? Can't she ever just leave something alone and quit worrying it like a dog with a bone?

"Are you saying they're too short?"

"It's your life. Wear what you want."

"Mom?"

"If you want them ogling you."

"Ogling?"

"Starin' at your ... legs."

"Mom. It's hot now. It'll be hotter later. Rain or no rain."

"They used to stare at me. You wouldn't know about that. You never think of me as havin' had a life before you came along."

"Mom, what are you—"

"I wore these tight jeans, so tight the seams would pop, and I felt them watchin' on the street and I flipped my hair back, just like you do, and I said, 'Go ahead and stare, you go right ahead and ...' "

I glance at her, puzzled. "Okay. Okay. I'll change."

"Did I say that? Did I ask you to change?"

We both hear Sky calling from the front of the house and turn at the same time.

"I phoned Allen," I say, "my boss in the city. Like you've been bugging me to. And my landlord, to tell him I'm coming for my stuff."

"Don't want to give Indians a bad name," Ada says. I look at her to see if she is joking.

chapter 49

"Mom, can you come over for coffee?"

"I'm busy, Katherine."

"What're you doing?

"I have to start cannin' tomatoes."

"Mom."

"What?"

"You can do that anytime. You haven't started even? I mean, it's not like you've got a big pot of tomatoes on the stove?"

"No, I was just thinkin' they look pretty ripe."

"I want you to see my new place, Mom."

"It looks like all the other HUD two-bedrooms, don't it?"

"I bought your favorite coffee cake—apricot with almond paste. And I just brewed up a pot of strong coffee."

"Okay. Maybe for five minutes."

I stand looking into the buzzing receiver. Five minutes? Well, that's something. I grab the sponge and wipe off the counters one more time. Everything looks so bare, compared to her house with its layers of rugs and afghan-draped furniture and books and pictures and carvings and the table covered with beadwork. I run out to the yard and pick a bouquet of daisies and am stuffing them into a drinking glass when she walks in.

It seems odd to see her in any home other than her own. She sweeps the living room with her eyes and takes a quick look into the small bathroom and both bedrooms.

"You've still got a lot of unpackin' to do," she says, and sits down on the chair I pull out for her at the kitchen table. I spin away to hide anger. Can't she say even one nice thing about the house? I pour coffee for both of us, letting it slosh out onto the clean white surface of the stove. I don't wipe up the spill. The brief act of defiance lifts my spirits. I carry the mugs over and plop them down on the table. Then I set a plate with two slices of coffee cake in front of her.

"You're really goin' to be stayin' here, I guess this means." She drinks her coffee in steady sips, as if hungry for it, not setting the mug down until it is half-empty. She stares out the window, distracted, thoughtful. Probably can't wait to get back home. I sip my own coffee in silence, unable to think of a thing in the world to say.

She tips her head back to get the last mouthful of coffee.

"Mom? You're not eating your coffee cake." She has pushed it away. Her elbows rest on the table and her hands hide her face as she massages her forehead with aching slowness.

"Gee, Mom. I had hoped we could have a nice talk." Why did I hope that? Have we ever had one, ever in our lives? Did I think that somehow having a house near her would make a difference? That finally we would approach each other as human beings? Yes! Yes! I hoped that. I plunge my own forehead into my hand and rub it back and forth inside my palm.

My mother looks up and I look up at the same instant, and there are tears in her eyes. They spill out and run down the smooth, brown cheeks. I have never seen her actually cry. I don't know what to do. There is an awful ache in my throat, a longing to do something to ease the pain that I feel seeping out of her pores. It's as if I could reach out and touch waves of pain. I stretch my arms across the table and grasp both of her hands. There is no resistance. She raises piteous eyes.

"What? What, Mother?" My voice comes out a plea.

"Katherine. My beautiful girl." I feel my body draw back in amazement, hearing those words come from her mouth.

"There is so much I should tell you. I've never been able to. I've always wanted you to think well of me." Her voice breaks. I start to get up. I want to go around the table and comfort her, but she hangs on tight to my two hands, her face a grimace of pain.

"I am so ashamed."

I am not sure I heard right. The words emerged as a whisper.

She rasps out a sigh, hanging onto my hands so tightly it hurts, and turns her head toward the refrigerator as it lurches into the loud, humming part of its cycle.

"You think I was always dull and strict and hemmed in like I am now. But I had a wild side." I remember what she said on moving day when we argued about the shorts. It made me wonder. It didn't fit my picture of her.

"I did something you never did, Katherine, even in your wildest days. I ..." Her lips tighten and almost disappear, as if they don't want to let the words out. Her eyes close down and the eyelids shut over the words when she finally says them. "I had a baby you don't know about."

I keep hold of the worn, old hands. They loosen their grip on me, but I hold on, not wanting her to feel abandoned. Her eyes and mouth are creased in agony. I yearn to say something to let her know it's all right.

"Did you ... did you give the baby up for adoption?" I put all the gentleness I can into my voice, but her reply rings out like a scream of pain.

"It wasn't me that did it!"

I wait, afraid to speak.

"It was my mother who adopted him out," she says, finally.

"He? The baby was a boy?" An awful thought hits me. "Was it Mark?"

Ada's face shows her rare brand of humor that comes at the oddest moments. "No! I'da had to tell you a little sooner if it was Mark."

I let out the breath I've been holding. "Do you know, Mom, what happened to the baby? That was crazy just now, wasn't it, me asking was it Mark? You don't know, do you, where the baby went?"

She watches my face as if she is studying it, learning it by heart. Or searching for something in it that she's lost.

"When I saw you side by side with him at the meeting we all had about the trees, Katherine, I was so proud of you both. There he was with his briefcase bulging with papers, showing all that hard work he done. He's always like that, not just standing up for what he thinks, but he's got the papers to prove it! And you too, Katherine. You're the same."

"Mom? Look at me, Mom." I see the answer in her eyes, but I ask anyway, not able to believe it. "You don't mean Richard Dillon is your son?"

She lets her eyes give back the answer.

"But he's *black!*"

"Gosh, Katherine, are you just now noticin' that?"

"Richard Dillon is my brother." I say it slowly, trying the words out.

"Katherine, I've learned so much from you, watching how proud you walk around here, your head held high, just as proud as can be of those boys of yours. I never knew how to do that. I was so afraid the tribe would all just turn on me and call me evil names and think I was worthless—it was pitiful, Katherine, what I did, makin' a poor orphan outa that dear boy—"

"Wait, Mom." I can't believe I am interrupting her, can't believe Ada would ever talk so much I'd need to. "Wait! You were in love with a black man?"

She looks startled. "In love? I was just a girl, Katherine. Fourteen years old. The missionaries took me and my sister Betsy and put us in different boarding schools. What did I know? It was all so stiff and strange there—nothin' but rules to follow. And no love in the place at all. Except for this one man who worked there, and I thought he was so friendly and fun to be around, and you don't know how little there was of fun or friendliness in that godforsaken hellhole. I hated it so much, Katherine, bein' away from all my folks and not allowed to talk Indian or say anything about bein' Indian. All of our ways, they wanted us just to forget it all, forget who we were. So yes, I got a little love, before I even knew what it was, and a little baby grew out of it and when I wrote and told my mother I had to come home—why, she brought me home all right, but before I knew it she'd told the minister and he'd arranged for me to go to a home in Kansas and have the baby there, and when the little baby was born it was so obvious who the daddy had been ..."

"Were you all alone when he was born?" I ask. I'd had Larry out in the waiting room each time, so eager to see our babies that the nurses had to keep sending him back—he came down the hall trying to get in every chance he got.

253

"My mama came," Ada says, so low I have to lean nearer to catch the words. "The way she looked at that baby ..." She shakes her head, and there is more pain in her eyes than I have ever seen. Finally she's letting it come out from where it's been hiding, deep inside. It's what Arethea sensed in her that was frozen, and I watch it emerge. "Mama told me to forget I'd ever had a baby," Ada says. "She told me to go back to the boarding school and just never think of it again. 'We'll never speak of it,' she told me." Agony sits on her face as she repeats her mother's words. "And we didn't."

I am afraid to speak, afraid of stopping the flow, afraid of trusting my own instincts. Too much lies naked on the table between us.

Ada sighs, a long, slow sigh, as though the worst of what she had to tell has been released. "For a long time I really didn't think about it. Not in any part of my mind I knew about. Can you imagine that, Katherine, how that's possible?"

I try to think what it would be like to have my baby taken away. What comes to mind is Larry's body, carried out on a stretcher by strangers, and guilt strangling my grief. "Yes, I think I can," I say.

"I came home from boarding school, after all those years there, and I hardly felt like I belonged anywhere anymore. They'd killed so much of what I was, and they hadn't given me anything to put in place of what was gone. They killed Betsy outright. She got TB there at the school they put her in, and she came home and died of it." Her eyes touch mine. "She died so young, Betsy did. Do you remember at all?"

"I remember hearing about her, Mama."

"She took my secret to her grave. I've never told anyone else, Katherine. No one! It's just stayed on my heart, like something crushing and weighing me down."

"How did you find out, Mom? Who your son was?"

Her eyes stare out across my kitchen into the past. "I stayed close to home when they finally let me come back. It wasn't till Pastor Dillon died, and then a few years later his wife—they were elderly, you know, and they left this little boy who was sixteen, and he stayed on, living in that little house of theirs

254

where he's still livin'. Folks started callin' him an orphan and that got me thinkin' about him. And I knew he wasn't all Indian, that he had black in him, and then I remembered hearin' he'd been adopted as a baby."

"But how could you be sure, Mom?" I want it to be true and am afraid somehow it won't be—we'll find out she's been wrong all these years. Victor would be so proud to have Richard Dillon as his uncle. The thought comes like a wild card in a poker hand. Like suddenly there's a way to win.

"At first I wasn't, Katherine. And I tried to not even think about it or wonder. I was so humiliated, afraid of what folks would think if they knew. He's always been so isolated, Richard has, going his own way. Went off to college for years. But I went on thinkin' about him in that part of the mind that goes its own way, you know? And one day at the tribal office, I went through the enrollment records when Sadie was out to lunch, and I found out they'd enrolled him through the BIA. They'd certified his birth mother was four-quarters Indian from our tribe, without giving a name. And then I saw his birth date." Tears gather in my mother's eyes. I go to the cupboard and get out a package of paper napkins and put one in her hand.

"He's got no family at all," I say. "We could give him that."

Ada looks at me. "How would Harry take it, do you think?"

"Harry's solid. He can take anything. Cut the trees, save the trees, help out a friend. He does what needs to be done."

"Poor breed boy," she murmurs. "Always tryin' so hard to make a place for himself here, and he made his way right to the top, he worked so hard." Again, a touch of humor lights her eyes. "Choppin' wood at the crack o' dawn for that sweat lodge he built."

I remember Sky said almost the same thing, and I smile.

"We have to tell him, don't we? I'm so scared, Katherine, that he'll hate me."

"He'll have an instant family, Mom." Yearning for family is written all over Richard Dillon. "He and Victor already love each other. I've seen that. With Dillon as his uncle, Victor won't care if I ever find him a father! That man has been so alone, Mom. But it's not how he wants to be."

"Katherine, will you go over there with me? One day—
when I'm ready? To that little house of his? I couldn't do it
alone."

"Okay, Mom. We'll go together."

The clock ticks loudly. It seems to go faster than normal. I
wait, seeing in Ada's eyes that there is more she needs to tell
me.

"I'd been warned by Mama about keepin' away from the
boys. Somehow I just thought nothin' like that could happen
with him." She pushes her fingers back through her hair and
seizes handfuls as if she wants to tear it out by the roots. "I can't
bear to think of our sin creatin' an outcast orphan child!"

"You were just a child yourself, Mama!" I reach over and
stroke her arm, wanting to give her comfort. "You've been carrying this all alone, not understanding it even."

"There was a time after it happened, a year or so, when I
acted real wild and stuck-up. I never let a boy come near me,
though. I was awful confused. And then I found church helped.
It helped me know how to behave, but, oh, it made me so
ashamed. I just lived full of shame inside, like that worm in the
hymn. I felt just like that, and I'd sing out so loud and strong,
'Oh, what a worm am I!' Mama looked at me real funny once,
when I was standin' next to her and we were all singin' that
hymn."

What to say? Anger seethes in me against the church that
encouraged this burden of guilt and shame, made it larger and
heavier and never, ever helped my mother let it go.

"I tried to give my sorrow to Jesus." She lifts puzzled eyes to
the ceiling. "It never left me, though—every time I tried to
give it to Jesus, I just felt it all come down on me again, pushin'
me into the ground."

She lowers her head and stares at the floor. "It was hard on
your father. I couldn't hardly ever enjoy the physical part. I
loved him so much, Katherine, but it didn't seem right to me,
what we were doin'."

The blonde woman, touching my father, flashes through my
mind, and his responding, as if he couldn't help himself. I have
blocked that out until this minute, his delight at being touched,
so evident in his eyes.

256

"I never knew if Mama told my father. She wouldn't speak of it—she'd just give me those looks of hers." Ada is backing away already from the memory of Big Jim, but I see him clearly, his ghost evoked by her naming him, standing in the doorway now as he did then.

"Did Dad ever try to come back?" There! I have done it, thrown myself against the wall! Something in her face cracks, regroups into familiar lines of pain.

"We weren't neither of us ready, Katherine. Not you or me."

I look away from her mute agony, which I have looked at all my life, not comprehending. I walk with her to her house and, for the first time, we sink into the embrace of each other's arms.

Back in my own kitchen, barely conscious of having returned, I pour more coffee and sit at the small table, feeling what my mother has been holding inside, the hugeness, the unending confusion. I walk into the living room and stretch out on the one rug in the house, staring at the white ceiling. It is a blank, waiting up there, watching. I lapse into a kind of stupor in which black babies float through the air like balloons going higher and higher, and I struggle to pull them back down to earth but there is nothing to catch hold of and only the misery of them floating, motherless, fatherless, not belonging to anyone.

"Mom! What are you doing?"

Victor stands over me, puzzled and demanding, as if he wants me to get up and be myself. I'm not ready.

"I'm dreaming, Victor. I'm lying here with dreams floating over me."

"I'm hungry, Mom. Do we eat here or at Grandma's?"

"Here."

"Okay. What's for dinner?"

"Victor, just sit down and shut up, okay? For a minute? I don't know what's for dinner. We just moved in, for god's sake."

"Well, so, we don't ..." He stammers, not used to being reprimanded by me.

"In a minute I'll make a list and send you to the store."

"Do I have to *walk?*"

"You just walked home from soccer practice. The store's closer than that."

257

He groans aloud and throws himself full-length on the couch. I want to tell him, and can't, about his grandma and the man at the boarding school. I'll have to let her tell him in her own good time, in her own way.

"Victor."

"What?"

"Grandma Ada—has it ever struck you she's a woman who keeps a lot to herself?"

He hoots with laughter. "Struck me? You kill me, Mom. Sometimes you kill me."

I raise myself to a cross-legged sitting position. "Why do you say that?"

"You're off in some world of your own. A poet, I guess. I don't mean it sarcastic, either. It's just that nobody's ever seen a woman who keeps more to herself than Grandma Ada. I can't believe you'd think you're the only one who notices!"

"Someday, Victor," I try to cut through his and my own carrying on and covering-up. "Someday, ask her to tell you about your Grandpa Jim."

"She does." He says it defensively, and I know right away it was the wrong way to get a dialogue going. "She's told me I'm a lot like him."

"Well, she loved him an awful lot. So I guess you can be proud."

"Oh shit, Mom. How could—just make your list, okay? I'll go. Can I take my bike?"

"You don't have a bike."

"Grandma said I can use that one she's got on her back porch."

"It doesn't have air in the tires. Probably no brakes, either."

"You sure don't want me to have any fun, do you?"

I jump up and hug him before he can roll off the couch and get away from me. "No, I don't want my big boy to have any fun. What do you think?"

"Don't tickle me, Mom! Don't tickle me!" He looks about five years old.

"Can't you take it?"

He is laughing now, reveling in being tickled, loved, noticed. I don't want to let walls grow up between us. If it takes tickling to keep the space open, then that's what I'll do.

"Just a little more tickle to get you going to the store," I laugh, and he flees from me, then dashes back into the room, grinning.

"I'll make up my own list. Just give me the money." He dances from one foot to the other.

"Where's Tony?" it suddenly occurs to me.

"Down at Turnipseeds' playin' ball."

"Bring him back on your way home."

"He's not gonna like that!" Victor's face is open, eyes shining. Money in hand, he bounds out the door.

I search through a box of items retrieved from the city until I find a half-empty spiral notebook and a ballpoint pen, then I pause to gaze out the open window. I can see the clear, running water of the creek and hear its bright song.

Sitting in the middle of the room, notebook on my knees, I write:

> I sought spirit and spirit sought me
> I didn't hear its flutter of wings
> I drank and danced and rolled in dirty sheets
> I didn't hear the music of love
> The secret, daring whisper of love
> I almost didn't hear.

I turn to the next page and begin a list:

> Get AIDS test.
> Learn Lushootseed.

I close my eyes and wait to see what comes next.